Traveler

ALSO BY RON McLARTY

The Memory of Running

Traveler

RON McLARTY

VIKING

VIKING
Published by the Penguin Group
Penguin Group (USA) Inc., 375 Hudson Street, New York, New York 10014, U.S.A.
Penguin Group (Canada), 90 Eglinton Avenue East, Suite 700,
Toronto, Ontario, Canada M4P 2Y3 (a division of Pearson Penguin Canada Inc.)
Penguin Books Ltd, 80 Strand, London WC2R 0RL, England
Penguin Ireland, 25 St. Stephen's Green, Dublin 2, Ireland
(a division of Penguin Books Ltd)
Penguin Books Australia Ltd, 250 Camberwell Road, Camberwell, Victoria 3124, Australia
(a division of Pearson Australia Group Pty Ltd)
Penguin Books India Pvt Ltd, 11 Community Centre, Panchsheel Park,
New Delhi–110 017, India
Penguin Group (NZ), Cnr Airborne and Rosedale Roads, Albany,
Auckland 1310, New Zealand (a division of Pearson New Zealand Ltd)
Penguin Books (South Africa) (Pty) Ltd, 24 Sturdee Avenue,
Rosebank, Johannesburg 2196, South Africa

Penguin Books Ltd, Registered Offices:
80 Strand, London WC2R 0RL, England

First published in 2007 by Viking Penguin,
a member of Penguin Group (USA) Inc.

10   9   8   7   6   5   4   3   2   1

Publisher's Note
This is a work of fiction. Names, characters, places, and incidents either are the product of
the author's imagination or are used fictitiously, and any resemblance to actual persons, living
or dead, business establishments, events, or locales is entirely coincidental.

Library of Congress Cataloging-in-Publication Data
McLarty, Ron.
   Traveler / Ron McLarty.
      p.   cm.
   ISBN 978-0-670-03474-1
   1. Irish Americans—Fiction. 2. Rhode Island—Fiction. I. Title.
   PS3613.C573T73 2007
   495.6'83421—dc22   2006046763

Printed in the United States of America
Set in Bembo with Lomba
Designed by Daniel Lagin

This book is for
Kate Skinner McLarty
Beloved wife

Acknowledgments

Special thanks to Paul Slovak for his warm editorial guidance—and, as always, to Zachary, Lucas, and Matthew for being in the world.

Jan. 6, 2001

Dear Jono,

I am writing to tell you that Marie has passed away. I know she would want you to know, as she always mentioned your Christmas cards.

I was with Sis and her husband, Chip, and their kids a few days before New Year's. She took a nap and did not wake up. Her funeral was two days ago, and mass was at St. Martha's. I have enclosed her mass card. Father Gallo buried her in a very nice service.

We do not know why she has left us. Rhode Island requires an autopsy, but we haven't heard anything yet.

I am so sorry to tell you such sad news. How are you? My mother is still alive and is eighty-seven years old. God bless her.

Your old pal,
Cubby D'Agostino

1

In 1961 I fell wildly in love with Marie D'Agostino. She was tall
and graceful and had a smell that was as if she had just toweled off
after a bath in rose water. Her skin was a shiny light olive, and
while everybody else in her family had this Sicilian peasant thing
working, Marie always seemed smoothly elegant and gracile. I viv-
idly remember her long fingers and how she would rub them
through her amazing, curly, ink-black hair. Her neck, like her arms
and legs, was long, and you could see that she had to concentrate
to keep her head high. When she got excited about something,
which was quite often, her head would bob around madly. Even
that was lovely. It was that one little comma in her otherwise perfect countenance. But the thing that caught me, hexed me—
engulfed me, really—was her deep, round voice. It seemed to roll
out of her small mouth and burst onto your face. And it was with
that full, sober, and dependable sound more than any other facet of
this astonishing human being that I have compared all women since.

In 1961 Marie was nearly twelve years old, and whatever happened to her happened quickly, because I noticed she was suddenly
different, and as I said, I fell hard. I was an eleven-year-old porker
from the mick section of East Providence, specifically Cardinal

Avenue behind the foundry and two blocks away from St. Martha's Catholic Church.

At that time I ran with Marie's brother, Cubby, their cousin Billy Fontanelli, and Bobby Fontes, who was a Portagee, but that was okay with us. We'd walk to places together and generally mess around. It was pretty good, and the rules were simple. Cubby was sort of the leader, because he looked older than the rest of us even if he wasn't and because at eleven he already sported pegged pants and a modified mondo flattop with high crew cut and swept back Vitalisized sides. He also had access to Marlboro cigarettes, which we preferred.

It was early fall, I remember, and I had just gotten my traditional back-to-school flattop Ra-Ra haircut, which I felt made me appear thinner for some reason, even though several photographs of me from that period show what looks to be a sack of flour with ears. We were watching Bilko with Cubby's old man, Big Tony, and it just happened. I smelled something, and I decided it was roses. I actually smelled her before she walked into the room. She was with her mother, and they'd just come home from the Outlet Company in Providence buying her school stuff. She had on red corduroy bib overalls over a checkerboard long-sleeved cotton blouse and brand-new black Chuck Taylor high-top sneakers. The ensemble was set off by a red comb in her hair. I about had a stroke. She said something to Billy. I think she asked if his sister, one of her girlfriends, was going to Catholic Youth Organization that night. I think that's what she said. I can't be sure, because for the first time since I knew her, I noticed that voice. It was like an echo down a well. A voice that hung around the room even after she had stopped talking. I stood up tall and tried to suck myself inside me so I would appear thinner. I also looked over her head, a technique someone had told me would add age and a certain maturity. Marie D'Agostino paused. It was as if time were frozen for a split second. Those black-pearl eyes beheld no one else but me. Her voice was slow, solid, and acute.

"Why don't you take a picture, Riley," she boomed.

Yeah, that was me all right. Jono Riley. No middle name. Not for the Rileys. We were first- and last-namers only. According to my old pop, there was a constant unbroken chain of Jono Rileys dating back several centuries before the birth of Christ. Which made sense to me, as pyramid building, especially the part where you pulled huge blocks of stone with rope and then died, was not unlike the kind of work the Rhode Island Rileys specialized in. But from that initial pertinent exchange with her, I could think of nothing else, imagine nothing more wonderful, than to be somehow included in the all-encompassing orbit of Marie.

I lived just around the corner from the D'Agostinos, but to the geniuses who had drawn up the elementary-school grids, I might as well have lived in Seekonk, Massachusetts. Marie was starting sixth grade at Kent Heights, and I was assigned to the Brightridge School, about a mile down Pawtucket Avenue. It didn't take Einstein to figure out that if I had any chance at all of impressing myself on her, it would have to come at CYO and weekends with Cubby. I hit upon a strategy of consistency. By being around consistently, I found it was difficult for Marie to avoid the occasional social interaction with me. For example, along with the CYO, which met on Tuesday and Sunday nights, I found that by walking to school a roundabout way, cutting in back of the foundry and up Chester Street, then over to Canton and up King Philip Street, I was able to casually saunter past Kent Heights at the exact moment that Marie and Cubby were walking to school from their house.

"What's going on?" I'd say to Cubby.

It was important, at that time, to coolly not acknowledge Marie at all.

"What's going on?" Cubby would reply.

Marie usually looked bored.

"Bozo," she'd say, if she said anything. Bozo was the nickname that their father, Big Tony, had given me. Big Tony gave everyone nicknames. Billy Fontanelli's nickname was Big Billy and Bobby Fontes's was Bobberino, and I was Bozo. Her mother used to call me Riley. She also used to like to say I had the life of Riley.

Anyway, I don't remember much about anything, really, so let me get right to that important day, two days after Christmas 1961. There was a lot of snow on the ground from a blizzard on Christmas Eve. Some of the high-school kids had gone down to Kent Woods, which was behind the Kent Heights School, and shoveled off Kent Pond and set up the hockey rink. The hockey rink had been set up on the same spot for as long as anyone could remember. My old man had played there, and "Pile On" Pendergast, who was an enforcer for the Providence Reds, cut his own vicious teeth at the very same place.

Now, I hope this doesn't seem self-serving or show-offy, but it's important to the progression of events of this particular day—or, more specifically, afternoon. I was, even at eleven, an extremely good hockey player. On skates I embodied a certain grace that escaped me in virtually every other facet of my early life. I could handle the stick dangerously, and when I was picked to fill out a game against the high-school kids, I would attack the net with an aggression that always surprised me. I could never have put it into words, much less understood the transformation that overtook me when I laced up the skates, but, looking back the way we all do, I now realize that I became an arrogant little prick on the ice. I always wore a pair of corduroys tucked into my high socks, with the *Providence Journal* stuffed over my shins. I also always wore my old man's East Providence High School hockey jersey with the number sixteen on it. I wore that jersey until I got my own and powered EP to the state title over Mount St. Charles with what would have been a hat trick if the chintzy refs—who were also French-Canadian Christian Brothers, by the way—hadn't disallowed the second one when I was clearly behind the line. But that's beside the point.

On this particular afternoon—two days after Christmas, as I said—I got picked by Denny Cunha to fill out his squad of cronies. Denny and his team were all Portagees and played the kind of finesse game I like, with great emphasis on puck movement and shot generosity. We were pitted against the Irish-Italian mob of Poochy Ponserelli and Jack Crosby from Riverside Terrace. I hated them for a lot of reasons, but the main one was, because I was only eleven, Crosby used to make me call him "Mr. Crosby." These guys played like the thugs they were, with an artlessness that even casual fans of the game could recognize. So while Cunha, his brother Jim, Gene Rezendes, and the other Gees played with some savoir faire and imagination, these goons brought a sort of mundane belligerence to the rink. Not to mention that I had to be very careful not to show up this monstrous dago-mick mix. I mean that Jack Crosby might have been a big talker, but Poochy Ponserelli exacted an awful price for any goal that got by him.

I hung back, like usual against these guys, concentrating on defense. Every now and then, Crosby would skate by and bump me and call me a faggot, but it was still nice to be out on the ice, even if I had to contain my game. That's when I saw Marie. She had walked down to skate with Billy Fontanelli's sister, Peggy, and they were twirling around on a section of ice separated by the rink's cleared snow. She saw me and waved and smiled. I waved my hockey stick. Marie and Peggy skated over to the low wall of snow, and she said something to me. I was straining to hear when Crosby slid by and elbowed me in the back of the head. I fell forward, more embarrassed that Marie had seen me pushed around than I was hurt. I popped back and went for the puck. I easily took it from Mr. Crosby and flew into a full rush from one end of the rink to the other. As I closed in on Poochy Ponserelli in the net, I could hear him threatening me.

"You better not! You better not!"

When I think back, I can understand Ponserelli's rage at being scored upon, not once but twice by the Pillsbury Doughboy in corduroys, yet I have to think his breaking my stick on my head and quitting a slight overreaction on his part.

I was rubbing my head and trying not to cry. Marie picked up the two pieces of my Gordie Howe–autographed scoop-molded stick and brought them over to me.

"That guy looked really stupid beating you up and everything," Marie said.

I didn't say anything, because I was trying hard not to cry.

She handed the two pieces of hockey stick to me. "But you played great."

I smiled, or I tried to. A knot was coming in fat on the top of my already formidable head.

Marie scooped up some snow and held it to my noggin. "C'mon," she said.

I followed her away from the pond and into the field next to Kent Heights School and across from St. Martha's Church. I realized that Marie was walking me home.

"Keep holding that snow on the bump, Riley."

Under the shadow of the East Providence water tower she stopped and made a snow angel. It wasn't show-offy or anything. It was as if she absolutely had to because the snow was untouched. There weren't even footprints anywhere. I watched her, and then I got down and made one, too. When we stood up and looked at them, hers was exactly like a butterfly, which is the way snow angels are supposed to be. Mine was a sort of snow moth. One of those round ones that are always banging into the kitchen windows to be near the light.

Now, you may think these are unimportant details of this disturbing day, but I feel that the mystery here is confronted by somehow gathering as many components as I can remember and arranging them in a kind of order. A relationship to one another. A semblance of something. Because she was standing on my left, as I say, admiring our handiwork, when the bullet struck her just above her left shoulder blade and drove her headfirst onto my angel.

2

I had taped Cubby's letter onto the small mirror over my dressing table and reread it as I pulled up my black tights. I've never gotten used to tights, to be honest with you. They always bind at the toes no matter what size they are and catch almost every leg hair on the way to your crotch. I pulled a maroon tunic off its hanger and slipped it over my head. Then I put on the black combat boots.

Marie would have been . . . what . . . fifty-two? A year older than me. I think she was eighteen the last time I saw her and already engaged to be married. I was still spending a lot of time with Cubby and the guys then. I had joined the army the day after high-school graduation on a program where you wouldn't have to go for three months and you'd still get a stipend. I thought I had outsmarted them, but, like everybody else I knew, I got outsmarted. By the time I got back home from Vietnam, I only had two months left on my enlistment, and they really didn't know what to do with an already used infantryman with no reliable skills and a piss-poor attitude. So they assigned me to Special Services. Special Services at Fort Lee in Petersburg, Virginia, was a loose configuration of sports activities, canteens, general entertainment, and a community theater.

It was to this strange, dark little theater that I was specifically assigned as a kind of ill-defined, unskilled laborer.

The people who ran it and the civilians who constituted the Fort Lee Community Players were generally the kind of eccentric outsiders that give pause to others in the regularly conducted order of life. To be drawn into a world of quasi-creation, where the constant is an overwhelming desire to pretend, isn't for the practical person and almost certainly not for an East Providence mick who would have been content just to ogle them like everyone else. But the local acting legend playing the Common Man in *A Man for All Seasons* had wrenched his back at the car wash he owned and operated, and I was the right size for his costume.

There were several—more than several, really—lovely southern young women volunteers who exulted in various theatrical disciplines. At any given time, they might be found sewing costumes, building sets, acting, directing, and generally filling a portion of their day with the feeling of artistic interplay. I'm cynical now, of course, but I remember those girls and their hopeful, noble purpose. It seems so odd to me to think that for a while I also came to share that hopefulness, that inner thrill that the plays we made had an affirming influence on our audience. And while I no longer linger over the nuances of Molière or Williams and have become discomfited by the whole procedure of acting, I do recall the contagion spawned in that dark theater and how it infected me and sent me out into the world looking for a remedy. Now my stage manager, Jeff Cornish, stuck his fat head inside the curtain that separated my dressing area from the performance space.

"Nobody's here," he whispered.

I looked up at Cubby's letter for some reason, then swung my look to Jeff. He was a nice, hardworking kid. Pasty-looking, with a damp sag of brown hair on his head. His jowls flabbed when he spoke.

"Nobody's here," he repeated in his exaggerated whisper.

I continued to stare at him, my mind at least half on Cubby's letter.

"I called Robert at his home, and he thinks we should perform anyway. Or you should perform anyway, but it's up to you."

"Why are you whispering?" I said.

"What?"

"If there's nobody in the audience, why are you whispering?"

Jeff didn't answer and waited for my decision. I turned toward the mirror and sighed. My little mind is like a bog these days. Sometimes I swear I can hear sloshing up there. Nothing is easy. Nothing is clear. Like most actors my age, I have an absolutely infinite capacity to feel sorry for myself. I reexamine details over and over and become more and more confused. After my discharge I followed one of those southern girls, the startling Beth Stein, to New York, having allowed the Fort Lee Community Players to convince me of some deeply hidden artistic gift. Beth was a sophomore at the University of Richmond, and we had been talking about going to New York since we costarred in the Players' Readers' Theater presentation of a local playwright's adaptation of *Atlas Shrugged*.

We took a fifth-floor walk-up on East Eighty-ninth Street and Second Avenue. In order to make rent and pay for acting lessons, Beth got a part-time sales job at Gimbel's, and I was the night bartender at Lambs, a few blocks down from our place. It's what you do, I suppose. You work and study and keep hopeful.

Six weeks after we arrived, Beth moved out of the apartment and moved in with Thom Satter. Thom was an extraordinarily handsome actor who had wowed them in his New York debut at the twenty-two-seat Societal Theater. The play was called *Hedder-off*, and the conceit here was that Hedda Gabler didn't really shoot herself offstage but was actually murdered by John Gabriel Borkman, who had been lurking in the shadows and was in reality the lover of Judge Brack. The *Post* gave it a polite dismissal, the *Village*

Voice essentially thought the rich bitch deserved it, and the *New York Times*, the one that counted, waxed poetic at the decision to play Borkman nude for the entire three hours and twenty-five minutes. Beth apparently agreed.

"I hear something, I think," Jeff whispered, and darted heavily out of my dressing room.

I heard that Beth returned to Petersburg a few years later, and she and Thom Satter married and opened a bakery. I hope it's true. I hope they're happy and maybe even doing a play at the Fort Lee Community Players every now and then. It's funny Beth should be popping into my head, but then heavy-duty nostalgia is another trait of the mature and borderline actor.

I married Fiona Donnelly in 1976. She was just over from Ireland, and we had met during Lincoln Center's revival of *Juno and the Paycock*. She had a small role, and I was standing by for a couple of actors. My mother loved her beautiful accent and her long auburn hair, and, really, I would say she resembled a very young Maureen O'Hara. I kept my night job, and we happily moved her stuff into the walk-up. We got a divorce in 1978, and she moved back to Ireland. I hope she's happy, too.

Jeff popped his big mug back through the curtain. "People are here," he whispered. "We'll go on in five minutes."

"How many people?"

Jeff hesitated.

"Five?" I asked.

He shook his head.

"Four?" I asked.

"There's two. We start in five minutes."

In 1643 a German by the name of Horst Gurnst discovered an ancient town on his small farm. He excavated it by hand and then displayed it for his neighbors. It was really an ancient Roman fort, but he called it a town because that seemed more romantic. Horst sort of went insane over his town. He stopped sleeping in his house and would sleep in different locations around the dig site. He started to talk to things that weren't there. He even stopped letting people in to see it, because he said the people in his town were tired. One day his neighbors hacked his head off and looted the town. They were Germans, too.

When I first read this play based on the Horst Gurnst legend, I thought it had great potential. I felt that the story of Horst gave itself over easily to the iambic pentameter that the playwright had selected to drive the action. I also liked that it was a one-man show and that, besides Horst, the actor chosen for the role would create seventy-one additional characters over the piece's two hours and thirty-seven minutes.

"Places," Jeff whispered.

I sighed and looked at my weary face. A Vandyke beard and some head hair. Not much, some. Light brown, thanks to Clairol for Men. Here's another thing: Actors spend an awful lot of precious time sizing themselves up. Identifying small but distinguishable quirks that set them apart from the crowd. These days I simply stare at the mirror to justify my confusion.

I got to my feet, attempted to touch my toes, did three pathetic leg bends, and took some deeps breaths. With any luck the show would be over by ten forty-five and I'd be behind the bar at Lambs for the midnight-to-four deal.

3

By the time my fat head could begin to process what I'd just seen happen to Marie D'Agostino, before I could even close my gaping mouth, she was back on her feet and running screaming toward Pawtucket Avenue, swatting at the back of her bloody coat. She crossed Pawtucket in full, wild stride, narrowly missing being pancaked by a cement mixer. I looked both ways and followed her as fast as I possibly could, which was not very fast. She was through the front door before I even got to the hedge. I ran through the hedges and into the house.

Her mother was removing her coat, and Big Tony was dialing the phone. Marie was shaking her hands and scream-crying. The house was filled with it.

"What happened? What happened?" her mother cried.

"Bozo!" Big Tony said, waving his hand at me. I ran over. He was about to say something when someone came on the line.

"Yes, this is Tony D'Agostino. 1114 Pawtucket Avenue. Our daughter's hurt. We need some help. . . . Yes. . . . 1114 Pawtucket Avenue." Big Tony put the receiver down. "What the hell happened to my daughter?"

"I don't know, Big Tony."

Mrs. D'Agostino had Marie's blouse and T-shirt off.

"Tony," she said, signaling to him and pointing silently so as not to alarm her daughter. "I think it's a bullet."

Mrs. D'Agostino patted a warm, soapy cloth around the small hole while Big Tony got on the horn to the police.

The police cruiser and the East Providence Fire Department rescue truck showed up together about five minutes later. It seemed like an hour, what with Marie's crying, her mom's cooing, and Big Tony's gnashing teeth. The medics went directly to Marie and laid her facedown on a gurney. The two cops came over to Big Tony. I knew them both. They were out in front of school every morning and were there when we crossed the street after being dismissed. They were big guys, and they knew most of the kids' names. Officer Kenny Snowden was a tall black man, very serious, never smiled. Officer Carl Rocha was older and always had a smile on his face.

"What the hell happened, Big Tony?" Officer Snowden asked.

"Well, Jesus, Kenny, me and Anita are talking, and in run the kids, and Marie's all bloody. Anita thinks she got shot."

"Shot?" said a stunned Officer Rocha.

Kenny Snowden walked back and whispered something to one of the medics.

"Looks possible," the medic said.

"Where was she?" asked Carl.

"Where were you, Bozo?"

"We were in the field across from St. Martha's, Big Tony. We had just made snow angels."

The medics raised the gurney.

"We're taking her to Rhode Island Hospital emergency."

"I'm coming," said Marie's mom, still cooing into her prone daughter's ear.

"Me, too," said Big Tony. "Bozo, find Cubby and tell him where we are."

"Okay, Big Tony."

I followed them out of the house onto the porch and stood between the policemen. We watched them load Marie and her parents, and then they were gone in a flash of red lights.

"Where in the field were you?" Carl Rocha asked.

"About the middle."

"What did you see?"

"Did you see anybody with a gun?" Kenny asked.

"Uh-uh," I said, shaking my eleven-year-old pumpkin head.

Later on, though, as my odd brain sorted and re-sorted through the minutiae of those minutes and seconds we spent in that snowy field, it struck me that we might not have been alone, and a blurry vision of something or *someone* coming hard and fast off the water tower gave me a lot of sleepless nights.

4

The Horst Gurnst piece is a two-act play designed roughly like this: In the first act, he discovers his town and loses his head; in the second act, he performs the monologues headless in a kind of ghostly reverie. I would accomplish this by means of some thin black gauze that blended perfectly with my tunic, which was yanked up over my ears. I was Velcroing the top closed when Jeff popped his big face back into my dressing corner.

"I think they're gone," he whispered.

"Who?" I said, headless.

"Those two older people. That couple. The audience. They went out for a cigarette at intermission, but they took their coats."

"Why are you whispering?"

Jeff ignored me. "Do you want to finish anyway? I was going to call Robert and ask him."

I pulled the tunic over my head and tugged down the tights.

"You don't want to finish?" Jeff whispered.

I rinsed my face and put on blue slacks and a blue knit shirt with "Lambs" across the chest pocket. Jeff waited. I put on some sneaks.

"Jono?" he whispered. "Should I tell Robert that we did the first act and not the second act?"

I put both hands on the kid's soft shoulders. I sighed, closed my eyes and opened them.

"Jeff, Peter Brook says that theater is like a communion between the audience and the actor. There's no audience. The audience has opted out of communion."

"Dario Fo says that the audience is a nuisance," he replied sincerely.

I took my hands off his shoulders and stepped back. "Mamet describes what happens between the actor and the audience in religious terms and essential for the experience of theater."

"Samuel Beckett said the audience was a distraction."

"Eric Bentley says without an audience it's just rehearsal."

"Molière hated to open his plays to the public. He said—"

"Stop. I'm not doing the piece. The play. The second fucking act. I am going bartending."

I grabbed my peacoat and slid past Jeff. He was right. There was no audience. Jono Riley had struck again.

"Don't forget, tomorrow's the last performance. Robert's coming to talk to you at half hour, and there's a cast party afterward," Jeff whispered loudly.

I turned back to Jeff. "I'm the cast."

"There's a party for you," he whispered.

I nodded and smiled at him, because, as I said, he was a good kid.

The space the play occupied was in the basement of a warehouse on Greene Street. I took the BMT up to Fifty-ninth and picked up the Lexington to Seventy-seventh. It was a nice winter night. Crisp but not terribly wet, so I hoofed it over to Lambs, where I had held down the fort, off and on, for almost thirty years. I say off and on because at one time or another I've actually fooled them enough to get some semiregular acting employment. Three road shows of Broadway musicals (I don't sing), two television series (I still get recognized for my continuing role as the autistic hospital orderly in *Blues and Whites*), and a seven-month gig as Benjamin Hubbard in the Carnival Cruise production of *The Little Foxes*. There's also been the occasional on-camera commercial or cartoon voice (I was Sandy, the left testicle, in MTV's maiden journey into animation, a half hour called *Chronic Conditions*). And I have performed in more than my share of live industrial shows, too, once landing the coveted role of Brian the Test Dummy for Ford's Las Vegas Safety Convention. But it is the living theater, the communal space, as I tried to explain to young Jeff, that has been the focal point of my alleged career, so I must be profoundly unbalanced. Whenever I'm asked what I do and I have relaxed my guard enough to say that I'm an actor, I'm usually met with such sympathetic head wagging that these days I say I'm a bartender. And I am. And I like it fine.

In 1987 Andrea Rosenthal moved into my little walk-up. Like Beth and Fiona, she was following the theater muse, but unlike my first two roommates Andie also brought a practical side to the garret. She was a producer/director whose plan it was to segue into film and television production as soon as possible. I admired this shrewd commercial bent. It seemed exotic to me that someone actually thought of making money in the game. We had met on a New Jersey local cable commercial shoot for Gonsalves Fish Market in Newark's Ironbound District. Andrea was assistant to the director. I was Carlos the fishmonger. I suppose when two people collide under such glamorous conditions, sparks are bound to fly. There's a kind of professional artistic connection that people who are not in the performing arts simply can't understand. A simpatico of spirit, if you will. A profound commitment that only those on the outside of everyday life can fully appreciate.

Andrea moved out six days later and moved to Los Angeles, where she became an incredibly successful producer/director. Her production company owns seven current television hits, and last year she was nominated the third time for an Oscar as Best Director.

I've been thinking of these women lately. The letter from Cubby about Marie's passing probably heightened this nostalgia, but the truth is, I've been in a period of reexamination for a while now. As if by the technique of recall I can make sense of myself. This is why I say I have an intimate relationship with self. Self-pity. Self-centeredness, and, of course, self-absorption. Actors. Wow.

I shake my head and cross Second Avenue at Eighty-fifth Street. Godfrey Kuroff, the night manager, is smoking under the Lambs awning.

He waves his smoke at me. "You're early. How was the show?"

Godfrey is another nice kid. A short, round, black guy about thirty-five, with the mug of a teenager and a Russian surname. He could smoke at the bar, but his elegant, fussy nature won't allow him to.

"Boffo," I said.

He nodded and offered me a drag of his cigarette. I was trying to stop, so I only had a short one. I'm a guy who keeps himself okay. Six feet and a fraction, 192, arthritic knees that I have to ice occasionally. I don't drink regularly, as I tend to get drunk and whiny when I do. A little grass if somebody is offering. My head is still big and square, but it nearly fits me now. I mean, the thing doesn't startle people like it used to when it sat on my eleven-year-old shoulders. I handed the smoke back to Godfrey and went inside.

Lambs is a long, wide floor-through. The heavy mahogany bar that runs the length of the front room had been brought over from a pub in London's Chelsea district when Lambs first opened in 1931. The dining section in back can seat seventy, and because Bob Riley (no relation) is a third-generation owner and offers pretty good food at pretty reasonable prices, it's usually filled up from about five-thirty to ten. My bar, of course, is six deep with young up-and-comers well past midnight.

I slid behind the bar and pulled a waist apron out of the small closet.

"You're early," Sheila Cimino said, squeezing past me for a bottle of house vodka.

She was one of three bartenders on this shift. I hired them, like I do the waitstaff for the front room. I go for speed and efficiency in a waitstaff, bullshit and efficiency in a tender. I'm pretty good at sizing them up.

"I'm a glutton for punishment. Also, I'm not officially on, so be sweet to me and I won't grab your tips. Ask Walt to bring me a tuna sandwich."

I pulled some beers, mixed a Tom Collins, and blended a frozen margarita. Getting the orders over the reverberation of the front room requires a great deal of concentration. I've become a passable lip-reader. I pulled two more McSorley's, and the sandwich was here. I squirted a glassful of club soda and took it to the end of the bar, where Randall Pound spilled over his usual stool.

"Hey, Jono," he said quietly.

Randall put a dog-eared paperback down on the bar and sipped an espresso. It's amazing to see the tiny cup on the edge of his fingers. Randall Pound is a shade over seven feet tall and proudly keeps his weight at 390. His neck is surprisingly long for a man of his great size. A contemplative, almost aesthetic Slavic face sits on top of it, with huge green eyes, long proportional nose, and thick shiny black hair combed tight into a short ponytail. At thirty he carries an agelessness about him. Seven years ago Lambs entered into a frustrating period where bar fights and loud, aggressive customers were becoming a nightly occurrence. After I tried to break up one fight, both the combatants turned on me. The next day, nose flattened, both eyes black, and reeling from a mild concussion, I ran an ad for a bouncer in the *Village Voice*. A lot of impressive men turned up (and one woman with a black belt in karate). But it was the quiet, dapper Randall Pound who won the job. The interview went like this:

"I'm Jono Riley."

"I'm Randall Pound."

"If guys start getting out of line or fighting, what would you do?"

"They won't."

"They won't what?"

"They won't get out of line or start fighting."

He always wears a tailored sharkskin suit. He owns seven of them. All metallic blue. He sits on the corner stool like he has every evening, without fail, for the last seven years. At the first sign of a problem, a waitress or a bartender will whisper to the offender and point down to Randall, who will slowly wave and smile. He was right. No one gets out of line. No one fights.

"You're early."

"We only did the first act," I said. Then I added, "Audience walked out."

Randall nodded thoughtfully. "I enjoyed it, Jono. I thought you rose above the limited material."

"Thanks."

"Theater, the printed word, language in the general sense has entered into a decline," he said quietly. "I attended a seminar at Columbia just last week where Bill Gates's futurist talked about the inevitability of fine and performing arts being marginalized." He held up the paperback. It was a copy of *Babbitt* by Sinclair Lewis. "Tell that to Lewis. Tell it to Hem or Billy Faulkner," he said.

"Is that the last one?" I asked through a mouthful of tuna.

Randall is a true eccentric. His life plan, as he has explained it to me, is to experience as many varied occupations as possible while devouring the whole of American literature.

"*Our Mr. Wrenn* is the last of Sinclair's canon," he said. "It was his first book. It's going to be the last one I read to complete it. After *Babbitt*, that is."

Randall's ten-to-four shift at Lambs is the only constant in an inventive and eclectic career that has included truck driving, construction working, hot-dog vending, supermarket stocking, bank telling, box-office managing, flower arranging, copywriting, street sweeping, census taking, and I forget what-all, but it's still only the tip of the iceberg.

"How come you never tried acting?" I asked.

He looked at me, concentrated and serious. "Because I'm an odd person doesn't mean I'm mentally challenged."

I nodded, took some fries and soda. He took a delicate sip of the espresso. I must have been wrinkling my eyebrows or something.

"What?" he asked.

"What, what?"

"You're pensive. Something's bothering you, all right."

"Uh-uh." I chewed.

"Look, it's reasonable to feel uneasy. You have chosen a dangerous profession. Peter Brook rather darkly ruminates about the deadly theater in *The Empty Space*."

"You read that?"

"I found it unsettling. I thought about you. It made me sad."

I held up my hand while I finished a bite. "Randall, I like it. It pisses me off a lot, but mostly I like it. Actually, there's something else on my mind."

I gave him a brief rundown of Cubby's letter and some background. When I finished, Randall sighed thoughtfully.

"O'Casey says it correctly," he said. " 'The world is in a terrible state of chassis.' "

5

My mother and Pop drove over to the hospital that afternoon. Me and Cubby sat in the back. Big Tony was having a smoke in the waiting room. He spoke the second he saw us.

"She's going to be okay. The wife is in with her."

Mother gave Big Tony a hug, and Pop lit up a smoke of his own to keep him company. Mother was the one who drew all the conclusions in our little family. She had an outgoing quality that everybody seemed to find comfortable. Pop foremanned a crew of tough guys who unloaded oil tankers on the docks of Socony-Mobil where the Providence River met the Narragansett Bay. He was quiet and shy except when he was running his men.

"Jono said that maybe somebody . . . shot Marie," my mother said quietly.

"Right here," Big Tony said, pointing awkwardly at the area of his shoulder blade. "She's twelve years old, for crying out loud."

Pop shook his head sadly.

"Cops find anything, Bozo?" Big Tony asked me.

"I don't think so, Big Tony. Officer Snowden looked around the field and stuff."

Just then Kenny Snowden, in civilian clothes, stepped out of the elevator. He nodded to Mother and Cubby and me. Shook hands with Pop and Big Tony.

"How is she? We called, and they told Dispatch it wasn't life-threatening."

"She's gonna be okay. She was shot, Kenny. Right here. Back. She's twelve years old, for crying out loud."

Big Tony, Pop, and Kenny Snowden all looked at the floor and shook their heads.

Mrs. D'Agostino came out of a room with a young doctor. Mother went over and hugged her. She'd been crying—you could tell by how sore her eyes looked—and when Mother hugged her, she started again. The doctor stepped over to Big Tony, who pointed to Kenny and Pop.

"Doctor, this is my neighbor and Kenny Snowden. Kenny's a cop. This is the doctor."

The doctor shook hands and turned back to Big Tony. He spoke loud enough for Pop and Kenny to hear.

"Well, we do indeed see a bullet lodged above the scapula quite close to the subclavian artery. Judging from the X-rays, it's a .22, for what it's worth. Marie isn't in any danger as far as I can tell, but I don't want to try to remove it today. I'd like to consult in the morning with a surgeon or two. No sense rushing anything. She's not in discomfort. I'm going to admit her tonight, and we'll play it by ear."

The doctor nodded at the men and padded away.

Big Tony headed to the examining room, and everybody followed. Inside the room were four examining areas separated by blue curtains. A single nurse sat at a small table by the door. She rose when we entered. She started to say something, but Big Tony directed his thumb at Kenny.

"He's a cop."

We followed Big Tony to one of the areas and walked through the curtains. Marie's long, thin body lay out belly-down, her head propped up on pillows. A double sheet covered her rear end. A reddish black stain leaked out from the large gauze bandage taped to her back.

Mrs. D'Agostino pointed to it. "It's not blood or anything. They just threw lots and lots of some kind of germ killer on her back."

Mother nodded, and then all of us nodded. Me and Cubby moved up close to her head. Marie smiled, and we did, too.

"I got shot," she whispered, still smiling a goofy smile.

"A .22," Big Tony said from behind us. Then he added, "She's twelve years old, for crying out loud."

"Who shot me, Jono?"

I shrugged.

"Do you think it was about the hockey game?"

"What hockey game?" Kenny Snowden asked.

"Jono scored a whole lot of goals."

"Two," I mumbled.

"And guys were mad?" Kenny pushed.

"I don't—"

Marie raised her beautiful head higher. "One of those high-school kids broke his stick over Jono's head."

"Which one?" my pop asked quietly. Not good.

"I . . . I play . . . You know, I'm pretty good and . . . and some-times the big guys let me play, and usually I don't try too hard, but today I . . . did."

I went out in the hall with Kenny Snowden, and he wrote down Poochy Ponserelli's and Jack Crosby's names. I told him I didn't think they would ever do anything like that. Kenny closed his pad.

"Ponserelli and Crosby. They're with that dago-mick crowd from the Riverside Terrace, aren't they?"

I nodded.

Kenny Snowden hit the elevator button.

31

6

It was three-thirty in the morning, and Randall Pound had left his barstool for the first time, stopping to chat at one of the tables on his way to the men's room. The long bar had thinned to two tired older guys nursing watery drinks. I was washing glasses when George Myer, the other night barman, waved the phone at me.

"Renée," he announced.

I dried my hands and picked up the extension. "Hey," I said.

"Hey."

One of the two customers at the bar got up and started out.

"Thank you," I said to him.

"Good night," he said.

"What's up?" I said into the phone.

"Are you coming over here or am I going over to your place? I forgot."

"What do you want to do?"

"Whatever you want to do."

"I'm pretty close to my apartment."

"It's convenient, all right."

"But it's not convenient for you," I said.

"Okay, so you come down here."

"You're not tired?" I asked.

"Are you?"

"No," I lied.

Renée Levesque once explained to me that everyone has been given two distinct lives that are going on side by side. One life is the screwup life, and one is the life that fixes screwups. I personally think, as philosophies go, it's a touch wacky, but it works for Renée.

Her screwup life flattened her with a divorce at twenty-five and a major-league addiction to alcohol. Several hellish years later, she sloshed her sorry ass (her words) to a church basement on the Upper West Side and threw herself into AA with gusto. She didn't miss a meeting for one hundred straight days. She wrote short, tight letters to everyone she knew and apologized to them all and asked their forgiveness. Then she forgave herself.

Renée Levesque wouldn't mind me telling you this—in fact, she told it to me the first time I met her four years ago. I was in another one-hander (a one-character play) entitled *My Own Personal Nagasaki* at the Performing Monkees Ensemble on West Eleventh. On the night she saw the play, she was the only audience member. I portrayed the misunderstood nuclear reaction, and again, as with the Horst Gurnst piece, I came into the project with enthusiasm for my portrayal of detonation and extermination. However, as rehearsals progressed, I began to see the play and my subsequent work in it for what they truly were. Shit. Three hours, six minutes of it. It's actually a little painful for me to recall those few Nagasaki months. I won't describe my costume, except to say that Reynolds aluminum foil ain't just for freezing chicken. The salary was nonexistent, and the Performing Monkees' space on West Eleventh was not up to the sanitary standards of that other monkey ensemble in the Bronx Zoo.

Then there was the question-and-answer after each performance. I was humiliated to stand out there, crinkly in foil, responding to things I knew nothing about and, really, had no interest in knowing about. But the truth is, inventive and phony little schemes are what drive the not-for-profit arts industry and push the government and corporate sponsors to ante up. So I would play Q&A and shudder each time.

ME
Yes, sir, you had your hand up?

EIGHTY-YEAR-OLD PROFESSOR EMERITUS TYPE WITH PATCHES ON HIS ELBOWS
Now . . . correct me if I am off beam here . . . but . . . the predisposition toward cataclysmic annihilation as suggested by your rather nifty turn into the nuclear winter . . . leads me to assume a certain atomic narcissism . . . a certain organic cosmopolitanism on the part of your chain reaction.

ME
Right.

The evening Renée attended, I couldn't see her in the shadings of the back row, and I was convinced that the stage manager was lying about someone being in the audience so I would act the damn play. Ninety minutes into the performance, I stopped in the middle of the Chain Reaction's monologue concerning platonic love at twenty thousand degrees Fahrenheit and began to peel off several layers of foil.

"Nobody's here. This is bullshit," I said off to the stage manager.

"I'm here," Renée said from the back of the theater.

I looked in the direction of her voice.

"Oh," I said quietly.

"But it *is* bullshit."

I actually started to replace the foil.

"I've really seen enough," she said.

"Everybody's a critic."

I still couldn't see her, but her voice sounded pretty good.

"Want to get a drink?" I asked.

"I'm an alcoholic."

"Uh . . . coffee?"

"Okay."

That was four years ago. I was forty-seven, and Renée was forty, or about to be in a month. She's medium height, with a slender and powerful body. Her oval face frames deep green eyes and goes perfectly with brown-blond hair worn long and often pulled into a ponytail. Oddly enough on that first evening, she reminded me of Marie's mother, who was short and dark but also very beautiful.

I waved good night to Godfrey and walked into the early morning with Randall. He'd just taken an apartment on West Eighty-fifth.

"I'm taking the Eighty-sixth bus to the West Side. I'll walk up Second with you," he said.

"I'm not going home."

"Say hi to Renée for me."

"Good night, Randall."

I watched him head uptown, hands in his black overcoat, head down in contemplation. I've seen him for years and never gotten used to him. He is as amazing and startling as he was the first time I laid eyes on him.

I treated myself to a cab into Chelsea. Renée lived in an Art Deco building on West Twenty-first. I used my key and rode the elevator to the sixth floor. When I walked in, she waved from the kitchen counter. She was watching CNN and eating some cold puttanesca. I gave her a little kiss on the head.

"How was work?" I asked.

"I'm trying to get Collins to drop about fifty pounds," she said between chews. "He's gonna go down hard. I'm worried about him."

"I thought you said he was a prick."

"He is. But he's a prick with a nice wife and two little girls. He told me tonight he's thirty-six. I honest to God thought the slob was forty-six."

Renée probably has good reasons to be concerned about her coworkers. She's a fireman with Engine Company 14 on East Eighteenth Street. She's been at it for eighteen years, and I would like her to pack it in, because, like every wimpy actor, I'm wary of real professions, and it doesn't get any realer than New York City firefighting. Usually our schedules don't run so parallel, but Renée has been on a shift that ends at 3:00 A.M. for the past couple of weeks.

I sat on the stool next to her, and she linked her left arm into mine and twirled the pasta with her free hand.

"Want a bowl?" she asked.

"I'm stuffed."

She shut off the TV with the remote. "How was the play?"

"Unbelievable."

"Many in the audience?"

"Two, but not to worry. I drove them out by intermission."

Renée chewed and shook her wonderful head. "You are such a great actor. You are really so wonderful as Horst."

When I'm tired, I try not to think about my alleged profession, so I didn't say anything. I just smiled.

"You think I say you're a great actor because I love you, don't you?" she said.

I kept smiling. She kept talking.

"My judgment may be clouded a little by that, I admit. Take this new fireman in the company. Big. Body by New York Health and

Racquet Club. Young—can't be more than twenty-three, twenty-four—and very nice. A very nice young man. Now, even though I think he's nice doesn't mean I can't see that he clearly is not cut out for the FDNY. He's not quick. He's not . . . what? Committed. Follow?"

"Finish your food. I'm tired."

Every now and then, when she's standing naked in front of the full-length mirror in the bedroom, I catch her in some personal, quiet evaluation. There's a raised scar running from the middle of her shoulder blades down to where her ass begins to mound. Her right ankle has surgical scars from when she, and the floor she was standing on, fell to the flaming floor below, snapping the ankle apart. To me these are like that chip Michelangelo hacked off the *David's* heel because he believed that only God could create perfection. Her shoulders are squared but narrow, and her arms and legs seem longer than she should possess, but they fit wonderfully onto a muscular torso. Her neck is long also. I call her my girl, but it's a woman's body, all right, and her soft oval face is a woman's, too. There are laugh lines and pain lines. Renée Levesque isn't hiding a thing. She probably looks her age, although I couldn't tell you that, because she's the only thing I am completely sentimental over. I love this woman shamelessly and appreciate the life she carries on her valiant face and in those fierce green eyes.

Renée made an easier turn into this relationship of ours than I did. Maybe "easier" isn't the word; maybe "braver" is. To me love is a complex deal, especially when you're not young and not trying to recapture something lost. That would be easy, I suppose, transferring that strange sensation from one person to another in a simple lurch for comfort and understanding. But what happens when a fifty-one-year-old guy who has successfully existed on the surface of things is suddenly confronted with a deep-diving sympathy? A fervor of need that is inexplicable? I'll tell you what happens. That

38

guy becomes the world's oldest teenager, contending with the exact same emotions and insecurities that turn younger, stronger kids into blithering idiots. I lost all sense of direction and was consumed with another new emotion previously unknown to me. I became jealous, even disoriented over the *past* of all things. How was it that this woman had lived a life without me? Why did fate or fortune or whatever let her marry someone twenty years before we met? Yes. I know. I was married, too. I had history of my own coming out my ass, but that was all part of the mystery. How did I become so dumb so quickly? It had to be Renée's fault, so I did what any fifty-one-year-old, half-baked actor would do—I sulked and squirmed and told her I didn't think we could possibly work this out. I said this even though I knew if we *didn't* work it out, I'd disintegrate.

"I just want us to be happy," she'd say sadly.

One Saturday we rented a car and drove up to an inn in Connecticut that Renée had read about. It was a beautiful sunny spring day. We walked some of the trails behind the inn, had a wonderful dinner in the cozy dining room, and retired to our suite. I got a fire going in the fireplace, and we sipped pretty good wine, compliments of the owner. Everything was perfect. There was a true sensation that all things might be right with the world of Jono Riley and the magnificent Renée Levesque. All the signs pointed to me being the luckiest two-bit actor who ever lived. I'm not sure what other men would do with all this positive karma, but I picked a fight, making a neat segue from the swell day into how I was sure Renée had had other swell days before she met me, and maybe they were sweller even. Yeah! You go, boy!

She became quiet. "Quiet" is not the right word. She became *still*. She was a statue, with only her eyes following the ranting idiot whose marginal self-esteem was dripping onto the floor with every word. When I stopped for breath, she began a low, dangerous synopsis of Renée Levesque. All of her sorrows and her joys and her disappointments and her relationships ran out of her mouth like a sigh. When she was finished, I couldn't move.

"I never think about it," she said, with the same small, almost disembodied voice. "It's just there. It's just my chronicle."

She looked up at me as if she just noticed me eavesdropping. She had caught this fool red-handed.

"Your turn," she said.

So that is how Renée Levesque saved Jono Riley. And us. And the world.

Renée ate a last bite, put the bowl in the sink, and took my hand. We walked into the bedroom, undressed, and climbed under the cool sheets. She snuggled up to me.

"Did you do any thinking about it?" she whispered.

"It" had to do with moving in together. I'm squirrelly about "it." Change and things.

"I've been distracted. A friend of mine died. I got a letter from her brother today."

I reached over her and pulled Cubby's letter out of my pants. She read it.

"That's so sad," Renée said.

We were quiet for a minute or so. I rubbed her back with my fingers. I told her about Marie and that day after the hockey game.

"She never had the bullet taken out?"

"I don't know. I saw her maybe once or twice after I got out of the army and was visiting with my mother. She already had a kid by then."

We were quiet again. I knew she was thinking. Renée Levesque is easily the most intuitive person I've ever known. She's not just smart, she has this nearly mystical insight into things. She rolled onto her back, and we both stared up at the ceiling.

"Are you going to Rhode Island?" she asked.

"I thought I might go up after the last performance tomorrow night. Just to see Cubby and his mom."

She snuggled back. "I'll meet you at the theater."

"You don't have to do that."

"I want to."

"What about your shift?"

"I already asked the captain if I could sneak out."

She snuggled deeper.

"You really don't have to come," I yawned.

"I know," she yawned.

I slept awhile, and when I woke, it was still dark and Renée hadn't moved. I asked her if she was asleep. I had to ask her five or six times before she woke up and we made love.

7

Marie stayed at Rhode Island Hospital two days while her wound was drained and cleaned. The doctor who admitted her consulted with several surgeons, and they all agreed that the small slug was too close to the subclavian artery and that removing it would not be worth the risk.

Big Tony and Marie's mom brought her home in the early afternoon, and I was at their house with Cubby when they walked in.

"I'm keeping the bullet in my back," she announced before she even took her coat off. "It's too close or something."

She was pale and for some reason seemed taller. Her red corduroy bib overalls were loose, and I noticed that one of her Chuck Taylor sneakers was untied. I thought she looked astoundingly beautiful. My mouth hung open idiotically, and my colossal head bobbed. I held out the bouquet of flowers my mother had sent me over with. Marie took them and looked at me.

After a minute she said in her deep, booming voice, "Why don't you take a picture, Riley?"

Big Tony gave the high sign to Mrs. D'Agostino, and she and Marie started toward the stairs and the bedrooms.

"Doctor said you got to rest up and eat and things," Big Tony said as they walked slowly away. "You be a good girl, okay? I got to get down to Tasca's." He pointed at Cubby and me. "Cubby. Bozo."

"Yeah, Pop?"

"Yeah, Big Tony?"

"You guys put a lid on it for a while. Doctor says she needs some peace and quiet."

"Okay, Pop."

"Okay, Big Tony."

My plan was to be there when Marie came home, then walk down to Kent Pond before all the big kids from high school got there and took it over. I picked up my skates and stick off the porch and felt in my corduroys to make sure I had remembered to bring a puck.

"You coming?" I asked Cubby.

"Nah, I'm gonna see if Ma needs help. I'm gonna watch cartoons."

Cartoons ruled those black-and-white afternoons. We got "Salty" Brine out of Providence and "Big Brother" Bob Emery out of Boston. Both were terrific cartoon hosts. "Big Brother" Bob Emery would begin each afternoon's festivities by telling us what was in store for us, usually an eclectic mix that included Tom and Jerry, Mighty Mouse, and of course Popeye. But before he'd flip on his projector, we would be invited to grab a glass of milk and join "Big Brother" Bob in a toast to President Kennedy. I liked his style, but we all really preferred "Salty" Brine, because his hosting was more direct: "Hi, shipmates. Let's watch a cartoon."

Cubby gave me two Marlboros and a book of matches out of his back pocket and went into his house. I crossed Pawtucket Avenue. When I got to the field in front of the water tower, I cut across it and headed up to where we had made snow angels. It was cold, and even though I was particularly good about cold weather, being a porker and all, I found that I was shivering by the time I got to the spot. Marie's perfect angel was still there; mine, too, although a thin cover of drifting snow had settled on the impressions. I stared at them and thought about how pretty she had looked doing that snowy backstroke. Then I thought of how hard she had been driven down by the push and surprise of the .22. I could see her running. I shuddered and turned back toward the slope leading to Kent Pond. I had walked about ten feet when this odd sensation washed over me that I was being observed. Not just watched, if I had to put it into words, but studied, measured. The mind plays games with itself, I know. My eleven-year-old mind roaming lonely inside that great, cavernous brainpan probably played games, too. I stopped and looked down at the pond, as if by doing that I could shake the creepy feeling of being looked at. It was exactly like a dream where you think you're moving but you're not, and you can't keep up or even fall behind, because your legs won't move.

Officer Kenny Snowden and his partner, Carl Rocha, had done a preliminary investigation of the snow angels and water-tower vicinity right after Marie was taken to the hospital. I know because I walked over with them and pointed out the spot. Later in the afternoon and early the next morning, Kenny and Carl, along with four other officers, met under the water tower, gave it another look-over, and then canvassed every house on the Kent Heights Platt. I remember Kenny telling Big Tony that there weren't even footprints under the tower's ladder.

That night I had the first of my bad dreams of the water tower and of something or someone coming off it. Coming off it fast. Coming off it like a black pirate flag down its pole. I started running back across the field toward Pawtucket Avenue. When I finally stopped and turned, there was nothing there.

8

I played Horst Gurnst for the final time before the largest audience of our sixteen performances. A near sellout of thirty-one assorted friends of the play's writer/director, Robert Allan Achur, and the fantastic Renée Levesque, still in smoky fireman blues, having recently finished fighting a fire in a small Chelsea bodega.

I received nice applause, and when I brought Robert up onto the plywood set, the audience, led by his parents and his lover, Raymond, rose as one to acknowledge his achievement. Robert is a young guy and loves the theater. He's a believer that it can save the world. Also, he's a nice kid, so I was happy to see the accolades. Then everyone was invited to join the cast (me) and crew (Jeff Cornish) for a wrap party. Robert had done the shopping, and the party featured white wine, Brie, and melba rounds.

"Keep your fingers crossed. I have a magical feeling that Horst is going to have an afterlife," Robert said to me, once he'd introduced his father and mother.

"I'll keep them crossed," I sincerely lied.

"Why not Broadway? Why not us?" he said with a joyousness that made you truly want it to happen for Robert, even though you knew "why not."

Renée listened quietly, and when Robert had circulated away, she held my hand. "You were wonderful. You are such a great actor."

I smiled into her green eyes.

"You were. But I don't like it when they cut your head off."

"Renée," I said, "nobody really cuts it off. I'm the only one in the play."

"I mean when you go off at the end of the first act to have your head cut off," she said, and kissed me quick on the lips.

"Do you have to go back to the station tonight?"

"Nope. We can have sex, sex, sex."

I looked down at her. "Well, sex anyway," I said.

A half hour later, I hugged Robert and Jeff, and then Renée and I strolled over to Astor Place and took the Lex uptown to Lambs. I got two coffees, and we went to an alcove behind Randall Pound. He swiveled in his chair, and Renée got tippy-toed to kiss him.

"How was it?" he asked quietly.

"The audience stayed," I said.

"He was great," Renée said in her sort of serious way. "He is such a wonderful actor."

Randall held up his espresso in a silent toast. He sniffed. "You been to a fire?" he asked Renée.

"Yeah, nothing much."

He sniffed again. "You smell like toasted raisin bread."

"Yeah?" she said.

We finished our coffee, and I asked George Myer if he could hold the fort without me for a couple of days. We walked up Third Avenue and over to my place. It's too small, and the bathtub is in the kitchen. The apartment has evolved over the years, going through three distinct renovations.

During Beth Stein of Petersburg's six-week stay, bricks were exposed in the bedroom and a sofa was purchased. Then, while my ex-wife Fiona Donnelly was in residence, a ceiling fan was installed and a removable heavy plywood top was cut and fitted over the bathtub for extra shelf space. Andrea Rosenthal, who endured nearly six complete days as roommate, had painted the bathroom ceiling. That was fourteen years ago and the last serious improvement of my living space. Occasionally I think I've been here too long, actually overstayed it, but the truth is, it's rent-stabilized. It's allowed me to save some money and even to accept those odd little plays in those odd little places that never offer a living wage, and not have to worry about losing my tiny piece of Manhattan.

We walked up, smelling all the good smells of the old building. Germans and Spanish filled the stairwell with the aromas of steaming bratwurst and rice and beans. When I put my key into the lock, I whispered to Renée, "Put the key in, break all the windows."

She grinned, but I could tell she didn't think it was too funny.

"It's a small place, all right," she said.

I didn't say anything. I knew where she'd been going lately.

"I know I've said it a lot, but if I got rid of my place and you got rid of your place, we could get a bigger place. We could get a place anywhere we wanted."

When Renée talks about us moving in together, she becomes like a young girl, hopeful, even wide-eyed. I enjoy seeing her like this, and I'm sorry when she gets the sad look because I don't say anything. She's extraordinarily patient, and even though the subject comes up frequently and I keep my big face flat to it, it doesn't seem to discourage her. It does, though, as I said, make her sad.

Renée knows about my history. How can someone slog it out for fifty-one years and not have crashed and burned or washed up on shore a few times? We both have. But what I haven't been able to verbalize is something I've just recently come to understand myself. When Beth walked out, I felt some serious relief. I was glad for her and even for the guy, because they seemed pretty well

49

matched. I was married to Fiona because I had heard that Irish accent and seen that red hair, and when she told me she chose Ireland over me, I was relieved all over again. I had become used to the voice, the hair. And Andrea? I often have difficulty even recalling Andrea's countenance.

All of which brings me to forty-four-year-old Renée Levesque, FDNY. How do I admit to her that if we scored that perfect apartment and moved in together, and if somewhere down the line she decided I wasn't up to snuff and moved back out of my life, I would not be relieved? That counterfeit actor, that night-shift bartender, wouldn't be able to stand up to it. Would, as sure as I'm standing in my minuscule kitchen, want to lie down and just stop. Marie D'Agostino and my mother aside, Renée Levesque is the only woman I have ever loved. Ever would, my instincts told me. So that's why I'm quiet. It's not the moving in that scares me. It's the moving out.

The next morning I rented a red midsize something from Hertz, dropped Renée at her place, then took the West Side Highway up to U.S. 95. Outside of New Haven, I remembered to call my agents to tell them I'd be gone for a few days. I left a message on my commercial agency's answering machine, then punched out the number for Marvin Weissman, who handles me for theater, TV, and films, or at least I think he still does. He answers on the first ring.

"Marvin Weissman's Theatricals, how may I direct your call?"

"Hi, Marvin. It's Jono Riley."

"Jono. Hang on."

I waited. Marvin was probably walking over to his desk to pick up the phone by the most comfortable chair. It's a tiny office that he used to share with a receptionist/secretary, but she walked out a few weeks ago. Marvin is the most full-of-shit person I know. He's eighty-one years old, and I like him very much. He gets back on.

"Look, I swear to God Almighty I'm gonna get down to that place and see that thing you're doing."

"It's over, Marvin."

"Honest to God?"

"Last night was the last performance."

"So you're available again?"

"I am available."

"I'm writing it down and sliding it over under the clear plastic part of my desk pad. There. Jono Riley available for film, TV. . . . Now, do you need a hiatus from the stage or should we just be discriminating on projects you'd consider?"

"That would be nice."

"I'm writing fast, and now I'm sliding it over."

"I'm going up to Rhode Island for a few days."

"I saw Ginger Rogers do *Annie Get Your Gun* in Rhode Island," he said.

"A friend of mine died, and . . ."

"Had a client playing Sitting Bull. Bullshit part, but a job's a job, am I right?"

"I better get going, Marvin."

"I'm writing you down. Riley: Rhode Island. I'm sliding it over right now."

"Bye, Marvin."

"Break a leg."

9

I spent seventh, eighth, and ninth grades at Central Junior High right on Six Corners and next to Bovi's Tavern. I don't remember an awful lot about this period, because I suppose thirteen, fourteen, and fifteen are lousy ages and because I was traumatized, although I didn't know it at the time.

It was 1964. I had just finished up with Junior Hockey, a Providence league that consisted of eight teams. It was a weekend league, and I took the bus in from East Providence every Saturday morning and Sunday after mass. I had fun in that league, because the players had to be recommended for membership. My old man had recommended me, and because he had been a really good player for East Providence High, they took me. Most of the players understood the game and could skate it. I was very lucky with our coach. Mr. Redmond had been the first black player for the Providence Reds of the American Hockey Association. Now he sold life insurance and coached as a hobby. Some of the other teams had rotten coaches. We shared ice practice time, and sometimes they would scream through the whole two hours. Mr. Redmond never raised his voice at our team, the Little Roosters. If your stick handling was loose or your defensive skating wasn't pinpoint or whatever difficulty you were having with our particularly fast game, he'd skate over and offer that quiet, confident physical example to follow. And with Mr. Redmond everybody played the same minutes. No favorites. He believed in individual skills and team strategy. The Little Roosters won all three years I was on the team, and I can truly say that we would've won even if we had players who weren't as good as we were, thanks to that wonderful coaching and teaching.

Cubby, Marie, and I usually walked the two and a half miles to school. Today was April Fools' Day. Me and Cubby were going to try out for Central Junior High's baseball team. I had my old small Spalding glove and Cubby had his catcher's mitt. Cubby was a great baseball player. He had all the tools of ignorance a catcher needed.

I was growing up in a kind of out-of-control way. Physically, I mean. I was taller and thinner, but my head still seemed, to me at least, as gigantic and out of place on my fourteen-year-old shoulders as on my eleven-year-old ones. I started to measure my head with a tape measure every night before bed and then first thing in the morning, absolutely convinced that by the look of things the old melon was growing out of proportion with everything else.

Anyway, after my last class I went down to the gym with the other kids. Mr. Pisacayne, the seventh-grade algebra teacher and Central Junior High's baseball coach, then walked us all over to Pierce Field for the tryouts. There were a lot of kids, and, to be completely honest, I was not a particularly confident porker off the skates. We broke into groups—infielders, outfielders, pitchers, and catchers.

I had long considered myself a third baseman, not coincidentally because Frank Malzone, the Red Sox third baseman, had a head the size of a Volkswagen, so I split out to the infielders. We did a groundball routine, worked the swivel to second for a double-play drill, and learned the basic bowlegged squat, glove-in-front stance that pretty much ruled Rhode Island ball.

We'd been fielding grounders for a few minutes when I heard Mr. Pisacayne screaming my name. Everybody looked over to me, and I thought I'd been cut, just like that. I assumed that my enormous noggin had so overbalanced my stance that the coaches had decided to end the torture there and then. I jogged over with my pumpkin hanging low. When I looked up, Big Tony was standing with the coach.

"Uh . . . Riley . . . Jono . . . Mr. D'Agostino needs to talk to you."

What is it about Italian men? Is it the eyes? It's always been a mystery to me how they can put into things a meaning that cuts through the complications of a moment and forms a kind of essence that in its simplicity is never forgotten. He walked over and wrapped his fat hands around my head and kissed my forehead. He squeezed me. It seemed like an hour before he pushed me away and held my shoulders at arm's length. His eyes were red.

"We got to go home, Bozo," he said.

I nodded like a stupe. He nodded, too.

"There's a problem at the oil docks."

That's what I remember most completely. That Big Tony was there. And even with me at fourteen and already several inches taller than him, as we walked across Pierce Field to the big Ford wagon, I reached out and held his hand. I knew that whatever had happened at my pop's oil dock was not going to go away.

10

Renée had made reservations for me at the Ramada Inn in Seekonk, Massachusetts. Seekonk is on the Rhode Island border and right next to East Providence. I checked in, stowed my stuff, then drove down to the Wampanoag Trail and took it into my old hometown. There wasn't a plan, really. I figured that I'd tool around a little, get my bearings, drive by some of the landmarks of my childhood before I made contact with Cubby and his mother. I took a left onto Pawtucket Avenue and stayed on it all the way into Riverside Terrace, doing the horseshoe in and out, slowing only when I passed the house that my high-school girlfriend, Sandy Minucci, used to live in. It was strange how small the place seemed compared to my memory of it. The whole Terrace for that matter.

My grandfather and Nana, Pop's folks, lived on Crescent Avenue off Pawtucket, so I detoured and stopped in front of the little square house for a while. I lit a smoke, which I usually don't do until evenings, in honor of my English Oval chain-smoking gramps, then rolled on up to East Providence proper. I stopped again, this time in front of the old entrance to the Socony-Mobil docks, which was gated and overgrown with weeds. I got out of the car and sat back against the hood, remembering some good things and some bad ones. Narragansett Bay glistened in the distance, and I thought about fishing it with the old man or with Cubby and the guys. How we'd catch fiddler crabs with a fish head and use them for bait, for flounder and tautog and even bluefish. I hadn't been back to Rhode Island since Mother's funeral nineteen years ago, but no matter how things change, there are always the constants to hold on to. Narragansett Bay is the East Providence constant. It was there like the air and the seagulls.

I drove to Cardinal Avenue and stopped in front of the house we lived in. New owners had put on a two-story addition by the living-room side. Pop always kept it white with black trim. Now it was kind of aqua. I left the car there and walked up the three blocks to where Cubby and Marie and their folks used to live.

It occurred to me that I probably should have made a few preliminary calls, like to Cubby maybe, to see if his mom was still there, or to at least alert someone that Bozo was on his way, but that's me all over. I rarely think things through. That's why I'm always ending up in projects like the Horst Gurnst play. If I called around, talked it out, chances are I wouldn't always end up kicking my own sorry ass all over the stage. I live, but I rarely learn.

Again, everything seemed smaller. The houses. The gardens behind them. Everything. Where the foundry had been, five small new ranch houses sat in a horseshoe arrangement. I turned right on Pawtucket Avenue. The D'Agostinos' house had been directly across from Kent Field. Now there was no field, just two rows of identical houses laid out gridlike. On a rise where the old squat black water tower had been was a new, white, flying-saucer-type tower. It loomed unnaturally among some cultivated pine trees. I hadn't paid attention to the weather, but for some reason I became aware of the darkness of the day, more of a sheen than an overcast, really. I looked up again at the water tower and wondered if the sun was behind it, hiding. I spotted the D'Agostinos' house and went up to it. The privet hedge that Big Tony loved and kept waist-high and full had been pulled up. A white picket fence took its place. I stopped at the front gate and turned back toward the flying saucer. I crossed Pawtucket Avenue and slowly strolled the quarter or so mile to the four-story mushroom structure.

While the old tower seemed to have been assembled out of a gigantic Erector Set, this new oval monstrosity appeared to balance precariously on its thin stem. A tall chain-link fence with barbed-wire topping still encircled East Providence's water dispensary. On the round, sloping side of the tower that faced Pawtucket Avenue, someone had painted in huge red block letters GO TOWNIES—KILL LA SALLE. So much for barbed wire.

I stood at the gates to the tower, alternately looking up and then across the new backyards to the D'Agostinos' on the other side of Pawtucket Avenue, like a man trying to make a decision or come to a conclusion. But what decision or conclusion? I stared in the direction of where we placed our snow angels so many years ago, about the middle of an aboveground pool in the backyard of a red-and-black mock Cape. I imagined the pool away and the fences of the other houses away and finally the houses themselves, until Marie D'Agostino and Jono Riley lay beautifully swimming on their backs in the snow. Marie and Jono stood laughing, even pointing to each other's creations. Hers breathtakingly perfect and his rough and round. I could see her putting more snow onto his swollen forehead where the fiend Ponserelli had shattered his hockey stick. Suddenly Marie was down, face first, on the snow. She rose almost immediately and began that mad run home, Jono following, waving his arms. I took a step forward, and something gonged, loud and hollow, above me. I looked back up at the tank but heard nothing else. That kind of soundlessness that follows a reverie. A deeply uncomfortable quiet. I moved away from the tower in the direction of the snow angels, hearing only the sound of my shoes on the roadside. About fifty feet away from the tower, I heard that cavernous gong again. When I turned, something had come around to the highest rail, something moving fast, moving now onto the ladder. A flow of something, flaglike. Coming down now like a pirate's flag. I began to run in the direction of Pawtucket Avenue. After a minute I stopped, winded and feeling stupid.

"Jesus Christ," I said out loud. "You're fifty-one years old."

I turned back to the water tower like I did so many years ago. There was nothing there. Nothing moving against the closed New England sky. I looked for a long time. Then I lit a smoke and moved toward the D'Agostinos'.

She opened the door on the first ring.

"Yes?"

Mrs. D'Agostino had lost a couple of inches off her already tiny body, but her face and hands seemed oddly young. Her hair was rinsed a deep black, and her olive skin spoke of octogenarian health.

"Mrs. D'Agostino, do you remember me? I'm Jono Riley."

"Jono? Of course I remember you."

She took my hand and led me through the familiar house to the kitchen. I didn't speak until I sat at the same table where I had feasted on countless bowls of macaroni and meatballs.

"Mrs. D'Agostino, I'm so sorry about Marie. She was such a beautiful person."

She closed her eyes and didn't speak. She nodded. I got up and hugged her, and she cried a little. I suppose I'm what could be called essentially a reticent New Englander. Not comfortable in physical contact unless some history is there. History was here, all right, and as I held her, I remembered how comforting her hugs had been for that little mick with the prodigious head.

When I sat back down and she began brewing some coffee, she spoke easily about her daughter. Cubby and Big Tony, too.

"The most difficult part, of course, the most . . . unnatural part is living longer than your child. It was so very hard. I thought losing my own mother was hard, and then . . . well, whoever thought that anything could have happened to Anthony? He was so strong. You remember how strong Anthony was."

"Big Tony was the strongest. In a lot of ways."

"Here and then gone. So I thought, well, losing Anthony was even more difficult than losing Mother, but . . ." Mrs. D'Agostino dabbed at her sweet black eyes. "But losing my little Marie . . ."

We hung on the thought of Marie, together. Silence is sometimes the only way to share the unsharable.

"Cubby wrote that Marie just took a nap and never woke up." Mrs. D'Agostino nodded.

I changed the subject as best I could. "How's Cubby?"

She smiled. "He's just like Anthony. The image of his father, and he's in charge of the parts and labor department at Tasca's, same as Anthony was."

"Maybe I'll drive down and surprise him."

She squeezed my arm. "He'd like that."

I steered my rental onto the Tasca lot. I parked over by Service and sat for a minute, looking out at the back of East Providence High School. When Big Tony ran the parts shop at Tasca, it was on about a half-acre tract at pretty much the intersection of Pawtucket and Taunton avenues. You couldn't see it from the baseball diamond behind the school because of a grove of trees and a swampy meadow. Tasca sold Fords then. Now it seemed to go on forever, acres and acres of every kind of car and truck you could imagine, and the ball field abutted it.

Some pimply kid was standing in front of a computer behind the parts counter, finger punching the keys with a surly expression. He looked up.

"Cubby around?"

He looked back down at the computer screen. "Service."

"I'm sorry?"

He looked up with exasperation and said slowly, "He's . . . in . . . Service."

"Where . . . is . . . Service?"

He pointed to his left.

The waiting area had a picture window that looked out over the service bays. The operation was enormous. I spotted Cubby talking to a mechanic. It had been years since I'd seen Cubby D'Agostino, but he was unmistakable. He'd thickened into an exact replica of his short, round, hard old man, and even though his hair had thinned dramatically, he still wore it in his signature, modified flattop with long, swept-back sides.

Renée has told me more than once that if she could change any part of me, it would be to make me less reticent and replace that reticence with a dose of sentimentality. I would, of course, change a hell of a lot more than that if I could, but she may be getting her wish in that department. For whatever reasons, Renée notwithstanding, I'm finally losing that diffident New England thing that seems so heavy in us Celts. I realized, standing there watching my old friend across the space of not only the car bay but our own little histories, that tears were welling up. I shook them off.

Cubby looked over as if he sensed me behind the glass. He waved happily and headed toward me. After our greetings we had some coffee in his office. Service awards and citations covered the wall, and the big old maple desk had a clear glass top that held hundreds of family photographs. He filled me in on his kids, two boys and a girl, picture by picture.

"I stopped by and saw your mom."

"Doesn't she look great?"

"Beautiful."

"Eighty-seven. Hey, we been seeing you. Commercials, that hospital thing . . . what was that show?"

I smiled embarrassedly. *"Blues and Whites."*

"That's the one. You were retarded."

"Well . . . an autistic orderly, actually."

"That's right. That's why you never spoke."

I gave a little shrug. A little smile. I didn't want to get into it, but I did speak in the first two episodes until one of the producers discovered that if they played the autism to the limit and I essentially became mute, they would not be forced to pay me at the union's higher speaking rate.

"You look just like Big Tony."

He smiled and pointed to another photo under the glass. There was Big Tony. There was Cubby and Marie and me, too.

"I'm so sorry about Marie."

"I know, Jono."

"How's the family?"

"They're coping, I guess. Her husband— Did you know Chip Cummings?"

"He was a couple of years ahead of us. Baseball, right?"

"Went up to the Sox for a cup of coffee. That'd be something if he stayed up, huh? He's principal of Riverside Junior High. He's a good guy. The kids were there for him—they're gonna make it."

"Marie was still at Providence Country Day?"

"Taught library science and ran the library."

We were quiet for a minute and sipped Cubby's good strong coffee. He answered my question before I asked it.

"It traveled, Jono." He sighed and took another sip. "State sent a copy of the autopsy to Chip. We both looked it over but couldn't figure out what all the mumbo jumbo meant. I called up Dick Roshone—he's our family doctor—and he told us to fax it over and he'd have a look. We were curious, you know. Your sister, your wife lies down and doesn't wake up. And she was never sick, Jono. Never. She jogged and lifted weights at the Country Day gym. She really took care of herself. Anyway, Dick calls back and says, 'Looks like a traveler.' It's rare, but it happens, like to soldiers sometimes. Fragments or, you know, bullets . . . move. Marie's just traveled over and pinched a big artery. Her heart stopped."

We both stared at the floor. My fists were clenched, and when I looked at them, my knuckles had gone white.

"Dick . . . Dick said it would have been painless."

I looked up at one of the most important people of my silly life.

"For Marie it was," I said quietly.

Cubby D'Agostino began to weep.

11

Big Tony drove me to my house in silence. Every now and then, he reached over and gave my shoulder a squeeze. There were about ten cars parked on either side of our place. Big Tony stopped on a side street. Officers Carl Rocha and Kenny Snowden were talking to our neighbor, Ethel Sunman, who threw her arms around me and cried. Kenny Snowden tousled my hair and whispered in my ear that my mother and grandmother were in the kitchen. I looked behind me at Big Tony, and he nodded that I should go in to them. The porch door opened onto the kitchen. Mrs. D'Agostino had her arms around my sobbing mother, and Mrs. Pacheco from across the street held my nana's hands. Nana—my father's mother—looked stunned. They all glanced up when I opened the door.

"Mom?" I said like a dummy.

Then they were all around me. A giant mick and Portuguese and Italian squeeze and kiss. I didn't realize then, of course, the absolute transcendent powers of these astonishing women. Comfort washed over me, and I accepted it fully, even if I didn't know exactly why. They were all still holding me when Sister Mary Agnes from St. Martha's rushed into the kitchen like a firefighter.

So this is what happened on April Fools' Day 1964.

My old man had been in the middle of a double shift down at the Socony docks. A double shift wasn't uncommon for a refinery foreman, because oil tankers would not always arrive in planned sequence. When that happened, it became high priority to get the hold of any ship already at the unloading dock pumped out fast, get it back to sea, and bring in the out-of-schedule one so that it didn't have to stay in a holding pattern in Narragansett Bay.

Pop's deal was simply to add another foreman with his crew to double-pump the docked tanker—in this case an English-flagged one named the *Lloyd George*—get it on its way, and bring in the Mexican tanker, the *Zapata*. Chucky Sorensen's crew was also working the docks, so Pop and Chucky would first make sure they were on the same page as to who was doing what. Then they started cleaning the crude oil out of the *Lloyd George*. Pop's crew was pretty representative of East Providence's working-class guys. Couple of Portuguese fresh from the Azores, three Italians (one of them a dead ringer for Dean Martin), and the Murphy boys, Timmy and Tommy. Pop was pretty tough on them, but he liked them all, and at Socony's annual clambake at Rocky Point he'd always introduce these hard, tough characters as "my kids."

About one o'clock in the afternoon, when the two crews were uncoupling the heavy unloading hoses, somebody smelled smoke. For about thirty seconds, the men stopped working, stood silently and sniffed. They stared at one another as the rancid aroma of burning crude and gasoline wafted over them. Not very much scared these guys. Fire did. Pop counted up his crew.

"Where's Tommy?"

Pop barely got the question out before someone started yelling.

"Fire in the pump house! Fire in the pump house!"

The pump house was set back a hundred yards from the dock. About the size of a two-car garage, it sat in red brick on top of a slab of concrete. In 1964 it had already been in use for nearly fifty

66

years and consisted of two huge, simple engines sitting side by side. One to take the crude out of the ships and the other to drive it up the slope of the bay and into the refinery tanks on the other side of Pawtucket Avenue.

Pop and Chucky's crews shut down the unloading and quickly disconnected the hoses from the tanker. The dock was cleared and all hands of the ship followed them out to a rise overlooking the docks, perhaps five hundred yards away. The last time there was a flame-up around the pump house was the day after the great hurricane of 1938. Twenty-three men lost their lives.

When they were all a safe distance away, Pop asked it again.

"Where's Tommy?"

Nobody knew, and Pop didn't ask twice. He jogged back down to the dock and started calling Tommy's name. He was jogging toward the men's room adjacent to the pump house when the flame-up came. The door popped off its hinges, and a sustained shoot of white-hot torch hit Pop midstride. There was only an idea of my pop to bury.

Tommy had driven over to Riverside for a sandwich.

12

I had dinner at Cubby's with his family. His mother was there, too. The kids were wild and sweet, and Cubby's wife made a bowl of fried calamari in hot red sauce and fantastic clam linguine. The kids laughed when I put Parmesan cheese on my clam pasta. Cubby explained I was Irish. I got back to the Ramada about eleven and called Renée at her firehouse. They were on a fire call, so I watched TV awhile, trying to get sleepy-tired.

I'm the kind of guy who relies on fleeting moments of clarity. I know that sounds like so much bullshit, but it's an absolute with me. It's something I can't call up at will, and sometimes it never shows at all. When it does, I feel a kind of order, a certain understanding that had eluded me in the past. Usually I'm rehearsing a play and my character is giving me no clues on how to act it. The role lies on the page in a sort of opaque flatness. Without shape, is what I mean. And that's when I get this occasional vivid insight. This view of my role in its most complete simplicity. I don't get these overviews in most other areas of my civilian, my nontheater, life. It's why I spend an inordinate amount of time banging my head against doors that won't open and generally doing everything the hard way. They're a mystery to me, these brain tingles. They won't come if you try to conjure them up, even if you hope for them. The cleanness of thought just has to happen, like a breeze or a sigh.

This one came into the bottom of my feet as I sat nodding in front of the Ramada TV. It slid its way up my legs, into my chest, and popped out the top of my head. My eyes opened quickly, and I stood and shut off the television and saw it clearly, stored as it was in the shaded corner of my mind.

The summer after Marie had been shot was my first time at Boy Scout camp. Our troop was scheduled to go for two weeks beginning the Saturday after the Fourth of July. We were pretty excited, because we were all going together—me, Cubby, Billy Fontanelli, and Bobby Fontes. We had all just advanced from Tenderfoot to second class and were feeling pretty full of ourselves. There were forty-two kids in our troop, and we were divided into four patrols. Our little gang all got to stay together in Patrol Number 3. Mr. Da Silva was our scoutmaster. He accompanied the troop for the first week, and then a committee of Big Tony, my pop, and some other fathers would take turns filling in for the second week. It was a pretty easy assignment, because Mr. Da Silva's philosophy of scouting was "boys leading boys," and he had a complicated network of assistants and junior assistants and junior-assistants-in-training to run the show. Plus, he liked to schedule us chock-full, so that from reveille to taps there wasn't enough free time for us to screw up and get into trouble.

While it was our good fortune to be together in Patrol 3, it was our bad fortune that Patrol 4 consisted of the Riverside Terrace rogues, including the younger brothers of Mr. Jack Crosby and the fiend Poochy Ponserelli. My old head aches just thinking about that hockey stick snapping over it. There were nine kids in Patrol 4, although when you knew them the way we knew them, you wouldn't exactly think of them as kids. Youthful offenders, maybe. Thirteen-year-old Howie Crosby and fourteen-year-old

Allie Ponserelli were the patrol leaders. They were also the capos of these Future Mobsters of America. Even though they were a few years older than us, what allowed our guys a little distance from the bullying and shakedown operation Crosby and Ponserelli presided over was our own personal monster. Bobby Fontes was a wiry, quiet kid with a high-pitched giggle and had what my mother thought was the sweetest disposition of any boy she ever knew. He was polite to a fault and always happy to be anywhere but his father's house. We never talked about it, but we all knew that his old man used to beat him up pretty good, especially when Bobby got between him and his wife. Which was a lot. I remember one day Bobby showed up at one of Big Tony's barbecues with a broken nose and a cauliflower ear. Big Tony got the burgers and dogs all cooked up and left the party long enough to put old man Fontes in Rhode Island Hospital for three days.

Bobby would never think of fighting his old man back. He actually used to feel sorry for him. He had this gift for understanding, a true empathy for what made his father a bitter and, really, a terrible human being. He also had this empathy for other people, to a point. That point was being touched. Bobby did not like being touched. I mean, we could touch him, and our moms and pops could give him hugs and kisses, but that was different. Allie, Howie, and their gang had been outside the Newport Creamery when Sam Thatcher, a legendary ninth-grade goon, had tried to put the bite on the four of us for an Awful-Awful, that obscenely thick vanilla shake common to southern New England.

"I only got a quarter," the big, crew-cutted Neanderthal said. "If each of you assholes give me a quarter, I won't kick your ass."

The Riverside gang was laughing and had become a sort of unofficial Thatcher entourage for the evening.

We each dug deep. Thatcher was a thick fourteen or fifteen. We were twelve. When he had the money in hand, he still hadn't finished playing to his admiring minions. He swatted me out of the way, spit in the direction of Billy Fontanelli and Cubby, and then made the big mistake of his young miscreant life. He pushed Bobby Fontes.

Bobby's expression didn't change. He didn't seem angry or say anything, but his hard little hands shot out like a swarm of hornets at Thatcher's face. I won't even embellish it or make it seem larger than it was, but it wouldn't be stretching the truth to say that Thatcher was hit no fewer than thirty times. All pinpoint. All face. None of us had ever seen anyone actually knocked out in real life, and now this big kid was facedown on the sidewalk with only a little twitch from his feet to indicate life. Cubby didn't miss a beat. He looked up from Thatcher, over to Bobby, and then to the Riverside boys.

"Anybody else?" he said.

Anyway, at the scout camp we pretty much got left alone, except for the fat schedule of Mr. Da Silva. About three days into camp, a sogging rainstorm began that lasted a full day and a half and played havoc with Mr. Da Silva's plans. There really wasn't anything to do but put the tent flaps down and wait it out. By the early afternoon, I was antsy to do something.

"Anybody want to go fishing?"

The guys all laughed at me. Rain pinged off our tent like BBs. I didn't care. The fishing is always better in the rain, and the camp pond was a spring-fed beauty with no houses or anything around it. I pulled my spinning rod out from under the bunk, rigged up a daredevil, and headed down to the pond. I passed Patrol 4's tent. All nine of them sat inside whittling with what looked like ten-inch switchblades. They watched me closely, identical sneers playing across their faces.

Crosby nudged Ponserelli. "Hey, look, shithead doesn't know it's raining."

Ponserelli yelled out at me. "Hey, shithead, it's raining!"

Crosby nudged him again and gestured toward our tent with

his pointy head. Bobby had pulled the front flap aside and was watching them. They went back to whittling.

The rain fell extraordinarily hard at the waterfront. Rowboats and canoes were filling fast. I turned left and made my way a few hundred yards down the shoreline to a flat, smooth glacial ledge that met the pond over deep water. On my first cast, a little bass hit the daredevil, and I brought it in. I put it back and threw around five more times in an increasing arc. My pop had said you'd cover a lot more water with this technique, and he was right. Especially since warm-water fish rarely darted away from their narrow territory. When I got my next hit, the rod bent and the drag on my reel screamed like crazy. I played the big fish so intently I didn't even notice that the rain was no longer pinging off my huge forehead. Then I was holding it by the lip like my pop had showed me. A fat, long largemouth bass with beautiful green lines down its side. I raised it up to eye level and marveled at it. I knew I couldn't keep it, because there was no place to cook it, and, really and truly, I wouldn't have wanted to eat it anyway. Except if I let it go, who'd believe I caught anything this big? That's when my fish exploded.

Almost instantly I found myself holding half a bloody bass. I dropped the thing and fell back on the ledge. I stared at it with my mouth open. It started pouring again. After a while I snapped the line that still held my daredevil and mutilated fish. I kicked it, daredevil and all, off the ledge and into the black water. I ran back to camp, stowed my fishing gear under my bunk, then sat there dripping, looking at the floor. Cubby was reading a comic on the top bunk.

"Catch anything?" he asked.

"Yeah," I said. "A big bass."

"Where is it?" Billy Fontanelli asked from his own bunk.

"It exploded," I said.

They laughed, and I shrugged. Now, sitting in the Ramada Inn, forty years after the fact, I remembered that beautiful fish on the end of my lure. I saw it clearly disintegrating and realized something I had subconsciously not allowed to seep into my mind: that someone or something had shot my prize as surely as someone or something had shot my sweet little Marie D'Agostino.

I tried Renée again.

13

So at fifteen or almost fifteen, I became the proverbial man of the house, although Mother continued to really run things, just as she had before the pump house got my pop. I grew to about an inch under my adult height, my head settled into my neck and shoulders in an almost natural way, and my hockey career started in earnest with a hat trick against mighty Mount St. Charles to open my sophomore season.

While the older Ponserelli and Crosby had long since been out of high school and pressed on to whatever criminal career they chose, their respective brothers, Allie and Howie, were still with us, Howie a sophomore like us after having been kept back twice in junior high for gross stupidity and Allie a senior.

Marie was more astonishing than ever, if that was at all possible. Now her long, lithe body had acquired those specific arcs in specific places. Her hair still tangled and flew out over an increasingly cool face. She'd smile with her eyes and show her teeth in small measures. She favored knee-length skirts and bright blouses. She also started to wear small gold hoop earrings. I wasn't carrying a torch anymore, because I saw her so much she was more like a sister. But probably the real reason was that she knew the essential big-headed eleven-year-old that loomed just beneath my outsize fifteen-year-old surface. Knew him better than he knew himself. But she was fun to be with in that way old friends have of routines and habits. I was still "Bozo" or "Riley," and she was still Cubby's sister.

It's funny how early years blur by, only slowing a little at those singular moments that are determined to stick out in memory. The rendezvous at the A&W root beer stand, the girls I followed around like a puppy, or even games lost and won seem like a prospect or an expectation rather than something that has actually happened. A cloudy dream, maybe. The frantic teenage life seems to me hard to believe that I ever lived it. What I do see clearly, remember enough to actually place myself there, are never the joyous, thrilling, maddening hours of my youth but rather the jolting and, thankfully, very occasional traumas. Marie's bullet, my pop's accident, my destroyed bass, and in 1967 the murder of T. B. Holt, an East Providence High School shop teacher. People just didn't get put down in my town, but one morning, two days before Christmas break, the entire school, students and teachers alike, was asked to report to the auditorium. Even the school nurses, janitors, and lunchroom staff were there. Officers Kenny Snowden and Carl Rocha were sitting on the stage with Principal Nels Blair along with two state patrolmen and a man in a black suit. When everyone was in and the doors were closed, Mr. Blair nodded to Miss Case of the music department, who was seated at the organ, and she began the intro to "The Star-Spangled Banner." We sang it and then followed Mr. Blair in the Pledge of Allegiance.

"Please be seated," he said.

We all sensed that something was up. Me, Cubby, Billy, and Bobby were sitting together as usual. I scanned the hall for Marie and spotted her with Billy's sister, Peggy. I never had been in the auditorium when it had been so quiet. Mr. Blair cleared his throat.

"Ladies and gentlemen, boys and girls, I have some very bad

news to share with you. Mr. Holt of the woodworking department was killed last evening."

A compressed, rolling roar swelled as we all mumbled to our neighbors. Mr. Blair held up his hands, and the place went quiet again.

"I have assured Captain Moniz"—Mr. Blair gestured to the man in the suit, who held up his hand in a tight wave—"that we would all be happy to be of some service to the police during this difficult time."

Mr. Blair stepped back, and Captain Moniz stepped up to the microphone. He was flat and clipped and clearly uncomfortable. He had a tone of blanket accusation. I thought I saw Kenny Snowden, looking crisp in his uniform, roll his eyes. Moniz cleared his throat.

"All right. We're going to have a locker search, so nobody gets anything out of their lockers until we say it's okay. Everybody who had"—Captain Moniz consulted a small pad—"Holt, Mr. Holt for any classes, I want you to go to that classroom right now for questioning. And remember, just like when President Kennedy was assassinated by the Russians or the Cubans, precious time was lost in the investigation. So thank you for your cooperation. And also, Jack Ruby, who gut-shot the assassin on television, screwed things royally because now we'll never know. So be careful."

I stayed in my seat as the shop kids filed out of the auditorium. The entire Riverside mob rose as one and slinked up the aisle. Howie Crosby saw me looking at him and gave me the finger.

Nothing came of the daylong interviews with Mr. Holt's students. Officers Snowden and Rocha netted sixty-one knives in the locker search, but nothing to do with the killing.

Fifty-seven of the knives were found in Allie Ponserelli's locker.

14

Renée's call woke me around 5:00 A.M. I was glad it did. I'd been sleeping light, rehashing an ancient experience in my dreamy head for clues to why things always fall apart.

I'd been in New York about ten years, in between girlfriends, making rounds, serving drinks at Lambs, and generally leaving as little wake as a person can when my old acting teacher, Heathcliff Hornsby, came up with an idea for a bus-and-truck tour of small colleges across the Northeast. He remembered me as a "big guy" who could "say it and mean it" and called to offer me multiple roles in what he called *The Portable Macbeth*. It would be tricky, he said, but as consummate performers we might make a lasting impression on young scholars and share equally in the bonanza, although Heathcliff would be sharing equally three times as the writer, director, and producer.

"As writer, too?" I asked him.

"I'm making cuts," he said rapidly. "There may be some additional dialogue."

The first rehearsal was at his apartment in Alphabet City, but his wife's book club was having a meeting, so we marched over to Tompkins Square Park for a read-through. There were three actors. Myself portraying Duncan, Banquo, Macduff, Menteith, Angus, the Earl of Northumberland, and an English Doctor, while Simon Fraser took the pivotal role of Macbeth and all the other male roles. Frances Solstice was cast in the female roles.

We sat in a circle on dirty grass. Heathcliff passed out copies of the Folger editions. "I like this format," he said.

"I prefer the Penguin edition," Simon intoned in his quasi-British accent.

Heathcliff smiled knowingly and waved his copy in the air. "I'll tell you who's playing whom, and then we'll read."

When he finished with the role assignments, Frances, a tall, bosomy southern girl with a heightened sense of the gracious, raised her hand.

"Yes, Frances?" Heathcliff asked.

"If I'm Lady Macbeth, how can I be my own gentlewomen? Why, I'd have to be in two places at the same time. I'd practically have to be Superwoman."

Heathcliff smiled and nodded. "Of course, that's why I thought of you."

"Most of the gals are incidental to the text anyway," Simon sniffed.

Frances ignored the remark, and we prepared to read. She was silent a long stage beat, then looked up from her script. "And I'm to play all the Witches?"

Heathcliff nodded.

Frances looked back down at the script. She opened her mouth but was cut off by an old female panhandler.

"I'm a . . . Vietnam vet, and I'm not mugging people or selling drugs or any of that shit, and so give me some money."

We watched our toes, New York style.

"No?"

We shifted our look to our scripts, and she waddled off.

"I didn't know there were women soldiers in Vietnam," Frances said.

"There weren't," sighed Simon.

I never know when to shut up. "Actually, there were. Nurses. Administrators. Logistical officers. Supply pilots."

Simon stared off into the bowels of the park. Frances began again.

"When shall we three meet again?
In thunder, lightning or in rain?
When the hurlyburly's done,
When the—"

"Obviously I was referring to women in *combat* positions," Simon hissed at me. And, pointing to Frances, he added, "I understood that the play was to be done in English."

"It *is*," Heathcliff said patiently.

"I mean *English* English. Correctly accented. The accent that Frances just employed for the Witches would hardly do for Lady Macbeth."

"It's just the first reading," Frances said softly.

"Let's continue," Heathcliff said.

"From the top?" Frances asked.

Heathcliff nodded.

"When shall—"

"The reason I interrupted at all, Heathcliff, is that if Frances insists on making Lady Macbeth into some southern whore, then what's the point?"

Frances left our rehearsal in tears and Heathcliff Hornsby's idea for a really portable Macbeth fizzled before the third witch could kick in. That's what I mean. Things fall apart. I picked up the phone.

It always surprises me how young Renée sounds on the telephone. Don't get me wrong on this—I think Renée's a knockout—but on the phone her disembodied tone is like talking to a kid.

"I'm pooped," she said.

"Long night?"

"We're throwing water nonstop. Apartment in the Village and a pet shop in Chelsea. Got the animals out okay."

"Get into bed."

"I am."

"Put the light out and go to sleep."

"In a minute. What's going on?"

I told her. Who I saw. What I was beginning to remember. "I'm going to stay up here a few more days. Put something on the graves of my folks—"

"And remember some more?" she asked in her softest girl voice.

"I'm improvising."

She went quiet for a moment, and I thought she might have fallen asleep. Then she said, "I got two more of the night shift, then three days off before getting on a human schedule. Want me to come up? I don't have to, so don't feel obligated or anything."

"Of course I feel obligated."

"I mean you don't—"

"Renée," I said formally, "is there any chance at all of you getting on a bus or a train and hauling your perfect little rear end up to this world-class Ramada Inn?"

"Yes, there is."

"Good."

"I'll call you with the times. I love you."

"I love you, too."

"You don't have to say you love me just because I say I—"

"Renée?"

"What?"

"Go to sleep."

15

Anyway, my sophomore year in high school was a mixed bag of good and bad. My nana, Pop's mother, died in April. She had moved in with us when she broke a hip at Christmas. Mother and I converted the dining room—which we rarely used anyway, because we were informal people and liked eating in the cozy kitchen—into a bedroom–sitting room for Nana.

As these kinds of arrangements go, ours was pretty good. Mother had lost her own mother very young and had transferred powerful parental status over to Nana. This was a good choice, because even in the clouds of memory and sentiment I believe that my nana was an extraordinary and wonderful addition to the planet. She was hopeful and positive and joyous, all the traits I struggle for but rarely attain. Even when stomach cancer started its endgame, she would sip her Irish breakfast tea and happily talk about tomorrow.

Several days before she entered the hospital on a permanent basis, I came home early from school and found her going through stacks and stacks of postcards at the kitchen table. I was stunned to see her out of bed. The doctor had visited the night before and couldn't rouse her. She hadn't been out of her room in well over a month.

"Ho, Jono," she called out to me with a big smile and a thick Northern Ireland accent. "Give us a kiss."

I did, and she pointed to the chair across the table from her. I sat down. She held her small, thin hands apart to display her cards.

"When my friends would leave Stewartstown for Belfast or Londonderry or over to Scotland or England even, I would give them these and I would stamp them, too. I collected them, you see. These. The postmarks from where they were sent. Annie Daly went with her da to Liverpool April twenty-second, 1905, and mailed this one . . . can you see?"

I looked at the fading mark. "At five P.M., Nana."

"Five P.M.," she said with enormous satisfaction.

She turned the card over, and a beautiful Victorian girl stood in profile.

"Miss Minnie Baker," she gushed. "Sang on the London stage and played Hamlet. I saw her with my da in Belfast. She took mass at St. Catherine's and sang communion."

I listened to more cards. Johnny Hewson in Lisburn. Bernadette Keating in Swansea, Wales, for holiday in 1903. And Mary O'Toole in Glasgow, Scotland, where she and her mum had gone to visit her oldest brother in jail for murder and who wrote, "Train leaves for coast 9:45. Arrive Ireland 8 or so next. Kill the fatted calf and don't forget the kettle."

Nana winked at me. "Oh, that Mary O'Toole was the naughty one. Kettle indeed!"

We went through two stacks before Mother came home from work. We both sat at the table with Nana and her cards until well past dinnertime. Finally, waving a postcard of Miss Ellaline Terriss and a Beeston Humber bicycle that Nana's girlfriend Jennie Middleton had sent from London, England, July 6, 1902, she said she was tired, and we helped her back to bed. Her doctor said Nana had a "surge" and that it's pretty common in cancer patients toward the end of the ordeal. They get temporarily stronger and focused. I guess my nana focused on her postcards and her friends at the start of the century. A few days later, she went into the hospital and died. It was nice visiting that one last time with her.

That summer we all had to get jobs, because that was what kids did in Rhode Island. Cubby, of course, got a job in the parts department at Tasca's. Billy Fontanelli pumped gas at Woody's Mobil station. Bobby Fontes worked on his uncle's deep-sea trawler out of Warren, Rhode Island, and yours truly snagged the cush job of lifeguarding at the Boy Scout camp. The job came with room and board, a salary of eighty dollars a week, and one day off every other week, which I usually spent at the Misquamicut State Beach on the Rhode Island–Connecticut border. I'd get a ride from Father Jimmy Dunny, a priest from Westerly who said mass and heard confessions at camp. He'd drop me and my sleeping bag off at the beach and pick me up in the morning on his way in. Sometimes Billy or Bobby or Cubby would show up, too, and we'd sneak some smokes and beers and watch the girls. We used to call Misquamicut "the Roman beach," because the people there were mostly Italians from Providence and New Haven. We all agreed that there was nothing like an Italian girl at the beach. They'd turn a kind of mahogany brown and kept their hair piled high on their heads. We were very easy to please. None of us had girlfriends yet but were too cool to show the beach girls any of the real interest we sincerely felt.

Marie D'Agostino waited tables at Asquino's Restaurant. She could walk there, and her new boyfriend, Mike something, could pick her up after work. When my camp ended two weeks before school started, Cubby and Big Tony came up to Rockville to bring me home. Marie came, too. I remember Big Tony backing the Impala down the small hill to my waterfront and popping the trunk so I could throw my footlocker in. Then I gave them a quick tour of the area. Marie looked very beautiful and held my hand and talked a blue streak. I knew that the other waterfront guys were watching and were wondering who that amazing girl was holding my hand. I didn't tell them she was sort of my sister. If they wanted to think she was my girlfriend, they could.

Two days later I was mowing our front lawn when Billy ran up to me, breathing hard.

"I thought your job at Woody's wasn't over till Saturday," I said.

Billy gulped some air and said, "Bobby's in the hospital."

"What?"

"He had another accident in his house. It's real bad. His mother's in the hospital, too, but Bobby's worse."

I put the lawn mower in the garage, and then we took a bus into Providence and walked over to Rhode Island Hospital. We didn't say anything on the ride. We were thinking about all those "accidents" Bobby and his mother would have.

We were directed to the same waiting area we went to when Marie was shot. Officers Kenny Snowden and Carl Rocha were sitting there in civilian clothes. When we walked in, Kenny stood up, holding his hands palms out in a "calm down" gesture. I suppose we must have looked pretty upset.

"He's got a few broken ribs," he said quietly. "One of the ribs snapped and punctured a lung. One of his eyes is in bad shape, and he's got a concussion. His mother has a broken jaw, but they're going to release her in about an hour, so it's not that serious."

Kenny paused and watched us. "He's going to make it. Why don't you guys sit down?"

We sat, and Bobby did make it. He came home wearing a patch over his eye. Later on, around Christmas, the eye acted up, and they had to take it out.

Two weeks after the "accident," Bobby's father dropped dead of a heart attack.

16

I couldn't find a phone listing for Kenny Snowden. I called the East Providence Police Department but got transferred so many times in a half hour that I decided to drive down and find some cop who might know him. Or *had* known him, I guess, because after all, I hadn't seen Kenny in over thirty years. The desk sergeant was a pretty, dark-skinned woman about forty years old. I waited in front of her until she looked up.

"Excuse me. I'm trying to get in touch with a former policeman here. An Officer Kenny Snowden? I couldn't find a number for him, and—"

"Kenny Snowden?"

"Yes, Officer."

She punched some computer keys and shook her head.

"Nope. I know he partnered with Manny Furtado his last couple of years on the force. Manny should be in."

She ran her finger down the list of phone extensions, got it, and was about to punch it in when she looked up.

"You look familiar."

I shrugged. After a certain age, having achieved only modest success at best, an actor embraces anonymity with the same determination with which he used to embrace the dream of celebrity.

She studied me. "Did you ever make a commercial?"

I nodded slightly. She snapped her finger and pointed.

"You just got off the toilet, and your family is lined up outside the bathroom waiting for their turn. Right?"

"I don't—"

"And you spray this spray so the smell goes away, and you hand the spray to your wife when you walk out, and she takes it back in. You said something. You said . . . what was it? What?"

"I said . . . I said . . . 'Smell-Away.' "

"That's it," she said happily. "Smell-Away. You did the Smell-Away commercial. You're the Smell-Away man."

I smiled slightly, and she punched Officer Manny Furtado's number.

"Manny? . . . Nancy. Hey, got the Smell-Away man down here. Guy who did the Smell-Away commercial. . . . Smell-Away. . . . No, the guy's on the toilet and his family's lined up outside the bathroom for their turn and he . . . Yeah. . . . Exactly. . . . He sprays the sprayer and he says 'Smell-Away.' . . . Yeah. . . . He's down here. He wants to talk to you. . . . Cross my heart. . . . Okay."

She punched out and looked up with a grin. "On his way."

Manny Furtado was short, with a weight lifter's body that he showed off in his tailored uniform. His baby face was topped with thick, curly black hair. After he insisted I repeat my dialogue from the toilet epic, I followed him up to a squad room on the second floor.

"He doesn't list his number 'cause he's pissed off. Been pissed off since they run him out."

"They run him out?"

"Fuckin' New York RICO shit made it all the way to Little Rhody. They called it 'cleaning house.' Cleaned Kenny and a couple of others. All bullshit. Here it is."

He read me Kenny's number, and I wrote it down.

"Tell him to come down to the department for a visit. He won't, but tell him we miss him. Know why the cocksuckers fucked him? He had to go to a wedding in Boston and didn't think the piece-of-shit Ford would make it, so he borrowed one from the motor pool. For that they run him out." He shook his head. Then looked at me. "How do I get into commercials?"

I crossed the street on the outside of the station house and ordered two dogs and a coffee milk at the New York System. Then I dialed Kenny's number. He picked up on the second ring.

"Who?" he said, flat and crisp.

"Uh . . . Officer Snowden, my name is—"

"It's definitely *not* Officer Snowden."

I waited to see if there was more.

"What?" was all he said.

"My name is Jono Riley. I'm sure you don't remember me, but my—"

"Of course I remember. My beat was the schools. I remember all of you. It was what I did."

I waited again. I wasn't sure why I even called. He didn't wait for me.

"Your friend died. I read it in the paper. I remember her, too. Pretty Italian."

"She was, yes. I guess the reason I called was—"

"Bullet shifted, is what they told me. I got a copy of the autopsy. A goddamn traveler."

I waited again. Why would Kenny Snowden have been interested enough to study the results of an autopsy?

"Sorry about that language," he said.

"No, that's fine. I guess that's why I called. I'm surprised you were interested enough to—"

"Happened on my watch, young man. Unresolved and on my

watch. That woodworking teacher, too. That priest, too, I think. They gnaw at you. They get to you. You remember them."

Father Al Persico, associate pastor of St. Martha's, had disappeared after the 1969 Easter sunrise service and was never seen again.

"Father Al," I said.

"Didn't know from anything. FBI, everything. Had some supposed sightings. Got a call saying they thought they saw him in Fall River. You remember those things. But it's the D'Agostino girl brought you back, wasn't it?"

"Yes, sir."

"Well, let's see. I'm no good today. I'm only good weekdays until eleven. Coffee tomorrow morning? Say, eight? Too early?"

"No, sir, eight is fine. I'm at the Ramada Inn in Seekonk. Want to meet me in the coffee shop?"

"Tell you what, Jono Riley. I'll pick up the coffee and you meet *me* at the new water tower."

I drove back to the Ramada. I always run out of ways to fill up my day. It's a true dilemma I have. This sense of time wasted. I felt a great urge to organize whatever the hell I was doing here. Catalog events. Something.

I sat at a little desk next to the TV, took a piece of hotel stationery, and wrote "Marie" across the top. Then the phone rang.

"Hello."

There was a slight pause.

"Jono?"

"Yes."

Another pause, as if it were part of the process of preparing to speak.

"It's me. It's Bobby. Fontes."

"Bobby," I said happily. "How are you?"

Another quick pause, and I remembered now that Bobby

would always wait before he spoke. Obviously wait. Ascertaining before letting out his words.

"Really fine. Really. I'm with a cable outfit. I moved over from the phone company."

"I remember when you got the job at New England Bell."

After high school Cubby had gone to Rhode Island Junior College. Billy and I went into the army. Bobby, because of his one eye, was classified 4-F and took the Bell job.

"I see you every now and then. The acting stuff."

"It's pretty silly."

"It's good. You're good in the stuff I've seen. That hospital show . . . what was that?"

"Blues and Whites."

"That's right. *Blues and Whites.*"

Another pause. This time I didn't jump in.

He said, "I was very sorry about your mother."

My mother had died of kidney failure nineteen years before. "It was a long time ago."

"I came to the wake. I saw you, I guess I should have come over to talk, but—"

"I'm glad you were there."

"My mother's in the Ide Nursing Home. I guess her and Mrs. D'Agostino are the only ones. Billy's old man died a couple of years ago."

"Hey, listen. Want to get a drink or something—after your work, I mean?"

He paused and thought. "Okay. Sure. How about six-thirty? How about Merrill's Lounge?"

"Where's that?"

"Across from where Asquino's used to be."

"Used to be?"

"Everything's gone now," he said. "See you later."

I had promised Renée I'd exercise, and the truth is, I felt like a jog. Usually I have to talk myself into it, but I needed the relief of tension that a reasonably decent workout can give you. As I must have mentioned, I try to keep myself up. "Try" being the operative word.

It was pretty cold and gray when I walked out of the Ramada in my sweats. I stretched a little, started walking to the street, then fell into a slow, ponderous jog. I crossed the overpass of I-195, passed the Howard Johnson's where I short-order-cooked one spring, continued on past the Grist Mill Restaurant, which was my old man's idea of the Ritz, and followed the Taunton Pike to a side road and took it into Rehoboth.

When I move my body parts, I do it slowly. I figure my old self will instinctively fall into the proper pace. I'm not looking to get back on the skates. I'm looking to free up my often confused and disorganized mind. A light snow began, and I started to loop back toward the Ramada. I was moving mechanically now; my racing thoughts slowed to a crawl. That's what a little exercise does for me. For a while I become uncluttered. There's room for other things. Sandy Minucci took the room and filled my head.

Sandy was my first real girlfriend. She was a tiny and extraordinarily vivacious girl with light blond hair that placed her people in the north of Italy. Most of the East Providence Italians, even the ones who'd been there since the Revolution, were from down below Naples or from Sicily. Sandy lived on the Riverside Terrace with her folks and eight brothers. She was the baby of the family, and when I picked her up for our first date in Mother's old Buick, I was threatened nine times.

First her dad said, "Ten o'clock. A one and a zero. Ten. Not ten-oh-five. Ten. Or else."

"Yes, sir," I said.

When Sandy went to get her jacket, her brother Larry, the

spokesman for her eight brothers, got up from the TV and walked over.

"Hey, Jono."

"Hi, Larry."

"If you touch my sister, I'll beat the shit out of you. Alex and Hank will, too. They told me to tell you. Brian and Dougie and Eugene told me to tell you if you touch her, they'll kill you. Jimmy and Billy . . . well, you never know what they'll do, because they're crazy."

I always felt very comfortable and welcome at the Minuccis'. Mama Minucci, the grandmother, was a wonderful cook, and of course I knew the parameters of my relationship with Sandy, even though she didn't. The main thing was to get her home at the given time.

The part I liked best about Sandy, the attribute I admired above all her other obvious qualities, was that she didn't seem put off by the size of my head. She never did a double take when she saw me in the hall—at least I don't think she did. Anyway, she was very nice, and the picture in my mind of her in her cheerleader outfit, laughing with her friends after a game, was so pleasant I didn't notice how hard it was snowing until I turned into the Ramada parking lot.

After a shower I sat in a chair and tried to meditate. That didn't work, so I lay on the bed and tried to meditate prone. That didn't work either. I fell asleep for a couple of hours. I woke at six o'clock. The snow was piling up. I dressed and drove to Merrill's Lounge, a one-story bar where Bobby said it was, across the street from the spot Asquino's, the greatest Italian restaurant ever, had been. Bobby was right. Everything was gone or going.

There were pool tables, all of them in use, to the right of the entrance. Most of the dining tables had somebody at them. The walls of the place were a light green, and so were the tiles on the floor. A long, plain bar with simple metal and red-cushioned bar stools ran pretty much the entire length of the back wall. No pictures hung on the wall, just beer ads and Red Sox pennants. I sat at the least occupied corner of the bar and ordered a bottle of Narragansett. While the little round woman behind the bar fished it out of a cooler of ice, I caught a look at myself in the mirror. My Vandyke beard was looking scraggly, and my slight ponytail protruding over my collar seemed downright silly.

"Jesus," I said out loud to my reflection.

"What?" a sixtyish man sitting a couple of stools away asked.

"I . . . Nothing," I said.

He nodded and looked back at his cigarette. The beer arrived.

"Tab?" she asked.

"Sure."

It was about a quarter to seven, but I didn't see anybody that looked like Bobby. In fact, nobody looked familiar. And they wouldn't, would they? East Providence used to be home; now it was only a place. I watched some of the pool players in the bar mirror, then swung my look to a pregame Boston Bruin hockey show on the big TV.

"They stink, huh?" the bartender said.

I looked to her. "I don't follow them."

"They stink big time. They let Bourque get away. They don't go after Jagr. They don't care. So how you been?"

"Uh . . . I been . . . fine."

"You don't know me, huh? I probably wouldn't recognize you either if it wasn't for TV. *Blues and Whites*. You were the retarded guy."

I didn't correct her. I suppose the way TV presents things now, the way it manipulates us, being retarded or autistic or blind or walking with a limp—they're all about the same thing. She held out her fat little hand.

"I'm Sandy. Sandy Minucci."

I kept a flat smile, but behind the façade was all the trepidation of coming face-to-face with the unrelenting reality of the human aging process. Sandy? My adorable little Sandy Minucci, who I had risked life and limb to date? Who had been my steady until I went into the army how many years ago? She was saying something, but I wasn't listening. One moment I'm jogging in the snow and we're young and crispy, and the next we're cracking like eggshells. Actors should just never ever confront their past.

". . . what's his name? The cop on that soap you did?"

"Soap?"

"You did that soap . . ."

"As the World Turns."

"Yeah. Who's that young cop? Mmmm. Cute."

"You know, I can't remember his name."

"Lawrence something."

"Lawrence St. Angeline," I said, snapping my fingers.

"St. Angeline. That's it. Cute, cute."

She smiled, and I nodded. My sweet little cheerleader in her new, robust body. She waddled down to the end of the bar and mixed a quick highball for a big man in a black suit and poured a shot and a beer for his companion, a smaller man in a blue shirt and whitish tie. They looked dour and fiftyish. Both were balding, and the taller one obviously had run some black color through his thin hair. Under the bar's fluorescent lights, it looked purplish blue. Sandy waddled back up to me.

"So, yeah, I got married and had a kid—well, he's a man now—and I got divorced. I never got hitched again. You know. Brian, that's my baby—well, he's a man now—he's a dealer in Connecticut at one of the Indian casinos. Ever been there?"

I shook my big head. "Uh-uh."

"We named him Brian for my brother. He got killed in 'Nam."

"I remember."

"You got hurt, too."

"Nah. I got some scratches."

"They reported it in the *East Providence Post*."

I shrugged. I knew we'd go there tonight, Bobby and me, for other reasons. I didn't want to go there now. I changed gears.

"I can't believe Asquino's is gone."

"Tell me about it. So what's new? What are you working on now?"

"I just finished a play."

"Broadway?"

"Well, off, you know. . . ."

"Off-Broadway, yeah."

"Yeah . . . off- . . . off-Broadway."

"Married? Kids?"

"I was, but it didn't work out. No kids."

"Most of them don't work out. Marriages, I mean. I read where more than half of them don't work out. My mother was married to Papa for fifty-three years, and the only reason it wasn't longer is because of the stroke and then the heart attack and then the cancer, which is what finally got him."

She crossed herself and got another Narragansett out of the cooler. Tapping on the bar twice when she set it down to indicate it was on the house.

"Hey, Sandy? Who's the ponytail?"

I instinctively looked down the bar to see Mutt and Jeff staring at me. The tall one sipped his highball, put it down and gestured with his head.

"Who's the new boyfriend?"

His friend laughed a familiar high giggle that seemed incongruous with his squat, drooping face. Sandy snickered at them, shook her head, and turned back to me.

"Some things never change."

"Huh? You say something?" the shorter one said.

"I'm talking to a friend here," Sandy said dismissively.

"That's what I said. Who's your friend?"

I've had a lot of experience with bars. Lambs, I mean. Most people getting belligerent will respond to a friendly smile and a non-aggressive tone.

"I'm Jono Riley," I said easily, even though for some reason these two had made me uneasy. "I used to live around here, and . . . well, I haven't seen Sandy since high school. What a coincidence."

The tall one smiled into his drink. "So you're here for the parade, right?"

"What parade?"

"The parade in honor of the big-deal actor we're supposed to give you because you're so fucking great."

"You might think you're so fucking great, but you ain't fucking great," his partner snarled.

"Knock it off," Sandy said disgustedly.

"Who's gonna make me knock it off?" the taller one said. "Ponytail boy?"

"Yeah. How about it, ponytail boy?" the shorter one said.

"Tom Hanks," the tall one said with some menace. "He's a big deal. What's his name? Cruise."

"Pacino, De Niro," his friend chimed in.

"Billy Crystal, Robin Williams . . ."

"Williams ain't so hot, though," the short one said.

"The point is, they're all stars. They're somebody. This guy thinks because he did a shitty television show, we got to give him a fucking parade."

"Can it, Allie," Sandy said.

Allie? Allie Ponserelli? Then the short one had to be Howie Crosby. Well, sure, this is what they'd grow up to be, all right. A two-headed asshole.

"What are you looking at?" Allie snarled, and walked down the bar. He got close enough I could smell his English Leather.

I put my hands up. "I'm not looking at anything."

"He says we're not anything," Allie said to Howie, who slid off his stool and joined his looming partner.

Do you know how much I want to report that unbeknownst to these fools I was a twenty-second-degree black belt and former heavyweight boxing champion of the Sixth Army and handled them with the skill and ease of a ninja? But, of course, I'm an actor and have no skills, fighting or otherwise.

They were on either side of me now. Three old boys twenty years removed from the shuffleboard courts.

"Did you say something?" Allie said in a lousy imitation of Clint Eastwood.

"I said I'll take a 'Gansett," a soft voice said.

Bobby Fontes stood at the center of the bar and was looking at Sandy. He was wearing jeans and a gray shirt with a New England Cable logo. Over it was a black motorcycle jacket. He was as tall as me, but so spare and hard-looking he seemed much taller. Full, long brown hair fell wildly across his hawkish face. His black eye patch seemed natural. I knew how old Bobby was. He looked thirty. He didn't move a muscle.

"Hi, Bobby," I said, a good imitation of controlled breathing.

He took his odd prespeaking beat. "Jono, sorry I'm late. The snow."

"No problem. You know Sandy?"

"Sure."

"Allie Ponserelli? Howie Crosby? Remember these guys?"

Bobby moved only his good eye and took them into his stare. Allie and Howie didn't say anything, and it wasn't as if they didn't want to. I got the real feeling they couldn't speak. Finally Bobby nodded. They nodded reflexively and walked carefully back to their drinks. A few minutes later, they left the bar.

★ ★ ★

Bobby signaled Sandy for another one.

"Anyway, my mother doesn't remember anything. Every time I visit, and I visit every day, she's in the same chair by the same window. She don't recognize me, but she always asks for him."

"Him," I knew, was his father.

"Go figure," he said to his empty glass.

Sandy put two new ones in front of us. I was feeling the other beers. Bobby wasn't. I glanced over to him. He was staring ahead, most likely still in the nursing home with his mother.

I said, "It's common, you know. People getting older . . . Alzheimer's, that stuff."

He looked back at me. I smiled and nudged him.

"I mean, it's okay to be turned around by your mother's confusion."

"I'm not turned around," he said after a moment. "I was thinking about Billy."

I nodded. We drank our beer.

17

Billy and Peggy Fontanelli's father was Marie's mother's brother. Bill Sr. worked with Big Tony at Tasca's. He was a transmission man. His wife waitressed at Eileen Darling's Restaurant in Rehoboth on the breakfast-lunch shift so she could be home when the kids got out of school. I suppose all of us were spoiled a little. I mean, even in our self-centered teenage years, we knew that whatever the folks were up to, they were up to it for us. Even Bobby's mother. But the Fontanellis took the cake. They doted on those kids like they were royalty. Every Christmas and birthday, their gifts became more and more elaborate, culminating with a late-model DeSoto, sitting in the Fontanellis' driveway with a huge red ribbon around it, on Billy's sixteenth. I remember Big Tony telling Cubby and me, "Don't you guys get any ideas."

Also, there were wonderful vacations that required complex planning and saving by Mrs. Fontanelli. Mother and Pop and me used to head up to North Conway in the White Mountains of New Hampshire each and every early August for Pop's two-week vacation. We always went to the same spot and did the same things. It was simple and suited us pretty well. Big Tony used to go to the shore for his two-weeker. He loved Sand Hill Cove and always took the same shack near the inlet. But Mrs. Fontanelli would plan and save, and somewhere in the middle of July, Billy, Peggy, and the folks would be off to astonishing destinations all designed to "broaden the kids' horizons," as Bill Sr. explained to Big Tony. I remember one summer when Bill Sr. had an extra week, earned by working through the Christmas holiday, and they all went to Italy, which was really something for working-class East Providence.

Anyway, it stood to reason that Billy and Peggy's mom and pop wanted the best for them. College. Career. Things like that. Important things that would allow them to transcend their cottage class and rise, I guess, like you're supposed to rise in America. So when Billy came home one night and told his folks that Jono Riley had "joined up" on the army's three-month deferred plan and he thought he would, too, they reacted in a pretty predictable way. They went ballistic. This was a week before senior prom, and it sort of threw a small wrench into Billy, Bobby, Cubby, and my plans. We had each saved thirty dollars from our summer jobs, pooled the cash, and had taken the unprecedented and extraordinarily cool step of renting a stretch limousine and driver for the prom. The parents all thought this was a very good idea, because getting drunk at a post-prom party and totaling your father's car tended to piss them off. Billy's mother had invited our folks and our dates' folks over for a kind of cocktail/picture-taking party and to see us off to the prom.

"You're disinvited, I guess," Billy said as the four of us huddled next morning in the school parking lot.

"Huh?"

"I just told them I was thinking of joining with you, and the old man takes off on the Irish."

"What about the Irish?" Cubby asked.

"He said that the army was all the Irish were good for."

We were shaking our heads, and Bobby said, after his beat, "That's not nice."

"He was just pissed, you know," Billy explained. "So I guess you have to wait in the limo."

"What about my mom?"

"I think it's *all* the Irish."

I thought about this. Mother was Scottish.

"What about Sandy?" Cubby asked reasonably. "Jono's girl is a dago."

"I'll have to check."

"Wait a sec," I said. "If my mom can't go and I can't go, how's my mom gonna get pictures of the tuxedo and shit?"

We all thought about it. Cubby snapped his fingers.

"We'll stop over at my house first and have Marie take our picture, and then we'll drive over to Billy's."

Cubby lit a Marlboro, and we waited until Bobby said, "It's still not nice. I wish I could join the army."

"Wait a minute," I said. "How can Marie take our pictures if she's at college?"

"She's coming home to see the tuxes and shit."

"I'm sorry," Billy said to me.

I was, too, but I said, "I don't give a shit about having my picture taken."

There's a lot more about the prom to tell, but not right now. Right now it's about how Billy's folks always blamed me completely. It's about those sad twenty minutes smoking Marlboros in the limo while the rest of them laughed and posed in Billy's backyard. It's about how a year and a half later I stood on crutches outside the Mello Funeral Home in my army uniform, alone again.

18

"I wish I could have joined up with you and Billy."

I had driven back to the Ramada shamefully tipsy. Slept poorly and met up with Bobby again at six-thirty the next morning for coffee. Then we made a stop at the Riverside Cemetery. We sat in Bobby's minivan looking over a field of snow and marble.

"Lots of snow," I said.

"I don't have to be at work till eight-thirty," he said after a moment, and got out of the car. I followed him, my loafers sinking in the snow. I followed Bobby across the field to a small rise. I remembered the spot. Remembered visiting it after the family had left. Remembered grudges silly and permanent.

Bobby brushed snow away from the stone. Billy was between his grandparents and mother and father. The stone said WILLIAM MATEO FONTANELLI 1950–1969. Under the dates it said BELOVED. I nodded. Bobby, too.

It would be whipping a dead horse to repeat that I had nothing to do with Billy joining out of high school except for that one conversation at Cubby's about what our plans were for the next year. The four of us were eating some leftover lasagne Mrs. D'Agostino had heated up and just shooting the breeze like we always did.

Cubby said that Big Tony had set him up at Rhode Island Junior College by arranging for the admissions guy to get a Tasca cream-puff used car at cost. Bobby had already been accepted into the phone company's apprentice program, and so I mentioned the army deal. Billy's father had gone to Boston College on a football scholarship but ended up quitting his first year because of the war, and now he was hot for Billy to go to college and "broaden his horizons." But Billy wanted to wait for school. And it wasn't as if we were being patriotic or anything like that. We just wanted out of East Providence. At least for a while.

We did our basic at Fort Dix in New Jersey. I then got assigned to an infantry program, because I didn't have any idea what I wanted to do. Billy had a real knack for keeping his things neat and organized, so he got assigned to quartermaster school. I shipped out to Vietnam, where three months later I was wounded in my thighs and feet by mine fragments. Two days after that, Billy was killed in an automobile accident just outside of Fort Gordon, Georgia. It's what made the Fontanellis' grudge even harder to understand.

"He would have been fifty-one," Bobby said.

I nodded. I missed Billy like I missed all of us at eighteen. But I did not feel responsible. I never felt responsible. I checked my watch. It was almost seven-thirty.

"I probably should be getting back to my car. I'm meeting somebody at eight."

Bobby looked up at me. "Something to do with Marie, isn't it?"

It struck me that this was the first time either of us had mentioned her.

He shrugged. "You never came back. I mean, after your mother passed away. Now you're back, so I figure it's because Marie died. I used to see her, you know. At the Dunkin' Donuts sometimes. At the drugstore. She always smiled. But we weren't young anymore."

We walked back to Bobby's car. My feet were getting those

little pins from the damp snow and cold. We drove back to the diner where my rental was. Bobby hadn't said a word. I opened the door and stayed seated for a while.

"Listen, my friend is coming in a couple of days from New York. I'd like you to meet her. Maybe we can have dinner or something."

I waited for his essential pause.

"Is she an actress, too?"

I shook my head. "Renée's a fireman. Fireperson."

Bobby smiled. "I'd like to have dinner or something."

I drove back into East Providence proper, getting up to the new water tower at five to eight. No one was there. No footprints in the clean snow. In the dull early light, the saucer-shaped thing looked exactly like a cream-colored mushroom. I got out of the car and stared up. The pump house, a small cinder-block replica of my pop's huge Socony-Mobil pump house, whirred through the otherwise silent morning. I thought I heard a clanging sound and looked up sharply at the tower.

"Jono Riley?"

I jumped a little, turned, and tripped on a snow-covered rock, nearly falling.

"Careful," Kenny Snowden said.

"I . . . I didn't hear your car," I said, embarrassed.

"I live just off the Wampanoag Trail. I walked. Only a couple of miles." He extended his hand. "Kenny Snowden. Jono Riley?"

I took it. "Yes, sir, Mr. Snowden."

"Kenny."

Except for heavy wrinkles around his eyes and mouth, Kenny Snowden was little changed from his knife-thin, taut, younger self. His full hair was trimmed tight, and clear black eyes took me in from a rich, dark face. We both looked up at the tower.

"Old one fell down," he said, shaking his head. "Two welders were working up on the back side. They broke for lunch, sat in their truck, and the thing buckled and fell. Over a hundred thousand gallons of water down the drain. Lucky welders, though."

I hadn't noticed a thermos he had tucked under his arm. He began to unscrew the cap. He looked at me.

"I put a little skim milk and an Equal in here. Okay?"

"Perfect," I said.

He poured the thermos cup about half full and handed it to me, took a small porcelain cup from his coat pocket, half-filling that, too. We sipped the coffee.

"This is very good, thanks."

Kenny Snowden looked back at the tower. "Soon as I heard of the passing of your friend, I began to separate and arrange my notes from '61. Probably because I always viewed it as unfinished business. December twenty-seventh, 1961, is when Marie went down over there."

Kenny pointed to the vicinity where we had made the snow angels. I nodded.

"Curious, though. Always left me shaking my head how anyone could take down a twelve-year-old. A girl. I'd give anything to have had a close look at the slug."

"It was a .22. At least that's what the doctor said."

"But, understand, without the actual fingers on the metal, the forensic people could never possibly draw a match."

I sipped the good coffee and thought about this. "A match to what?" I said finally.

He looked at me. "A match to the others. Walk with me a bit."

He marched into the snow, high-stepping around the perimeter of fence. Some pine and oak separated the sides and back of the tower area from adjoining ranch-style development homes. I was chilly, but Kenny Snowden seemed oblivious to the weather.

"That woodworking teacher . . ."

"Mr. Holt," I said.

"That's right. Ted Holt. They dug two .22 slugs out of him in '64. Father Persico—"

"Father Al just disappeared, right? Nineteen—"

"Nineteen sixty-nine. Said a mass at St. Martha's, then disappeared."

I nodded.

"Until this new tower went up," he said casually.

I stopped, calf-deep in the snow. "What?"

"When they were digging the foundation for the thing, they found a canvas duffel bag about five or six feet down—1987."

"You're not saying Father Persico was in the bag."

"No, but all his things were. Clothes, wallet, ID, car keys, even his collar."

"Jesus," I said, and shook my head. "What do you think happened to his body?"

"We dug hard after we found the clothes." He swept the air and pointed. "Dogs, everything. Best guess was he was killed here, then disposed of somewhere else. Not many people know that the woodworking teacher wasn't killed at home where we found him either. He was moved there."

"You think he was killed here?"

Kenny Snowden sipped his coffee and then smiled at me. "*That* is the sixty-four-thousand-dollar question."

We started walking again in silence until he stopped about halfway around the fence perimeter.

"It's no secret that, contrary to popular belief, many, many crimes go unsolved. Assault, burglary, even the more heinous ones. Rape. Murder. This is usually put up to the perpetrator being a one-time-only malefactor. Crawling out of the mud into regular society after their one act is completed. FBI has a psychological profiling kit I've worked with from time to time, and let me tell you, it's discouraging at best."

I nodded like a dummy. My feet were freezing. Kenny looked at me hard.

"But what really loads you up with an empty feeling is when you know for sure that whoever did these crimes has done others and maybe isn't finished yet."

I'm a bartender and an actor. The information, like Kenny Snowden himself, suddenly felt like a thousand pounds of reality. My shoulders sagged. He piled on more weight.

"Before the computer could cross-reference criminal scenes in minutes, you had to use your noggin and your connections. I used the old tower as a center point, because that's really all I had, and canvassed other municipalities for similarities. To Holt. To your Miss D'Agostino. Even Father Persico's clothing. I made arcs on a map like vibrations. Started with Seekonk. Nothing. Rehoboth. Providence, Barrington, the same. Then I made another arc. North Providence. Taunton. Like that. Nothing."

I was starting to feel some relief for some reason.

"Till I got to Warren. A man named Soares. Bunny Soares got shot about the same time the priest disappeared. Body was recovered, case never solved."

He started moving again, around the fence, and added casually, "Bullet came from the same rifle that got Holt. There was a postal worker in Rockville, Rhode Island. Same thing. Same rifle."

"So the person that shot Marie may have killed four other people?" I asked weakly.

"The boys from the FBI came in when whoever it was crossed state lines. An insurance salesman in North Stonington, Connecticut, disappeared—and guess what? They found his clothes and wallet buried in a duffel bag."

We arrived back at my car.

"This is unbelievable," I muttered. "Look . . . uh . . . Kenny, can I give you a lift?"

"I always take a long walk about now. My wife is ill, and we have a visiting nurse from seven to eleven in the morning. Then I'm on full-time duty till seven next morning."

He sighed and rubbed the back of his neck.

"I haven't really troubled myself about the thing in a long while until I read about your friend. I should have, though. I should have troubled myself. I didn't leave the force under particularly pleasant circumstances, and then, of course, there's Lila, my wife. But that young lady got hurt on my watch, and no matter what's gone on, it will always be my watch."

I didn't say anything. Kenny Snowden was in a sort of sense-memory exercise now, like an actor might use to prepare a scene or a moment. The only difference was that Kenny's feelings were ascendant and bona fide.

"I need a favor," he said. "It might be an uncomfortable one. It's very, very important we get our hands on that .22 slug. The one that was inside your friend. You know the husband? He'd have to give permission."

"You mean exhume Marie's body?"

"I wasn't thinking, or I would have tried before she was buried. You still at the Ramada?"

"Yes."

He shook my hand and pushed off for the long way home to Wampanoag Trail and his sick wife. I drove over to St. Martha's, sat for a while in the parking lot, then drove into Providence.

19

Father Al Persico didn't like me. At least not after my pop was killed at the pump house. I more or less became a pumpkin-headed prick, and that lasted throughout most of my sophomore year until the great macaroni-and-meatball threat. I'm pretty sure I was okay with Mother, though. I tried to be a good boy and be attentive and all that, because I knew, without having to be told, that since my pop was gone our life was not going to be the same. But to most of the world, "prick" would be the word. When I look back, which I often do now, it surprises me, because I'm fundamentally pretty nice. Anyway, I became difficult to teach and impossible to coach. As a matter of fact, I was jettisoned from both the football and baseball teams in my sophomore year for conduct unbecoming a Crimson Townie, and, really, the only reason I was allowed to keep my surly ass on the hockey team was that I was a great player and Mr. Eblemyer, who coached the varsity team, overlooked some of my peccadilloes, such as not practicing. So this would pretty much illustrate why Father Al didn't like me. Why he didn't like St. Martha's was another thing altogether. Because we were a working-class parish, it goes without saying we didn't have a pot to piss in, with pledges and offerings barely keeping the three-priest, two-nun operation on its feet. As most of the men had to work two jobs, volunteers were limited to older female parishioners with interests in altar floral arranging and a twice-a-year thrift-shop sale. So it was to Father Al Persico, the forty-year-old associate pastor, that the lion's share of responsibilities fell. At least those responsibilities that required mobility. The pastor, Father Conlin, was pushing seventy, and just saying the mass about knocked him out, and his assistant, Father Bouvier, while a parish favorite, was also wheelchair-bound due to a childhood case of bubble polio.

From the moment Father Al plugged in the coffee at five-fifteen, a half hour before Mrs. Delaney the housekeeper arrived, to when he helped Father Bouvier into bed eighteen hours later, his minutes were spoken for seven days a week. He said early mass, visited the shut-ins, coached the girls' CYO basketball, swim, and softball teams. He also somehow coached the boys' CYO basketball, swim, and baseball teams, organized the talent shows, was present at the Boy Scout and Girl Scout troop meetings that met once a week, and said afternoon mass when Father Conlin was too exhausted to do it, which was often. He said mass regularly at the Ide Nursing Home, which was chock-full of ancient Catholics, and he rounded off his religious duties with a heaping helping of church custodial work. What I remember most about Father Al was his amazing thick black hair that he wore in a high flattop and, of course, the bags under his eyes.

Mother was devout, I suppose, in that we never missed Sunday mass. We used to go when my pop was here, too, but I knew he never liked getting up on his only day off and getting dressed in a suit and tie. All these Irish and Portuguese and Italian men would stand outside in the parking lot talking and sucking down one last cigarette while their wives took the kids in and saved them a seat. It was strange and good. Strange because a lot of the Portuguese and Italian men were newly arrived and didn't speak much English and the Irish spoke a curious Rhode Island form of it. But good because the last smoke before church drew warm and smooth, and their wives had saved them a seat, so it didn't matter that they couldn't understand each other.

Unlike most of the adults I knew, Father Al did not embrace the position that it was okay for me to be a jerk because I had lost my pop. Even Big Tony tended to give me leeway. My "poor me" attitude just pissed Father Al off. I can't remember how many CYO meetings I was kicked out of or how many times, when he'd be greeting the parish on St. Martha's steps after Sunday mass, he'd give me the brush-off. I didn't care. I didn't want to be at the stupid CYO anyway, or go to stupid mass. I only went because of Mother. What I did care about, though, was the CYO baseball league.

It was the middle of May, and the high-school coach, Dee Metz, had already bounced me from the team for giving the double finger to a tollgate first baseman who I thought put the tag on my wrist a little too hard during a failed pickoff attempt. Initially Coach Metz just removed me from the game, but when I explained that the stupid dago tagged me too hard and also was a fucking son of a bitch, I suppose I placed Coach Metz in a situation where he had no choice but to have me turn in the uniform, leaving the St. Martha's Martyrs, coached by the Jono Riley–hostile Father Al Persico, as my only spring sports team.

The truth is, CYO baseball was vastly better than most high-school clubs. Especially those teams coached by the Jesuit brothers. Not only did the Jesuits frighten the boys into playing all-out, they also combined modern coaching techniques with physical abuse. I once saw a catcher lose the ball in the sun, drop it, and get slapped in the back of the head by a Jesuit priest who was only filling in for the regular coach. Our club was pretty solid, with a steadily improving yours truly at third, Billy and Bobby making up a serious second and short combo, and Cubby anchoring it all behind the plate. It was wonderful to play with them. Memorable, I suppose. I was getting tired of my bitter-prick act, but I didn't know how to just stop it. I was kind of in a rut. It's a lot of work to be an asshole—at least for me it was. Exhausting, if I had to choose a word. But out there after school with my best friends, just throwing the ball around, I could relax. They knew it, too, even if they never said it. It might have been the only nice part of my fifteenth year in East Providence.

It was a Friday night, and we had just knocked off practice. On Saturday we were playing Holy Ghost Brotherhood in Providence, and if we took that one, we were in the playoffs. The girls' softball team was finishing up their practice directly behind us. Father Al would position himself between us so he could coach both teams at the same time. The girls were no joke. I mean, they took the game deadly serious and, so far, had destroyed every one of their opponents. Father Al was thinking state title. We were twelve and two and knew that Holy Ghost had three outfielders and a pitcher that the *Providence Journal* had predicted would become stars. The girls broke with a cheer, and Marie jogged over to me.

Father Al walked up to her. "Great pitching, Marie. Keeping the ball high and tight is the key. What's the name of that Spanish girl?"

"On Holy Ghost?"

"Yes."

"De Herrera?"

"That's her. She's got some power, and she's tough on the base path. I was talking to Father Joe at Fatima, and he tells me she's got a weakness for risers."

"Thanks, Coach."

She yelled over to Cubby, "I thought Daddy was going to watch practice!"

Cubby thumbed over to the parking lot. "He watched from the lot with Billy's old man."

Marie waved, and Big Tony pushed off the car he was leaning

against and started over. Father Al stopped and signaled the boys over. He tapped Cubby on the top of the head.

"Good thinking on those throws to second, D'Agostino. They're gonna run on us tomorrow, and the one low hopper is the throw that's gonna get to Billy the fastest. Now, boys, I want to slant the infield tomorrow. By that I mean we all know that Bobby's got a lot more range at short than Riley has at third, so, Riley, you play closer to the bag, and, Bobby, you pick up the slack."

Father Al turned to Ronnie Nelson, our first baseman, but before he could say anything I opened my big mouth.

"That'll leave a big gap between second and short."

"We have to do what we have to do," Father Al said, still getting ready to speak to Ronnie.

"It'll screw up the whole infield," I whined.

Father Al turned back to me. "Hey, I'm just the coach, Riley. I'm not the one with stone feet."

"Stone feet?"

"Do I hear an echo?"

I want to say that I sucked up this monumental insult and went out the next morning and played like Frank Malzone, once and for all shutting up that mean, unforgiving priest. I want to say that, but that would be at variance with the truth.

"I quit," I whined.

"I'm not surprised," he snarled.

We stared at each other. Then I stormed off, walking past Big Tony and Marie without a word. I could feel them all watching me disappear. I walked to our little house on Cardinal but didn't go inside. My eyes were tearing with that rheumy combination of anger and guilt. I sat on the swing set in our backyard and pushed back and forth, my cleats scraping the grass, my mitt in my lap. I sat there a long time, not really thinking, just wallowing in the warm self-righteousness that always seemed to follow on the heels of a teenage confrontation. Our porch light came on, and Mother let Big Tony out into the yard. She looked at me, then at Big Tony, who nodded reassuringly and she went inside. Big Tony strolled over to the swing set, lighting a Marlboro as he came. He squeezed onto the next swing seat. The set itself seemed to settle and moan under his great weight. He puffed a little in silence, the good fat smell of tobacco filling the cool evening.

"I'm sixteen, right? I drop out of EP, lie about my age, join the Corps, okay? I get out after the war, come home, no idea what I'm gonna do. You listening to me, Bozo?"

"Sure, Big Tony."

"I bump into a guy says they're hiring at Tasca's. Parts. Now, I don't know nothin' about cars. What parts they need, that stuff. But guess what? There's an older guy running the parts department who knows everything, but instead of helping me he goes around complaining that I don't know nothin'. Old Man Tasca calls me on the carpet. He goes, 'What about it?' I go, 'It's true. I don't know nothin'.' He goes, 'How can you do parts, then?' I go, 'I guess I can't if nobody'll teach me.' You know what the old man did? He honest to God sent me to Ford headquarters in Michigan to parts school. See?"

I nodded, but I didn't know where he was going.

"You think I should go to baseball school?"

"No, I think you should shake it off. What the priest said."

"He said I had stone feet."

"I know. Cubby told me."

"I don't."

"I know."

"He wanted me to play close to third and have Bobby cover everything else."

Big Tony put the last of the cigarette out on the bottom of his foot and flicked the butt.

"You know what, Bozo? A lot of times a man's got to do things he doesn't want to do."

He let this sink in.

"I want you to call Father Al and apologize. The guys need you."

"He should apologize to me. I don't have stone feet."

"That's true."

"I'm not slow."

Big Tony stood up. "Bozo?"

"Yeah?"

"Yes you are. Now, it don't mean you can't get quicker around the bag, but right now . . ."

"I am not slow."

"Just call him and say you're sorry. Think about the team," he ordered.

Now I stood shaking with rage. "I'm not gonna call him. I don't care about the team."

This last little gem got Big Tony's eyes wide.

"You better care, Bozo. Now, go in the house and call him."

"No."

"You don't call him, you won't be mooching no more macaroni and meatballs across the street."

"But, Big Tony, he's an asshole."

The slap knocked me sideways. I know it was a restrained slap, because if Big Tony had really whacked me, my big head would have landed somewhere between Tiverton and Newport. It surprised him, though, as much as it did me. We stared at each other until I ran into the house. I locked myself in my upstairs bedroom and had a good long cry. When I came out, it was past eight. Mother was reading in the living room waiting for *Perry Mason* to come on at nine. She didn't say anything. Mother was terrific like that. She had a definite and powerful point of view but never shared it until she knew it would contribute meaning to whatever the situation. I wandered into the kitchen and sat red-eyed at the table where Mother had laid out my schoolwork. I opened my math book, and all the numbers blended together into blurry symbols. I put my head onto the table.

Marie came into the kitchen. "I came in the back door. Here."

She put a large white porcelain bowl onto the table. Aluminum foil covered it snugly. I didn't have to look; I had smelled it.

"Daddy cooked it himself and told me to bring it over."

Marie D'Agostino was sixteen now and still wore her jeans and sweatshirt from the afternoon practice. Her hair was in pigtails, and tonight her perfectly oval face seemed to float on her square shoulders.

"He already put the Parmesan on, so it's all melted and stuff."

Marie came around the corner of the table and kissed my cheek, smiled seriously at me, and left by the front door so she could say good night to Mother. I got up and walked over to the phone in the den.

Half an hour later, I brought the empty bowl that had held maybe the greatest combination of macaroni and meatballs in history back to the D'Agostinos'.

Cubby thumbed me into the kitchen. "Pop's doing dishes."

Mrs. D'Agostino was washing, and Big Tony was doing the ritual drying. Mrs. D'Agostino left us alone after giving me a hug. I put the bowl in the soapy water and slowly washed it.

"That was great, Big Tony."

"I make the gravy like my grandmother, my Nona Pia, used to. Hey, don't scrimp on the tomatoes," he said softly.

I handed him my bowl, and he took it into the dish towel.

"I called Father Al and said I was sorry, and he said okay, I could play."

"You gonna stick close to the bag?" Big Tony asked sort of nonchalantly.

"Yeah."

He smiled at me. "Cubby's waiting for *McHale's Navy*. Call me when it's on."

I'm still not sure whether it was the slap or the macaroni and meatballs soaking in Nona Pia's magical gravy that knocked the black cloud off of Bozo Riley, but the next day, even though Holy Ghost Brotherhood battered us nine to three, I stayed tight to the bag.

20

I didn't know Chip Cummings very well. Actually I only knew Marie's husband by his legendary East Providence baseball career. He was already in Triple-A ball at Pawtucket when I was in high school. He started dating Marie the next year. Chip Cummings had not only made first-team all-state at third base three years in a row but went directly to the Pawtucket Sox and in 1967 performed the mind-boggling feat of making the Red Sox major-league roster. At least for three days, until the backup third baseman's groin loosened up. Now he was the principal of Riverside Junior High and a widower to boot. I didn't relish the task that Kenny Snowden had more or less assigned me. How do you ask a grieving person if you can exhume a recently dead spouse? Especially if that spouse is still running around in your head in pigtails and red corduroy overalls? I needed to think this one through before I pushed myself into someone else's life.

I drove across the Washington Bridge into Providence, got off 195 at Benefit Street coming into the city proper sort of sideways. I doubt if any city I know has changed the way Providence has. It used to look as if its function was to just sit there and wait for the next tidal wave to roll up through Narragansett Bay and lay it out, like in 1938 or 1956. Except for the Industrial Trust Building and the Old Stone Bank, the feeling of hopeless enterprise seemed entrenched. Now even the obnoxious Providence River looks worthwhile, sludging its way around new office buildings and under high-rise apartments. I passed the beautiful railroad station and the renovated Biltmore Hotel, parked the car at a meter, and walked up to the Trinity Square Repertory Theater. Renée would arrive day after tomorrow. My amazing firefighter's idea of a perfect evening is the theater and a long dinner discussing exactly what we'd just seen. She even liked the stinkers, and God Almighty we've seen a ton of them, and not just the ones I've been in, thank you very much. She has a theory that while TV and films are all right, they tend not to give themselves to any clinical analysis, because there's a vicariousness about the medium. A distance between us and them. Also, she's convinced, film and TV manipulate our feelings to the point where they tell us what we should take away from the experience. With live theater there's an immediacy (again Renée's theory) and a certain haphazardness that allows you to put your own spin on the event. I don't know, really, if she's right or not. But anything with that lovely woman is right for me.

Trinity Square Rep is a pretty impressive operation. I had seen a play there with Mother a few years after they opened, 1966 maybe. I'm not sure what it was, but there were musical interludes every ten minutes or so and the set was a dirty old living room. Mother loved it. I thought it was awful. I felt the cast was daring me to like it. Now Trinity Square had changed along with the rest of the city. It was housed in a renovated church with a large theater upstairs and a smaller one downstairs. I checked the signs in front of the box office. Upstairs was *The Seagull*. I've seen about twenty productions of it and was in one myself in Roanoke, Virginia, and I have never seen the kids, Trepleff and Nina, pull off act 4. Ever. It's discouraging. Downstairs they were presenting a two-character world premiere of a play called *Sandpilot*.

I bought two tickets after the girl in the box office told me it was good, and then I drove back into East Providence and Riverside Junior High.

My pop was from Riverside, which was really an extension of East Providence. He used to say he was from the good part, meaning the part that's not the Terrace. I never got the association, because even though the Ponserelli and Crosby swine festered there, I also had a lot of pals from the Terrace. My nana and pa, Pop's mother and father, lived on Cedar Street about a block from Narragansett Bay. The section of bay that borders Riverside narrows as it squeezes up against the Providence River. It's much cleaner now than it was when I'd visit my grandparents and walk down to the water. There has been a real effort made to soak up the oil and crap that contaminated the clam beds. When my pop was a kid, they'd swim there. I've seen the pictures. He said you could walk out twenty feet and see the bottom. You can't now.

Riverside Junior High smelled like a school. Musty and inky and nostalgic. I found the principal's office and tapped on the door. It opened almost immediately. Chip Cummings was closing in on sixty. His curly hair had receded to about the crown of his head, but there was still a lot more red than gray. He was shorter than me by a few inches and still had the rugged stance of a third baseman. When I saw he was wearing a starched white shirt and blue tie, I was uncomfortably aware that I had on an old bowling shirt under a gray overcoat.

"Mr. Cummings? I'm Jono Riley, and I was—"

He pulled me into his office and shut the door.

"You don't have to introduce yourself, Jono Riley. You're famous at our house. Sit. Sit."

Any compliment, any acknowledgment of my alleged career feels like an accusation these days. Renée says I have a self-esteem problem, but I think it's more of a chemical reaction than emotional.

"We have your picture from that *Hallmark Hall of Fame* show you did a few years ago on our refrigerator."

It was the story of a woman who finds new romance after her first husband dies of a massive heart attack. She meets a writer in a wheelchair, and it's a really sweet romance of words and ideas. I played husband number one. During the opening credits, I take my coffee onto the porch, breathe deeply of the good fresh air, and drop dead.

"Marie was so, so proud of you," he said. Then he added quietly, "So proud."

"I'm awfully sorry about Marie. When I was growing up, she was like my sister."

He nodded and smiled. "Well, I can tell you truly, the first time she saw you on TV, she screamed." He laughed at the memory. "She thought you'd be the last person that went into show business."

"I kinda fell into it, I guess. I'm a bartender, too. It gets slow sometimes."

"Things turn out funny, all right. I always thought I'd play baseball my whole life."

"You were the greatest."

He shrugged it off. "Big fish in a small pond. I found that out in Boston. But I love what I'm doing, all things considered. Although I can't get used to the new culture. Hip-hop. Drug-free school zones. Jesus Christ, they didn't have to put up drug-free school zone signs when we were in school. Somebody sold drugs and one of the parents would kill them."

"Big Tony," I said, and we both smiled.

"I'm sorry I missed . . . didn't get up for Marie's . . . service. Cubby wrote to me just after."

"Father Gallo said the mass. Lots of people were there. Lots of the kids from Providence Country Day. She was their librarian, you know. We were having a little get-together, and Marie said she was tired and wanted to lie down for a bit. Janey, that's our oldest, the married one, went in to tell her we were getting ready to eat. Couldn't wake her. We called 911, but . . . Doctors said it was peaceful. Brian's in graduate school, but he had come home for Christmas. Cubby and Julie were there, too."

Chip Cummings looked at the top of his desk, and one short sob came. He caught himself. I reached across the desk and put my hand on his arm.

"I'm all right," he choked with a smile. "I've had some doozy cries, though, I can tell you. She was loved for sure. She deserved being loved."

Now I had to catch myself. My head swam in the knowledge that someone had murdered Marie D'Agostino Cummings forty years after the fact. We were quiet in our own thoughts for a few moments, and then it was the time to get to it.

"Do you remember Kenny Snowden?" I asked.

"Sure. Great guy. Cop liaison to the schools department. Knew all the kids by name. I never could figure out how he did that."

"Took it seriously, I guess."

"I guess. We could use that kind of cop now. Of course, then it was predicated on respect for authority."

"Did you know that I was with Marie when—"

"The famous snow-angel story." He smiled at the memory. The smile faded. "Used to be a wonderful story. It's why she died, Jono, did you know that?"

"Cubby told me."

"A 'traveler,' is what our family doctor called it. A traveler. Jesus Christ on a cross."

"I talked with Kenny this morning. Where it happened. He told me some pretty disturbing things."

"Like what?" Chip leaned forward. We watched each other's eyes.

"Like there might have been at least four other people killed by the same .22 rifle."

He opened his mouth to speak but couldn't. He closed his mouth. I continued.

"Remember Mr. Holt, the woodworking teacher?"

"Sure. You mean . . ."

"Father Al Persico?"

"I thought he just disappeared."

"That's what everybody thought until they found all his clothes and his identification buried up at the water tower. A guy in Warren. Mailman in Rockville. An insurance salesman, maybe. They matched up the bullets, and three of them definitely came from the same rifle."

He looked at me, and his anger flashed. "Same rifle that got my wife?"

"Kenny thinks there's a chance. See . . . look . . . I don't . . ."

He watched me hard.

"Because the bullet . . . the slug . . . was never removed from Marie, there was no way for the police scientists to compare it to the others. Kenny says the only way to be sure is to . . . actually . . . have the thing."

He leaned back and looked off. I couldn't read what he was thinking. I was thinking of a coffin being raised, of medical tools whirring against her disturbed peace, of her family—of me, really—being violated one more time.

Chip tossed something onto the desk. "Better take it, then."

The small copper-coated missile rolled for a second and stopped. It had lived a life inside my friend. Now she was gone, and it went on.

"Don't know why I kept it. When I found out that it was a . . . a . . ."

"Traveler."

"Yeah. A traveler that got Marie. I called the medical examiner just to confirm it. A few days later, he sent another copy of the autopsy report and had Scotch-taped this to it."

Driving back to the Ramada, I couldn't be certain if it was that I had the damn thing in my pocket or that I never had to get to the part of asking Chip to exhume his wife, but I felt like taking a bow.

21

Even with Bobby's old man teeing off on her on a pretty regular basis, his mother was a very beautiful woman. I remember thinking that all of our mothers were pretty, and they were, but Bobby's was much younger, having gotten married to his father when he was twenty-eight and she was sixteen. They had both been born in the Azores and migrated to East Providence when the fishing business got tough in Portugal. Bobby used to mumble about it being an arranged marriage, but I don't know. The few times I saw them together, they both seemed happy. Like at St. Martha's. But Bobby's old man stopped going after Big Tony "spoke" with him about Bobby's black eye.

Anyway, nobody was surprised when six months after her husband's death Adele Fontes showed up at church with Bobby and a handsome man about her own age. He was particularly attentive to her. She didn't look pinched anymore, as if she were flinching, waiting for the next punch. She had grown her black hair long and might have even lightened it. I couldn't be sure, and I didn't want to ask Bobby. Whatever she did, though, set off that soft face in such a way that she appeared very young, maybe twenty-three and not thirty-three.

Bobby, as usual, got his mother seated, then came over and squeezed in next to Big Tony, Billy, Cubby, and me, where we sat impatiently waiting for mass to be over. The four of us walked home the long way, stopping at the Sunnybrook Farm convenience store for chocolate milk and Marlboros. We smoked as we walked. Billy shook his head.

"Fucking mass gets longer and longer. Especially when Father Bouvier gives the homily."

"No shit," Cubby agreed.

There was the requisite pause, and Bobby spoke.

"He's in a wheelchair. Poor guy."

"Just because he's in a wheelchair doesn't mean he has to talk so much. And how about all his pauses?"

"No shit," Cubby said, savoring the smoke.

"He pauses longer than Bobby does," Billy said.

We all laughed. Bobby, too.

"I'm thinking what to say, is all," he insisted.

"Father Bouvier was reading, for chrissake."

I had been thinking about fishing. "I'm gonna see if my mother can drop me off at Hunt's Mills. Fish the river. Anybody want to go?"

"I thought we were gonna watch the Giants," Cubby said.

"I been thinking about fishing. I don't like Tittle."

"Grow up," Cubby said.

"Well, I don't."

"You don't like him 'cause he's old and bald. I think he's better than Charlie Conerly was."

"You think your mom would take us?" Billy asked.

"Maybe. Then we could walk over to that ice cream place and call her when we're ready to come back."

"I'm going," Billy said.

We smoked silently for a while, then put the cigarettes out

when we turned onto Brightridge Avenue, where anybody who saw us smoking might very well call Big Tony.

"That sounds like fun," Bobby said.

"I'm watching the Giants," Cubby added stubbornly.

We lingered in front of Cubby's house.

"Who's your mother's friend?" Cubby asked.

Bobby looked up quickly. "He's not a boyfriend."

"I didn't say he was. I was just wondering."

Bobby paused. "He's just some guy. He's not from around here."

Billy put both his hands up and turned to Cubby. "Wait. Wait. Wait. Did you just say the stupidest thing of all time? Tittle better than Conerly?"

There's such a wonderful and warm, almost milky sensation that comes with arguing intangibles. An abstractness that actually gives nuance to memory. We argued the inarguable often then. We bounced Cousy versus Kerr, Chamberlain and Russell, even Teddy Ballgame and Mickey. Our debates went as unresolved as we were. As we would always be.

I think the American retrospective of small-town lives is a cleaned-up version of how we wished we could have been. How when we were teenagers the political future and raging Vietnam War should have been paramount in our thinking along with all concerns of racial equality and poverty. I can't place myself in another community's shoes. Maybe the kids in those places were mightily committed to world peace and prosperity. It sounds good. It sounds a lot better than what drove our East Providence conversations. The Beatles, large breasts, baseball, and hockey. Did I mention large breasts?

Bobby's mother continued her social life and even had her engagement to one guy printed in the *East Providence Post*. But she never remarried. Several years ago his exceedingly beautiful mother forgot where her car keys were, then where her home was, and finally where she was. Now Bobby visits every day and tells her. Who she is. Who she was.

My mother gave us a ride to Hunt's Mills, where we caught some nice little brook trout. Later she picked us up at the ice cream place. Cubby came with us, Y. A. Tittle or not.

22

I had called Kenny Snowden and arranged another water-tower rendezvous for the next morning, then left messages for both my legit agent and my commercial agent, saying I was still out of town. The truth is, agents don't care where you are if you're not a big breadwinner, but the calls are absolutely essential to the illusion of the marginal actor. Even if you're not really in the game, you have to pretend you are. I also phoned up Lambs.

I'm a reticent man. I know I've said it before, but it bears repeating, if only to help myself figure out how a standoffish person would ever end up on the stage. It's very weird indeed to be in this profession and to dislike having other people watch you. I think about this more and more. I think about it to distraction. I was thinking about it now. Even after breakfast with Bobby, meeting Kenny at the tower, getting tickets from Trinity Square and seeing Chip Cummings at his school, it was only four o'clock. I had to get out of the hotel room or go nuts.

Jono Riley's Rhode Island Sentimental Journey Tour: 2001 starts just across the Providence River at Swan Point Cemetery, where Nana and Pa, Mother and Pop are buried. Well, of course, not Pop due to the circumstances, but it doesn't really matter. They're all there, for all intents and purposes. The stones are a coppery granite and look out over the river. I stood with them and remembered the wakes, the services, the friends coming over to our house afterward. I remembered that when Pa died was the only time I saw my pop cry. Death is surprisingly interesting, because most people just never think about it. It's sort of like a five-hundred-pound gorilla in your living room. How can you not think about it? People are funny.

I drove over to the Brown University campus and Meehan Auditorium. I circled it a few times. Rhode Island held its high-school state hockey championships there, and while I never, ever dwell on past glories, I thought of the games I played there. The three hat tricks. The player of the year (twice). The two state titles. But I don't dwell on that. Although a lot of people would. Did I mention the player of the year (twice) and the two state titles? I steered back to East Providence, cut through Rumford past the Rumford Chemical Works, where my mother's father had worked, then took Newport Avenue into Pawtucket and spun through Goddard Park. Sometimes when I was a little kid, if the weather was okay, we'd have a picnic at the park after church. There were thirty-foot-long First World War cannons bolted to concrete slabs here and there, and I'd sit and pretend to shoot things. Hunt's Mills was just the other side of the park, but it wasn't there when I looked for it. I turned back through Seekonk and crossed the Palmer River that wiggled its way into Shad Factory, an artificial lake and a favorite fishing spot of ours. I had a beer at Sun Valley Golf Course, where we caddied sometimes, then got onto Taunton Pike for East Providence.

It would be easy for the general public to view East Providence as just an eyesore located approximately at the junction of Interstate 195 and Interstate 95. The place is laid out oddly, and there aren't really many going concerns. There weren't when I was growing up either, except for Socony-Mobil, the largest employer. While it's technically a city, there aren't any city-type buildings, unless you count Town Hall, which I don't. But it has a serious place in American history and some great Italian restaurants. The history of old EP is linked directly to Massasoit, who saved the Pilgrims. In 1674 his only son, Metacomet, who was nicknamed King Philip by the New England colonists, got angry when two Narragansett Indians were hanged in Plymouth, Massachusetts. He attacked Swansea and began King Philip's War. A couple of years later, he got caught and slaughtered, but before that happened, old King Philip and his Narragansetts burned East Providence to the ground and killed every man, woman, and child. Later the Narragansetts had a fine lager beer named for them, brewed from the clear water of the Scituate Reservoir. Today, while there is still technically a Narragansett beer, it's brewed by Falstaff in Indiana. But as I said, East Providence has to be taken in its historical perspective. And, by the way, Asquino's Restaurant was a particularly terrific place until it closed down.

The sun had set and some light snow had begun. I went to a McDonald's drive-through and cruised over to the Ramada. I had just shut off the ignition when something clicked against my driver's-side window. I turned to see Allie Ponserelli tapping on it with what looked like a German Luger. I rolled down the window.

"Don't roll down the window, fuckface, get out of the car."

I got out, and he motioned me to walk to a black Town Car parked directly behind. He opened the back door.

"Here's the big-fucking-deal actor."

I got into the backseat, where a tall, fat, bald man in a tuxedo was sitting. Allie got into the front seat next to who I guessed was Howie Crosby, the driver. Howie nudged him, and he laughed.

"Big-fucking-deal actor. Look at me. I'm an actor."

"Big-fucking-deal actor," Allie snorted.

"Look at me. I'm a big-fucking—"

"You two assholes can it," the fat man snarled, and they did.

We pulled out of the parking lot and got onto 195.

"Richard Nixon said he thought better when he could feel the wheels moving. You ever heard that?" he said without looking at me.

"I don't think so."

"Used to turn up the air conditioner at the White House in the middle of summer just so's he could light the fireplace. That made him think better, too. But we're doing the first thing now. We're feeling the wheels moving down there so's we can think better. I know everything about Nixon."

"You better believe he does," Allie said threateningly.

"Shut up, asshole," the fat man said. "You been on the grand tour today. We been following you since Swan Point. Know where I'm going? Know why I got the tux on? Huh?"

"No. No idea," I said quickly.

"I'm going to a fund-raiser for the governor's reelection campaign. I'm a big contributor. He's a close friend of mine."

"Where we going, Poochy?" Howie Crosby asked over his shoulder.

Of course. Poochy Ponserelli. The skinny teenage hoodlum who broke a hockey stick over my head was now a fat old hoodlum. He leaned forward and slapped the back of Howie's head.

"When I want some words from you, I'll rattle your cage." He looked at me. "I'm an independent contractor now, in case you didn't figure that out. I live on Blackstone Boulevard now, in Providence. I got a beautiful house—"

"Fucking unbelievable house," his brother said. Poochy slapped the back of his head, too.

"It's a beautiful house. Know who my neighbors are? Huh?"

"No. No, I don't."

"If you stand facing out on my front steps, on the left-hand side is the president of Brown University, an Ivy League school, and on the right side is some eighty-five-year-old bitch whose fucking people came over on the *Santa María*."

"The *Mayflower*," Allie said without thinking. Poochy just stared at the back of his head. He turned to me again.

"Point is, I'm right between them. I still got people back at the Terrace, but I'm on Blackstone Boulevard. So here's the question, actor. What the fuck is the matter with you anyway, you fucking shitty actor you? When that girl . . . what's her name?"

"Mary," Howie offered.

"Marie?" I asked. "Marie D'Agostino?"

"That's the girl. When she got shot, I remembered it. Know why? Huh?"

"A girl gets shot, I guess a lot of people would remember."

"Wrong. Jesus. I remembered it because that Zulu cop harassed me and Jackie Crosby like we were criminals. He thought we shot her, and we didn't shoot anybody. This afternoon here comes the old Zulu again, comes right over to Blackstone Boulevard to tell me that the bullet traveled and now she's dead. 'So what?' I said. He said, 'I thought you ought to know.' Look, we are not criminals. Period. I'm a contractor with a loan-out corporation and a 401(k), and Jackie's in jail, but it's a bullshit thing he absolutely didn't do. So tell the Mau Mau to get off my ass or else. And by the way, I know you been hanging around with that crazy little fuck, and, no shit, I am not fucking shitting you here, you tell him that he has to let that whole thing go, as I said I was sorry. That's the end of it."

"We can handle that," Allie whined. Poochy tapped the back of his head.

"I know. I know. You handled it great before."

The front seat got very quiet. Howie and Allie stared straight ahead. Poochy seemed suddenly aware he had hurt their feelings.

"But these two, these two guys are . . . the best. Underestimate them at your peril. Even big-time professionals like yourself can get hurt. Get it? Huh?"

"I get it. I do."

Allie and Howie nudged each other.

"Big-time professional," Allie said.

Howie laughed, and Poochy Ponserelli slapped the back of both their heads.

"Shut up and go back to the hotel, jerk-off."

23

In February 1967 I was almost seventeen and the East Providence Townie hockey team was deep in the hunt for a title along with Mount St. Charles and Woonsocket, two teams heavily tilted with French Canadians and, I still think, semiprofessional goalies. I don't know this for a fact, but I disguised my voice when the season was over and called their schools. Neither of them was matriculating anymore. So what do you think?

I was going steady with Sandy Minucci, and it felt okay not having to look around for girlfriends and everything. Especially with the season coming down to several rough contests. A guy could get distracted worrying about who he was going to take to the Newport Creamery, and the next thing you know, he'd be skating on his ankles. So it was me and Sandy, which was okay. She had those dangerous brothers, of course, and she understood that Cubby, Billy, and Bobby were equally important to me. Well, actually, more important, but it's something to do with knowing each other since we were five, and you just can't explain it to your steady girl, so I didn't.

A few months earlier, a Visigoth from Massachusetts moved into the Terrace with his divorced mother and began attending

East Providence High School midyear. Petey Maloney was a disturbing Irish-German blend of South Boston mayhem. He was a goon who gave even the Ponserelli-Crosby old guard pause. His great size and hyperactivity blended smoothly with his reasoning capacity, and at nineteen Petey was a sophomore. The Riverside mob moved quickly to assimilate him into their culture, and soon Petey Maloney was their chief enforcer. If somebody needed beating up, if some wiseass talked to one of their girlfriends, if some fool mistakenly sat at their lunch table, all it would take was a nod from the Ponserelli-Crosby brain trust and Petey would fly into action. I had nothing to do with him. With the hockey season coming down to the wire, I had bigger things to think about. At least I did until Petey Maloney fell in love with Sandy Minucci.

One sunny afternoon after school, while he was happily taking some kid's money so he could treat himself to an Awful-Awful, Petey spied the unbearably adorable Sandy running over to the bus that would take the hockey team to Willard Avenue pond for practice. Her short skirt swayed with her perfect bottom, and her breasts, though hidden under the white cheerleader sweater with the megaphone picture and EP in crimson over it, bobbed and pointed up to heaven. She had a red ribbon tying back her silky blond hair. I had just thrown my duffel and skates onto the bus. She leaped into my arms. We were leapers then. More leapers than lovers actually. She kissed me and told me to have fun at hockey practice. I told her to have fun at cheerleading practice. We did not have a complicated relationship. It was about to *become* complicated, though, because Petey Maloney had seen her kiss me.

The next day, right before my second-period English class, Petey began phase one of his South Boston courtship. I was at my locker with Cubby, Billy, and Bobby when he put his finger in my chest.

"Stay away from my girlfriend," he stated in an oddly high

voice. He was fidgeting and seemed to be fighting for control of his body. His feet moved when he spoke.

"Who's your girlfriend?" I asked, trying to disarm him with my winning Riley smile.

"You know who I mean. That girl. What's her name? She's my girlfriend now."

"Sandy?" Cubby blurted.

Now Petey put his finger in Cubby's chest. "Shut up, faggot." he said cleverly, and stormed away.

"Sandy's going with *him* now?" Billy asked incredulously.

We all looked at each other, and Bobby took his pause.

"He's that new guy from the Terrace."

"I heard he got expelled from Boston for beating up some cops," Billy added.

"Bullshit," Cubby said. "He's just a big stupid mick."

I didn't see Sandy until lunch period. We took our usual seats. She had bought me some chocolate milk to go with the peanut butter and grape jelly sandwich I brought from home. I waited until we'd each had a bite of food.

"You know that new guy from your terrace?" I asked.

"Uh-uh." She chewed.

"Big guy. Boston accent. He's with Ponserelli and those guys."

"Don't know him, why?"

"Well, he told me to stay away from you because you were his girlfriend now."

She looked up and laughed. "I'm his girlfriend and I don't know him?"

We both laughed.

"Maybe he just dreamed you were his girlfriend."

There we were having this funny little conversation, enjoying our funny little lunch. It's not an easy assignment being a teenager. Everything seems terribly important, and angst rules. But along

143

with the difficulties comes a sort of gift. An ability to enter into a moment for the sake of the moment. To not anticipate the next second. To enjoy exactly where you are. Of course, the gift is transitory, and as you mature, all you do is anticipate some future dilemma. However, now I was absorbed in merely watching her eyes and her smile and her softly chewing mouth. At least I was until the razor-cut, pimply face of Petey Maloney loomed over her shoulder.

"I told you," he said in that strange, upper-register voice, "I told you."

Sandy looked up at him. "Told him what?"

"Told him you were my girlfriend now," he explained reasonably, although his big, nervous feet shifted weight more or less constantly.

"I'm not your girlfriend."

"Maybe you don't think so."

"I don't think so."

"How about after I beat him up? Will you be my girlfriend after I kick the shit out of his ass?" he asked, high-pitched and hopeful.

"I will never ever be your girlfriend, and don't swear."

"Shut up," he snarled.

"Don't tell her to shut up," I said, and stood up.

Later I knew a guy in the army like Petey. He wasn't looking to beat me up, he was looking to beat up a couple of Puerto Rican kids who couldn't speak the language very well, which pissed the guy off. I would try to figure out why in the middle of a situation where people were shooting at us this guy wanted to beat other guys up. The conclusion I reached is that guys like that are hopelessly stupid. But now, standing on the other side of the table from this truly demented and experienced marauder, I couldn't think of anything but how stupid *I* was.

"What did you say?" he asked, as if he really wanted to get it right.

"I said . . . I said . . . don't tell Sandy to shut up."

He looked down at her. "Sandy? Your name is Sandy? I only knew one Sandy, and he wasn't a girl. Sandy Norton from Charlestown. Beat two dagos to death with a cobblestone. On you, Sandy is a pretty name. After I beat him up, I'm going to buy you an Awful-Awful. I'm sorry I swore."

He looked back at me. Howie Crosby and Allie Ponserelli materialized on either side of me.

"This fuckface giving you a hard time?" Howie said, waving his head at me.

"Hey," Petey warned, and gestured to Sandy. "Don't swear, okay? My girlfriend doesn't like swearing."

"I'm not your girlfriend."

"Her name is Sandy," he said proudly. "I'm going to beat this guy up, and then we're getting Awful-Awfuls."

"Beat him up behind the carousel at Crescent Park," Allie said. "My brother used to beat guys up there."

"Mine, too," Howie said proudly. "If you do it in the school parking lot, that spook cop always breaks it up."

"We didn't have spook cops in Boston," Petey cooed to Sandy. "Hardly any dago ones either."

Allie addressed me clearly. "After school. You better show up behind the carousel, or everybody'll know you're chickenshit, and Petey will still get you anyway."

"And bring enough money for me to buy Awful-Awfuls for me and what's-her-name," Petey ordered.

"Sandy," she said, exasperated.

He smiled at her. "I love you." And they walked away.

"Hey," I said. "I have hockey practice, and I can't miss it."

Petey, Allie, and Howie huddled together. Howie took a couple of steps toward me, stopped, and pointed. "Okay. Six o'clock."

"And don't forget the Awful-Awful money!" Petey shouted.

Practice that afternoon was generally uninspired. It was probably the way it should have been, as we reviewed the mundane portions of the game that add up to the whole. The Mount St. Charles game was two days away, and the coaches had us seeking a balance between high energy and knowing confidence. At least I think that was the gist of what Coach Eblemyer had said. I had trouble processing his before-practice speech, as I found myself a little preoccupied with getting killed at six o'clock. By the time I'd left the pond and bused back to the locker room and had walked home, it was five-thirty. I didn't bother going into the house, because I didn't want to be the one to tell Mother that her only son was about to die in a half hour, so I got my old three-speed out of the garage, pedaled to Pawtucket Avenue, and headed down to Crescent Park.

In 1967, *Walt Disney's Wonderful World of Color* rebroadcast their Fess Parker festival of Davy Crockett fighting Indians and politicians and riverboat thugs. But far and away the most memorable and moving segments were Davy at the Alamo. He rallied the odd assortment of frontier soldiers and fought to the very end. The night before a final attack by the Mexican army, Davy sat by the campfire and sang farewell to the land he loved. If I could have thought of the words to that song, I would have sung it on the way to the carousel.

The gray that preceded the black of New England nights had already descended when I pulled up to the carousel. It was placed at the entrance to the Terrace. Behind it eerily loomed the great wooden Crescent Park roller coaster that had been closed down for years. Wind gusting off Narragansett Bay moved through the coaster's wood slats and created a moaning lament that did not lift my spirits. It was cold. Icy. I walked the bike around to the back of the carousel. Three of their gang's cars were there. The doors opened, and four or five guys got out of each car, with a cloud of cigarette smoke billowing behind. Howie Crosby had on a porkpie hat and looked like a little IRA informer.

"Hey, look who showed up, Allie. It's the big-deal hockey star."

"He's so cool," yawned Allie. "Big-deal hockey player."

"He thinks he's so great," said Howie.

Allie nodded. "You just *think* you're so great. You're not so great. You know who's great? Bobby fucking Orr. *That's* great."

"No shit," Howie said. "He thinks he's better than Orr."

"He thinks he's better than Howe. Better than Bobby fucking Hull."

The other kids laughed.

"Wait a minute," Petey Maloney said seriously in his pinched tenor. "He thinks he's better than Bobby Orr?"

"He thinks he's better."

"That's stupid," he said to Allie, and looked at me.

Allie's big brother, Poochy Ponserelli, who I hadn't seen in a couple of years, got out of the back of one of the cars. He wore a black suit, white shirt, and narrow black tie. A Frank Sinatra hat sat back on his small head.

"You jerk-offs got me here to talk sports or see a fight?"

"It ain't gonna be a fight," Petey explained. "It's gonna be a slaughter. He's after my girlfriend."

"Who's your girlfriend?" Poochy asked.

"You know . . . that girl . . . that . . ."

I looked at Poochy. I was a vastly better talker than a fighter, even if I wasn't much of a talker. "She's my girlfriend. Sandy Minucci."

I couldn't see Poochy's eyes, but I heard a subtle recognition of certain potential difficulties.

"From the Terrace? Related to Billy and Jimmy and Dougie and those guys? Those Minuccis?"

"Uh-huh. She's their sister."

Poochy glanced at his little brother, and I thought I saw disappointment glide over his face, but he stopped talking. We were here now, and I guess it had to play out, whatever it was. Petey moved away from the others. He had a watch cap pulled low over his head. He'd changed from his cheesy school clothes to jeans and a black Irish fisherman's sweater. He wore tight leather gloves. I looked down at his thick engineer boots and felt my stomach roll. He started toward me, a dumb grin on the side of his face. He seemed much bigger than when he looked over our lunch table. I heard Cubby's voice.

"We got the Awful-Awful money."

Cubby, Billy, and Bobby came around the side of the carousel. Petey stopped and watched them, his face displaying the full measure of his thought process.

"Give it here," he said, holding out his hand to Cubby.

"Bobby's holding it."

I noticed Bobby had changed, too. Standing between Cubby and Billy, he wore an old pair of chinos and a tight black leather jacket. He had on his red Chuck Taylors. His hands and head were bare. A five-dollar bill wagged around the breast pocket of the jacket like spinner bait. Petey fixed his eyes on the cash and Bobby. "Wiry" did not describe Bobby. At almost six feet, "slight" would be the word, unless you experienced him day to day.

"This is my fight," I said to Bobby, although I didn't really think it was.

"Shut up, faggot," Petey said. He turned back to Bobby. "Give me my Awful-Awful money, or else."

"Don't touch him," Allie said quickly. "Just beat up Riley."

"I'm gonna beat them both up. I want my Awful-Awful money."

"We'll give you the Awful-Awful money. Beat up Riley."

"This is my fight, Bobby," I said, and meant it this time. But Bobby was not listening. He didn't move his body a flick and watched Petey Maloney like a cheetah watches a water buffalo. I walked over and stood in front of Petey. "This is between you and me."

Petey took two quick steps forward, and I was on the ground. I didn't even see him hit me. My nose had been broken before in a game, and I knew it was broken now. My stomach ached, and I struggled for breath.

Petey had turned back to Bobby. "I want my Awful-Awful money."

"Forget it," Allie said. "C'mon, don't touch him. We'll give you the money."

"I want that money."

Petey grabbed the front of Bobby's jacket and lifted the bill with his free hand. Bobby's fists snapped out at the ends of his long arms. It was a combination of precise punches, maybe eight or ten, all striking Petey Maloney's mouth or nose or eyes or cheeks. Petey screamed and tried to cover his face. The five dollars floated to the ground. Bobby stopped and slid to his left. Staggered, Petey rushed him, grabbing him in a bear hug. I can still hear the thumps like drumbeats against Petey's stomach and chest. He released his grip and fell to his knees, gasping and crying. He rolled onto his side and curled up. Billy and Bobby picked me up. Cubby picked up the money. He looked at Allie Ponserelli, then Petey Maloney's fetal shape.

"We're going to get Awful-Awfuls now," Cubby said. "We might even get two apiece."

We left the carousel, and then the Ponserelli-Crosby gang left, too. Petey's adventure wasn't over, though. We know *what* happened, but the *how* is open to interpretation. Here's mine:

Petey remained tightly curled in front of the locked merry-go-round for an hour or so. Breathing was difficult, because his lungs pushed heavily against some bruised and fractured ribs. The front of his black sweater was sticky with nosebleed. He couldn't see at all out of his right eye and had swallowed several teeth. He picked up his watch cap, pulled it low over his bruised forehead, and started toward his mother's tiny house on the far side of the Terrace, next to the marina. He thought how he hated the smell of the marina.

The diesel oil, the fish guts, shells. The smells that seeped into his crummy room. Why did they have to come here at all? Why couldn't he still be running in Southie with his people? The scent of beer from the bars and the wonderful smells wafting over from all the dago places on the North End. And his mother would say I told you so. She'd see him and say, I told you so. And it wasn't his fault. It was love, and this is what happened. The first girl he liked since the O'Brien girl, and he gets attacked. He hated Rhode Island and hated East Providence and hated love.

Petey was midway in his stagger home. He could hear TVs and radios on inside the close little houses. He could hear the bay licking the shore. He was as cold as he'd ever been. And then he saw her. The girl. What's her name? Sandy. The bitch who'd promised love and broke his heart and had him beaten up. She was getting out of a car full of other kids and walking up to a house. She wore a cheerleader's uniform and carried pom-poms. She waved, and the car left.

Petey crossed the street. When Sandy got to the front door, he yelled, "Hey!"

She turned around and looked at him. "Yeah?"

"I think you're stupid and ugly!" Petey shouted from the middle of her front lawn.

Sandy watched him like he was something odd under a microscope. He felt the strange and powerful pains of unrequited love. He felt that his heart had been broken for sport. He grew louder.

"I never liked you at all. I thought you were stupid and ugly."

She still studied him, pom-poms at her side, fine blond hair crazy in the cold breeze.

He breathed deep and screamed. "I think you're just a stupid, ugly dago bitch!"

Petey put his hands on his hips, satisfied he had made the point. Love was not going to break Petey Maloney. He might be aching from the vicious blindsiding he had gotten, but he was still standing tall and bold. And now he had made it clear to this cruel heart-breaker exactly what he thought. The porch light went on, and the door opened. Sandy disappeared inside. Larry, Alex, Hank, Brian, Dougie, Eugene, Billy, and Jimmy Minucci walked out, down the steps, and spread out in a line, facing Petey like gunslingers.

Petey Maloney was not able to return to East Providence High until April. He was healing nicely and needed only one crutch to get around. Because of the lacerated kidney and the loss of his spleen, the doctors had put him on a low-sugar diet heavy with healing vegetables and chicken broth, so by the time he was able to move about on his dislocated hip, his terrible acne had disappeared and he actually looked sort of handsome. He was a quiet and shy student, and teachers tried to speak into the ear that still had an eardrum. He wasn't the enforcer anymore; that job reverted back to Connie Dwyer, who was big and dumb as a bag of hammers but smart enough to stay away from the Minuccis. Petey would sit alone in the lunchroom and eat the lunch his mother had packed and not look up. This is what I remember then. Even bullies should think things through, because it's a strange world.

We beat both Mount St. Charles and Woonsocket for the first of my two state titles. I scored goals in the two games. I wasn't Bobby Orr or Bobby Hull or Gordie Howe, but I was pretty damn good for a guy with a head the size of a beach ball.

24

Early next morning, keeping with Kenny Snowden's strict schedule, we met at the new water tower, where I gave him Marie's .22 slug. Again I drove over to St. Martha's parking lot, only this time I went in for seven o'clock mass. The last time I took communion was in the service, where I was essentially motivated by superstition. I was hedging my bets against getting hurt, but I got hurt anyway, so I stopped going.

There were twelve people this particular morning. All elderly. I sat alone a couple of pews behind them. The priest was a very young, very fat little guy with rosy cheeks and a joyous voice. Whatever he was doing worked for him, because he was so happy it sort of rubbed off on you. We ran through the ups and downs and genuflections. The old folks were game, struggling up and down again in our wild Catholic ritual. The homily, delivered in the priest's gleeful voice, had to do with working hard and praising God. I had heard it before, I think. A theme repeated over and over to the ten-hour-shift blue-collar East Providence man who was just pleased that he had employment. Work and pray. I hope I don't sound like a typically bitter ex-Catholic. I'm not. Mother got great comfort from this place. I suppose my pop and I never worked hard enough at understanding the spiritual thing. We just never got it.

I cupped my hand, took the wafer, and returned to my seat. Someone else slid in next to me. It was Mrs. D'Agostino, who squeezed my arm and smiled. When mass ended, we sat and chatted for a moment. On our way out, she introduced me to the priest, Father Oscar Merrill, who studied my face when Marie's mother told him I was an actor.

"What have I seen you in?" he said happily. "Hint."

"Nothing, really," I said, embarrassed.

"Jono was the orderly who couldn't speak in . . . in . . ."

"Blues and Whites," I said softly.

"Steven Bochco produced that, didn't he?" he asked.

"Ted Goldman," I said.

"I love Steven Bochco," the priest gushed mightily. *"Hill Street Blues, L.A. Law, NYPD Blue . . ."*

"He's really good," I added lamely.

"He did that one where the police sing. What was that?"

I remembered something about it, but I forgot what it was called. He looked at Mrs. D'Agostino and tried to explain thugs and cops dancing and singing. His arms waved for effect.

"There'd be a scene, something serious, an arrest or something—or a shooting—and all of a sudden they'd start singing. I thought it was fabulous. Especially that singing forensic cop. He's played a lot of cops. What an actor!" He looked back at me. "You were in that?"

"No, no. I was in *Blues and Whites.*"

"Ahhh."

I walked Mrs. D'Agostino to her house and returned to the parking lot. Father Oscar was sweeping the steps. He smiled at me.

"Budget consideration. We're down to one nun and two priests. I'm on the go so much, I don't know why I'm such a fatty."

"This parish was tough on its priests even when I was a kid."

"This was your church?"

"Until I went into the service. They had one young priest who had to be like Superman. The pastor was sort of old, and Father Bouvier—"

"Wheelchair." He nodded with a smile. "He's over at the retirement home for religious in Olneyville." He looked around conspiratorially. "I'm afraid I'm in the same situation as your young priest." He gestured to his sweeping with a giggle. "I'm the designated sweeper. Morning-mass man. Nursing-home rep, CYO director, Boy Scout coordinator—"

"Coach, too, I'll bet."

"Girls' and boys' CYO basketball and baseball. I made the diocese hire a swim coach. I got a terrific girls' basketball team, and if I can keep the boys' baseball together, it could be a big year."

I watched him sweep for a bit.

"Did you know a priest named Father Al Persico?" I asked.

He kept sweeping. "Persico. Persico. Was he here?"

"He was the young priest I just mentioned."

"I'm pretty good with names, but I can't bring his up. Why?"

"Well, Father Al disappeared one day, and I was always—"

"Oh, that priest. Okay, yes, I didn't put a name on him. Weird, huh? I mean, it's not uncommon for a religious to go on overload and crack up, but disappear? It's a legendary story in seminary."

"Any theories?"

He leaned on his broom. "I think you have to have—and this is just me talking—I think you need to like being a priest. It's a ridiculous amount of work, of course, and you spend countless hours with the dead and dying. But there's also this inexplicable desire to serve. Like being an actor. You just have to do it."

I thought about it and shivered. He kept the thought.

"Anyhow, if you don't feel that way, it's easy to be overtaken. And if you're a depressive personality, then it's all too much."

"So you think he might have been depressed?"

"I don't know. Actually, the only thing I do know is that . . . who?"

"Father Al Persico."

"Yes. I only know Father Al had a pretty strange hobby."

I looked at Father Merrill, who was staring out across the housing development that used to hold our snow angels.

"What hobby?" I asked finally.

"He collected guns. Lots and lots of guns. They're still in two trunks in the basement."

Twenty minutes later Kenny Snowden pulled in to the parking lot in the passenger side of a police cruiser. Manny Furtado, his former partner, was behind the wheel.

"Home nurse agreed to spell me," Kenny explained.

I introduced Kenny to Father Oscar, who already knew Manny as a parishioner, and we followed him down to the basement.

Madonna Hall, as the basement was called, was a large, neat room with green tiles and white walls. The colors of the Boy Scout and Girl Scout troops were wrapped against one wall. There were also section dividers on rollers that formed Sunday-school areas. A large kitchen was off in another open room. Father Oscar led us to a room behind a small stage. This was the true basement. Concrete floors, heating and cooling systems, fuse boxes, and several large plastic storage bins.

"His footlockers are under all this crap," Father Oscar said, and we started removing the bins. The footlockers had combination locks. We dragged them under the only light source, a bare bulb in the middle of the room. Father Oscar started the combinations.

"I've got a great memory for numbers. When I got assigned to St. Martha's, I took a kind of unofficial grand tour. Curious, you know. These footlockers were unlocked, can you believe that? I bought these combination locks posthaste."

He opened the first of the trunks and moved to the other one. Manny Furtado flipped it open. There were three layered racks, each containing four rifles, all in soft cloth wrappings. On the footlocker's inside top, fastened by bungee cords, were four odd-looking old-fashioned pistols. A manila envelope lay between the first and second rifle racks. Inside were the descriptions of the weapons. The second footlocker held the same three racks of four rifles each, but four modern handguns were fastened to the inside hood. There was a similar descriptive envelope between the racks. We all silently stood back and looked at the stacks of weaponry. Father Al Persico drifted around in my head.

Manny Furtado looked at Kenny. "What think?"

"Department still work with Adelman?"

"Sure."

Kenny turned to Father Oscar and me. "Lou Adelman's the local president of the National Alliance of Stocking Gun Dealers. Got a shop at Six Corners. He'd know what's what."

Manny gestured toward the lockers with his head. "Okay if he comes over and takes a look?"

"Of course he can," Father Oscar said.

"He'll take serial numbers, et cetera," Manny explained.

"Might be helpful to pull any .22s in there, too. Have 'em look-see'd," added Kenny.

"Of course," said Father Oscar.

Before he got back into the cruiser, I mentioned Poochy Ponserelli's visit.

Kenny Snowden sighed. "It's sad, really. He's as slow on the uptake as he ever was."

"And you think he's responsible?"

"He's responsible for a lot of things."

"I mean Marie. He thinks you're harassing him."

Kenny thought about this. At least I think he did. He gently waved his hand.

"It's important that people such as Ponserelli and that bad mick of his understand that they are not acting in a vacuum. Actions have consequences. Let me ask you something. Did your family drink tap water?"

"I . . . uh . . . yes."

"Right out of the faucet?"

"Yes."

"And you feel all right? You don't get confused or anything?"

"I don't think so."

"How about your parents?"

"Well, my father died. . . ."

"That fire. I remember."

"Mother, too, but later."

"Was her memory okay? Her thoughts all lined up?"

"Sure. Why?"

"Just curious."

Kenny sat in the passenger seat and rolled down the window. "Water tower. Six-thirty in the morning."

I nodded, and Manny pulled out of the parking lot. Standing alone, some wind whipping around and gray clouds rolling in, I felt it seemed to be the perfect time to ask myself what the hell I was doing here. Rhode Island. East Providence. The bartender/actor sinking in memories and mysteries. Threatened by aging mondos, seeing shadows of assassins. I would be the first to admit to a few strange notions about the world, but I remain essentially a child of the working class, seeking at the very least a modicum of order. But where is the order in priests with trunks of guns and ex-cops obsessing about tap water? I needed Lambs and my fifth-floor walk-up and especially my wonderful firefighter. Renée would be in Providence at six-thirty. I hoped the train would be on time.

25

Roxanne Boneria took a swim off a granite ledge in front of Yaw-goog Pond's assistant camp director's cottage every afternoon at five-fifteen. I was the waterfront director of Three Point, a division of the scout camp, that summer between my junior and senior years. The cottage was fifty yards to the left of my dock and I never missed seeing her slowly exit from the screen porch in her modest black bathing suit and elegantly dive into the cold glacial pond, cutting into the smooth water with barely a ripple, which was re-markable given the size of her breasts. I was very glad that Rox-anne chose five-fifteen, because the last swim before dinner was over and I was able to stand unencumbered at the edge of my beach, smoke a Marlboro, and watch her. There was a kind of suspense, standing there. A sensation that something was going to happen. Something strange and wonderful and supernatural.

To tell the truth, everything that summer was strange or con-fusing or both. Big Tony had the first of a half dozen heart attacks that would eventually bring him down. Bobby's mother got en-gaged and got left standing at the altar. Hickey and Rickey, the two old polar bears at Goddard Park, were murdered. I suffered through the Troop 6 East Greenwich swim tag screwup and, of course, Roxanne.

Roxanne Boneria was a junior at Rhode Island College, and her roommate was the daughter of the assistant camp director. They were waitressing at a pretty fashionable place on old U.S. 1 near Green Hill Beach and, to save money for school, were sharing a room at the cottage. The two girls caused a stir at the all-boys' camp, but they were hardly around, and when they were, they always carried themselves demurely. They were both very pretty. Actually, Paula Webster, the assistant director's daughter, was the one with what you might call the classic sixties beauty. She was quite tall, and her blond hair, cut in the Jacqueline Kennedy style, always bounced perfectly on her head. There was also a peaches-and-cream complexion that spoke well of Rhode Island's English forefathers. I didn't hold that against her, though. She seemed lovely. Roxanne was shorter, with a dark Sicilian face, black pixie haircut, and the most unlikely blue eyes. While Paula favored knee-length shorts and always kept her eyes straight ahead, Roxanne wore short shorts and would occasionally look around and smile. Did I mention red lipstick? Roxanne had it on even for her afternoon swim.

After the last scheduled scout swim before dinner, I'd have my four lifeguards scrub down the docks and rake our beach while I would recheck the swim-tag board and fill out my day report, making special note of any merit-badge work or swim advancement. A Boy Scout waterfront is ferociously structured, and a system of checking and double-checking is always the order of the day. Then I'd release the lifeguards until after dinner, when we'd have evening swims for troops that had scheduled them. I hustled everything along so I could make my five-fifteen Marlboro rendezvous. I had been taking my smoke regularly for about three weeks when Roxanne, right before she sliced into the water, waved at me. I waved, too, hoping, in the shade of the late afternoon, that my head might appear a reasonable size to her. She disappeared under the water, and when she surfaced, she began to perform a luxurious breast-stroke in my direction. I walked out to the corner of my dock as casually as I could, drawing the smoke into my lungs and seductively shooting it out my nose.

"Hi," she said, treading water.

"Hi," I replied brilliantly.

"I'm Roxanne."

"I'm Jono. I'm the director of the waterfront."

"Want to go for a swim?"

"Okay."

I kicked out of my flip-flops, sucked in my stomach, took off my T-shirt, and dived. I had been working out and had a great tan, so I suppose I didn't look disgusting or anything. When my head popped up in front of her, I realized I suavely still had the cigarette in my mouth.

"You're funny," she said, pointing at the butt.

She swam over to the floating dock with the diving board and climbed onto it. I stayed in the water and watched her dive. She did it a couple of times, and then we kicked back to my beach.

"You want a towel?" I asked.

"Sure."

I found her a towel in our log-stockade waterfront staff house. I hoped it didn't smell too much of sweaty-sour boy, but I couldn't be sure. She wrapped herself in it, I pulled on my T-shirt, and we sat in the folding beach chairs I'd had my mother bring up for me. We were quiet. The sound of the dining room roared dimly in the distance. The sun was a half fire above the far side of the pond. Some bass broke the glassy surface of water, and bugs skittered over it.

"This is really pretty," she sighed.

"It is," I agreed.

"So what do you do?"

"I'm the director of the waterfront."

"I mean, when the summer's over. Like I'm waitressing and then I go back to college."

"Oh . . . yeah . . . well . . . I go back to school, too."

"Where?"

"Where?" I asked.

Roxanne watched me now, and I felt a chemical collision inside. An upside-down stomach roll that comes right before you ease into the dentist's chair for your root canal. Anticipation and imagination are constant and brutal teenage companions. I was already justifying myself before I spoke.

"I go to Harvard," I said, and lit another Marlboro.

"Wow. Harvard. That is so hard to get in there. You're, like, really smart."

I shrugged and smoked, looking coolly over the pond.

"I go to RIC."

"That's a good school."

"I'm going to be a teacher. Early childhood."

I nodded, but I thought early childhood was what *I* was in.

"What do you study?" she asked.

I shrugged. "A little of this, a little of that."

"Like, medicine?"

"Exactly."

"You're, like, going to be a doctor?"

I nodded.

"What kind?"

"It's kind of hard to explain."

She nodded seriously, so I expanded on the theme.

"See, first we look at all the different parts of the body, and then we . . . we decide . . . what it is . . . we like."

"A doctor. Wow."

We fell quiet again. I finished my cigarette and flipped it. It was a small lie. Maybe not even a lie. Maybe one day I *would* go to Harvard and be a doctor. That D in junior biology could present a problem, but who knows? Okay, a small lie. One tiny little lie. That was it. No more lying. But her perfect legs peeked out of the towel.

"I'm leaning toward brain surgery."

She looked at me.

"You know, people with brain problems . . . I could help them . . . with surgery."

"Wow."

The sun was almost all down, and with the dusk Roxanne Boneria became the most beautiful thing that ever walked, and she was sitting next to me.

"So you got a girlfriend in Boston?"

"Why would I have a girlfriend in Boston?" I asked, honestly for once.

"I mean, at Harvard."

That's right, I thought. Jesus, I was thinking Harvard was in New Hampshire.

"No, no, I don't have a girlfriend in Boston. New Hampshire either."

Now Sandy Minucci filled my head. I was meeting her at the beach on my day off, and my high-school ring was on her finger. I swallowed hard. I was lost and swallowing.

"Actually," I heard myself say, "I don't have any girlfriends anywhere."

We were quiet again. A good quiet. So good that even though I was a lying sack of shit, I didn't care. Dr. Riley. It had a good ring to it.

"I just broke up with my boyfriend right after second semester."

"I'm sorry," I said.

"I was sort of glad. I mean, he was a nice guy, and sex was great, but . . . I don't know. I don't care."

I lit another cigarette with a shaking match. Sandy and I didn't have sex. We had pawing. Until twelve seconds ago, pawing at each other was okay, especially with the Minucci men's rules factored in, but now pawing would never do. I tried to elaborate for her.

"I know what you mean. It's . . . great to have great . . . sex . . . but . . . you want . . . I mean . . ."

"Exactly," she said enthusiastically. "It's not everything. Sex is great, but you want your sex partner to be a great friend, too."

A friend? What? Jesus, this was complicated. I didn't want a friend. I had friends. I didn't want to have sex with them. I wanted to have sex with Roxanne.

"Exactly . . . friend . . . and . . . and sex."

"Exactly."

Roxanne stood and neatly folded the towel, laying it on the chair. I liked her bathing suit. Very much. I started to stand also, but my erection suggested that I stay in the chair. She held out her hand.

"Maybe we can get a drink one night," she said.

My day off was Wednesday at noon until Thursday at noon. I could see the day clearly circled on sweet Sandy Minucci's calendar.

"How's Wednesday sound?" I said.

"Great. I'll come over here around seven, and we'll take your car."

"Wednesday at seven. Cool."

I watched her walk away, her bottom bobbing joyously under her suit. I smiled deeply and thought about the drink we would have and the great sex we would have and the car I did not have. Billy Fontanelli came around the corner of the stockade.

"Jono."

Something had to be wrong. Billy should just be getting off his summer shift at Woody's gas station in East Providence.

"What?" I said standing.

Billy hesitated.

"My mother?"

He shook his head. "Big Tony. C'mon."

I threw on some dry shorts and followed Billy to his DeSoto. Bobby was in the passenger seat. He wore a fisherman's jumpsuit and smelled like Narragansett Bay. We stopped at the camp director's cottage, and I told him I would be at Rhode Island Hospital. Then we took the fifty-minute trip into Providence. We knew the hospital from the bullet in Marie's back and the beatings by Bobby's old man. The emergency waiting area was standing room only. Six or seven coworkers from Tasca's milled by the soda machine. My mother was there, along with Billy's folks and his sister, Peggy. Mrs. D'Agostino sat in a chair, with Marie and Cubby on either side. Cubby stood up and walked over to us. His eyes were bloodshot and swollen. It was 1966, and Rhode Island boys didn't hug, but the three of us stood as close to Cubby as a human being could. We were silent for a moment, and Bobby took the pause as his.

"What about Big Tony?" he asked slowly.

"I was working in Parts. I was getting something, spark plugs for some guy's Fairlane, and I could see Big Tony talking to a mechanic through the glass, and then he just fell, and the mechanic caught him. He just fell."

We followed him back to his mother and Marie. Marie got up and kissed us, but her mother stayed in her seat shaking her head. Every now and then, a small sob came out of her. Father Bouvier was wheeled into the room by Sister Margaret and asked us all to join in a prayer. We had our heads bowed when a young doctor in blue cotton came out of the emergency room. He waited until Father Bouvier had finished.

"Mrs. D'Agostino?"

She stood quickly and moved to the doctor. Mother held her shoulders, and everyone crowded around the family.

"Mr. D'Agostino has had a serious episode of the heart."

"Is that like a heart attack?" Mrs. D'Agostino asked.

"Yes, it is. It is a heart attack. There's some damage, and it will

165

be several days before we can assess the extent of it. We'll keep him in ICU for the next forty-eight hours. He's awake now, so the immediate family can visit for a few minutes."

Mrs. D'Agostino, Cubby, and Marie followed the doctor. The Tasca guys talked a little and left. Billy's dad fired up a Marlboro. By the time he put it out, the D'Agostinos returned looking pretty relieved. Everyone said something encouraging and left the waiting room. Cubby's mother told him that it was okay to go with us. Before we got into Billy's DeSoto, we had a Marlboro moment in the parking lot.

"He looks good. He really looks good," Cubby said.

"He say anything?" Billy asked.

"He said he was feeling lousy the last couple of days."

"He's gonna be great," I said.

Bobby smoked thoughtfully and looked up at the white brick hospital. "They were nice to me in there. I remember that they were so nice I wasn't scared or nothing. I'm glad Big Tony's in there."

We drove over to a liquor store that never carded us, picked up two six-packs of sixteen-ounce Narragansett lager, and drove to the Stop & Shop parking lot to drink them.

"What's the story on Wednesday? You gonna meet us at the beach after you see Sandy?" Cubby asked.

"I took Wednesday off, too," Billy said. "Don't have to be back till Thursday night."

"Misquamicut Beach babes!" Cubby shouted, and elbowed Bobby.

Bobby laughed.

"Bobby almost got laid the last time. She was hot for you, Bobby."

"Mine was hot, too," Billy said.

"Yeah, only she wasn't hot for you. So you gonna meet us there, Jono? What's the story?"

I gulped a mouthful of good beer and leaned forward.

"I got a date at seven Wednesday night with a college girl, for a drink and friendly sex."

Cubby snickered. "You lying sack of shit."

"It's true."

"What?"

"Both things. I got this date *and* I'm a lying sack of shit."

We all took a drag on our smokes and considered this.

Bobby looked concerned. "But what about Sandy?"

Cubby held his hand up. "Wait a minute. Wait a minute. Are you serious?"

"Yeah. She goes to Rhode Island College."

"She don't care you're in high school?" Billy asked, amazed.

"She thinks I go to Harvard."

After they stopped laughing, I filled them in on my logistical and ethical quandary. Logistically, I needed a car, and ethically, I needed a good lie to tell Sandy so I could have sex with Roxanne and not feel too bad about it.

Billy, with his great powers of organization, thought out loud. "Cubby's going, right?"

"Sure. I'm gonna call in sick."

"Bobby?"

We waited.

"Skipper has something going on next week. We'll be on the bay for forty-eight on and forty-eight off."

"So what about Wednesday, Thursday?"

"I can go."

"Okay. You're supposed to have sex when? Seven?"

"We're gonna have a drink at seven, then I guess sex after the drink."

"Like eight? Eight-fifteen?"

"Yeah."

"Okay. Me, Cubby, and Bobby will pack up my car with the

sleeping bags and shit and go to the beach. I'll drive the car over to the camp at six. You drive me back to Misquamicut, and we'll meet you after the sex."

"Really? You'll let me borrow your car?"

"You got to be careful and things."

"I will."

We lit up again and passed out more beers.

"But what about Sandy?"

We looked at Bobby. It was as though he needed this resolved as much as I did.

"I feel bad about lying," I said.

Bobby nodded.

Cubby stretched out in his seat. "It's not really lying. I mean, it's like that Tony Curtis movie where he pretended to be different people. See, you didn't actually lie—you assumed a disguise. So when you have the drink and the sex, it's not really you having it, it's this Harvard guy. You didn't lie at all."

"But what should I tell Sandy?"

"Tell her you got the runs."

It seemed like a month until Wednesday rolled around. I called Cubby every night, and Big Tony was feeling better each day. On Tuesday night, before I called Sandy, I got Big Tony himself on the phone at the hospital. He sounded tired but good. Then I called Sandy.

Jimmy answered the phone.

"She's around. How you doing?"

"I'm not feeling too good."

"Eat some cereal. I'll get my sister."

I waited. The breeze off Yawgoog Pond gave me goose bumps. Then she was on.

"I love you," she gushed. "I cannot wait to see you tomorrow."

"Sandy . . . I'm real sick." I coughed.

"What is it?" this sweet, sweet girl asked, all ears and concern.

"Well, I went to the . . . the camp nurse . . . and she says I'm sick."

"But what is it?"

I coughed and wheezed and thought. I was sorry that I specialized in general brain surgery and not specific diseases.

"She didn't tell me. She just said I should get right into bed. And I got a sore throat and things."

"Poor baby."

"I'm sorry, Sandy."

"That's okay. I want you to get better. I love you."

This was the great friend that Roxanne had talked about. A familiar and trusting confidante. But tomorrow I would have the DeSoto and the drink. My head was spinning. Jesus, I had really made myself sick.

"I think I'm going to puke."

"You go and do what the nurse tells you to do. And call me tomorrow."

"If I don't call tomorrow, I'll call Thursday."

"Okay. I love you, Jono."

I coughed again. "Me, too. Bye."

I didn't sleep at all that night and had an impatient attitude all day with my staff and the scouts. I wanted the workday to be over so I could properly prepare for my rendezvous. Drinks would be at the Pequot Wigwam, a Narragansett Indian bar in Rockville that made no distinction between serving a seventeen-year-old Boy Scout and serving a Harvard physician. Later Roxanne Boneria and I would cruise over to the parking lot at Acadia State Park that was adjacent to the camp, drop the DeSoto's front seats, and . . .

"Where's Troop 6?" my assistant waterfront director Johnny Mahoney yelled over to me.

"What do you mean, where's Troop 6?"

"Troop 6 East Greenwich. They were all just in the water."

"So?"

"They all left their tags on the board."

The last swim was over; my crew was raking the beach and washing the docks. Nobody was in the water.

"Run up to their campsite and tell those assholes to get down here and get their goddamn tags off the board."

Roxanne came onto her ledge and waved. I waved back. It was five-fifteen. In one hour and forty-five minutes, we'd be in the DeSoto. I smoked and watched her glide fetchingly in the water. I held myself tall and Ivy League. Johnny came charging back to the beach.

"Their campsite is empty."

"Jesus."

"They couldn't have all drowned, could they?"

"Of course not!" I shouted, but looked at the water anyway.

"There's forty-three of them."

A couple of times a year, some little sucker will forget the rules and leave his swim tag on the board. Until he comes back to claim it, we have to close the waterfront, call the other waterfronts for backup, notify the camp director and camp ranger, and begin a seriously exhausting line search. Now forty-three of the little shits all forgot together.

I called over to Roxanne that she'd have to get out of the water, called the other waterfront directors, camp director, and ranger, then ran up the all-boats-in flag and began the line search. The five of us, equidistant apart, beginning in the nonswimmer area, under the barrels to the beginner area and on out past the swimmers' raft. Then we'd search backward to the nonswimmer area and repeat until the tags were taken off the board by the little shits who put them in. By the time the camp director and ranger arrived, I was conducting the line search with eleven lifeguards. The sun was going down fast. Billy came up behind me on the beach, holding the car keys.

"Give me a ride back and she's yours."

"Wait in the cabin, Billy," I panted as we spread out on the beach for our twelfth line search. "I'll be there pretty soon."

By six-thirty, three of the lifeguards were vomiting on the beach and two state troopers from the Rockville barracks arrived on the scene. We kept on searching while they conferred with the director and ranger. That's when Troop 6 arrived en masse for their scheduled evening swim. The scoutmaster explained that since they had a troop swim scheduled for after dinner, he thought it would be more efficient for the boys to leave the tags on the boards and let us think that they had all drowned rather than bother to take the tags with them. The troop seemed to think it was funny to see eleven lifeguards collapsed on the beach. I ran quickly to change into a new pair of chinos and penny loafers, an outfit that Cubby had assured me was very medical-looking. White shirt, too.

Billy winced at my cologne. "That's a lot of English Leather. You smell like my father."

Roxanne knocked on our open door. "Hi," she said.

"Hi," I said. "Roxanne, this is my friend Billy Fontanelli. We're going to give him a ride in my DeSoto."

Roxanne had on a blue miniskirt with white calf-length patent leather boots and a tight beige sweater. Billy gasped but covered it with a cough.

She smiled at Billy.

"It's the same DeSoto Jono has at Harvard," he said sincerely, shaking her hand.

"Do you go to Harvard, too?"

"No, I go to . . . the University of Rhode Island."

"That's neat."

We swung by Misquamicut Beach and dropped Billy at the farthest corner of the parking lot. I could see the two tents the guys had put up and the fire sparks flying over the dunes.

"Ever been to the Pequot Wigwam?"

"No," she said.

"It's a little place I enjoy frequenting."

The bar was just off old Route 1, and the entrance was a wooden replica of a tepee. The Narragansett Indians were actually famous for their longhouses, but the tepee had a cheesy coziness to it and fit nicely with the general dishonesty of Jono Riley, M.D. I ordered a Narragansett, and Roxanne had a Black Russian, whatever that was.

"There's a bar in Providence, Corella's, that makes the best Black Russians," she said, sipping her drink.

"Yeah, that's a pretty good place."

I lit a cigarette, and she reached over, took it, sucked in some smoke, and handed it back to me. A little lipstick clung to the filter. It tasted very good. In the dark, smoky room, Roxanne's blue eyes reflected the bar lights and her skin became darker. She talked slower, and her voice dropped an octave. She smiled, and we both sipped our particular libation. Confidence flowed over me like a flaxen river of beer.

"One day," I said earnestly, "if there's anything I can do about it, there won't be any more brain problems. Anywhere."

I dragged deeply on my cigarette and looked off to a distant place of healthy brains and friendly sex.

We ordered a second 'Gansett and Black Russian but didn't finish them. We walked out to the DeSoto, and I put my arm around Roxanne. She stopped walking and looked up to her Harvard brain guy and sighed. I kissed her. I felt something rolling around my mouth, and Jesus God Almighty it was this wonderful girl's tongue. Girls' tongues are ascendant. You are instantly diminished, and the armor of a lifetime, knitted and pounded into chain mail by a boy's experience, becomes tissue paper. She pulled away from me and nodded knowingly and seriously. I stood slack-jawed and vacant. Her eyes burned bluer under the fluorescent lights of the full-figure billboard of "Salty" Brine saying "My beer is 'Gansett." The

Harvard doctor asking his scrub nurse for a scalpel and the East Providence high-school porker with a hockey stick collided head-first. I opened her door, and she eased gloriously into her seat. I got in my side and kissed her again. Yes, it was her tongue. Jesus, Mary, and Joseph. I drove to Acadia Park with Roxanne snuggled against me. We glided into the empty parking lot and kissed again. She pulled away, keeping her hands on my shoulders and looking at me with her azure eyes. I waited, my heart pounding in my ears.

"I don't want you to think I ever do this on the first date," she whispered.

"I don't."

"I don't. I really don't."

"I know."

"I just like you. Since the first time I saw you watching me swim."

She cuddled back against me. I stroked her fine hair and thought. Thinking and talking are the enemies of romance. I suppose they're the enemies of deceit, too. Now I held her shoulders at arm's length and looked at those eyes.

"What?" she whispered.

"I don't go to Harvard."

Roxanne tilted her head to the side but kept her soft expression.

"I'm not learning how to be a brain surgeon."

She smelled like lavender soap. Her shoulders felt strong and soft at the same time. I considered transferring my credits to the University of Rhode Island, where I would study rocket science with Billy, but I sighed and closed my eyes.

"I'm gonna be a senior at East Providence High School."

I opened my eyes and added quickly, "But I made first team all-state hockey and was the MVP in the Rhode Island hockey tournament, where I should have had a hat trick, but the refs were all French-Canadian Christian Brothers and were prejudiced."

I shut up and watched her. Her face gave away nothing. I expected the long drive back to camp to be a special kind of embarrassment. But I felt better. Stupider, but better.

She kissed me. "I'm glad you told me." She kissed me again.

"You're not mad at me?"

"You're funny. Paula's father told me you were still in high school."

"You knew I didn't go to Harvard?"

Roxanne put her hand on my belt, pulled it, and unhooked my buckle. "Yup."

I gulped for air. "And . . . and . . . I'm gonna be all-state again."

After I dropped Roxanne off, I rolled that big boat of a DeSoto back to Misquamicut and the guys. They were pretty pissed that I didn't give them all the details. All I would say was that she was a great girl, and she was. And that we played around. Which was true. We had become friends. We played like friends for most of the summer, although I did reserve my days off for Sandy. Roxanne didn't mind, and when she got back with her old boyfriend in late August, I didn't mind either. I continued to have some Minucci guilt issues but discovered that these feelings fade away when you're seventeen and your conscience isn't fully developed.

The last Saturday before camp closed, Bobby's mother was supposed to marry a guy at St. Martha's. It was going to be mostly a Portuguese affair, but of course we got invited. I got permission from the camp director to take off, and Billy and Cubby came up for me. We had some smokes and beer on the way into East Providence and sat in the back of the church on the side of Bobby's mother's friends.

Bobby was wearing a light olive green tuxedo that his mother had picked out. He seemed particularly uncomfortable that his job was to give his mother away. Her fiancé's best man was in a front pew, and Father Al Persico was busy preparing the altar for the marriage sacrament. Thirty minutes later some woman walked down the aisle and whispered in the best man's ear. He followed her up the aisle. A few minutes later he whispered something to Bobby's mother, and she ran out of the church. Bobby ran after her, and the place erupted in head shaking. Getting stood up at your wedding isn't like getting stood up for a date. Afterward we drove by Bobby's house a couple of times but didn't see him. We called from Cubby's but hung up when Bobby's mother answered. We saw Bobby the next week. He said his mother was all right and that the guy had actually called the best man from Portland, Maine, where he was on a three-day drunk.

The dual murder, on the last day of August—or night, to be accurate—was huge news in Rhode Island and front page center in the *Providence Journal*. Sometime between eight in the evening, when Goddard Park closed, and five-fifteen the next morning, when the zoo people arrived, someone had shot and killed Hickey and Rickey, the zoo's two polar bears. Because they were each shot twice in the head, the *Journal's* headline was MOB-STYLE RUBOUT FOR HICKEY AND RICKEY.

This was not the first time the bears had been in the news. A few years earlier, Hickey, the male, had inadvertently eaten the nose of a drunken teenager who had tried to kiss him through the bars. This led to the discovery that the park people didn't really know anything about polar bears and were quite lax in such things as feeding them and keeping their pool filled with fresh, circulating water. So profoundly mistreated were these beasts that the *Journal* defended the nose eating as a form of polar bear self-defense. Rather than being punished, Hickey became a sort of hero. Elementary-school kids visited in busloads and drew pictures of the world's deadliest carnivore happily romping in his pool. Of course, after a while interest flagged, and Hickey and Rickey's keepers reverted back to muddy water and occasional feedings. Both bears developed open sores, lost teeth, and obviously suffered through their last horrendously hot summer. I'm not sure why I remember Hickey and Rickey. I'm not clear why they seem so important all of a sudden.

Big Tony recovered nicely and returned to Parts the same day we returned to school. Cubby, Billy, and me still had our crew cuts, but Bobby had let his hair grow longer and grew sideburns also. He was as thin as ever and dressed sharply. We knew he had been seeing a girl. We just didn't know who.

26

I checked my message service. There were calls from both Marvin Weissman and my commercial agent. I returned the calls, then drove into Providence to wait for Renée's train. It was actually early. We kissed, and she hugged me. "Clung" is really a better word for it. She holds on, and it makes me feel necessary and normal. We crossed the Washington Bridge into East Providence and stayed on 195 into Seekonk.

". . . so we throw about fifty million gallons of water on the flower shop, and I look around, and I'm thinking this is a pretty nice neighborhood."

I knew where she was going.

"Rents are high, but it *is* SoHo, you know."

I was quiet.

"I know. You don't like to talk about moving in together. I'm sorry. I love you."

"I love you, too," I said, and meant it.

"You don't have to say you love me just because I say I love you."

"I know. I've missed you."

She rubbed my leg. "Me, too. So what's happening?"

Sometimes, when one of my silly roles seems even sillier than normal, I'll bounce it off Renée for her insights, which are always helpful. I wasn't sure anybody could help me with this one.

"Renée, you won't believe it."

"Try me."

I filled her in, every little detail. Some things I had forgotten myself popped into my review. I had been so discombobulated by the surrealistic Ponserelli kidnapping that I forgot Poochy Ponserelli's strange remark about "that crazy little fuck" and wanting him to "let that whole thing go" because Poochy had said he "was sorry."

"Who was the little fuck?" she asked me as we entered the hotel room.

"It had to be Bobby."

"Why are they all afraid of him?"

I shook my head. We undressed and got into bed. When our heads were very close, I whispered, "I got theater tickets for tomorrow night. Trinity Square."

"You really know how to turn a girl on. What's the play?"

"I forget, but it's not *The Seagull*."

Roxanne Boneria was absolutely correct. The best sex is with a good friend. Especially if she happens to be your *best* friend and is a surpassing human being. Still, I decided not to share Roxanne or her theories with Renée.

We had dinner at a seafood restaurant, which was very plain and very good. Back at the hotel, we watched an old episode of *Law & Order*. It was about these three kids that entice a retarded girl into having sex with them. They get charged with rape, and the jury convicts them, but the judge, who's been hard on McCoy through the whole show, overturns the jury's decision, saying something like, "C'mon, she wanted it. She had a great time."

Renée popped out of bed, stood straight in front of the TV, and yelled, "You fucking prick bastard, you!" and shut the set off.

"You said that the last time we watched this episode."

"But why do they have to keep using that prick judge?"

"He's an actor," I laughed.

"Every time he's on, he's like a right-wing extremist. He's always overturning the jury."

"Renée, come back to bed."

"You'd never overturn that jury, would you?"

I looked at her and smiled. "No, Renée," I said, patting her side of the bed. "I'd be a good, loving judge."

She got back into bed and did her snuggle.

"I got a callback for an on-camera commercial next Wednesday," I said.

"A good one?"

"A regional bank. I'd be the guy who gets turned down for a loan, and Marvin called about a show at the Denver Center Theater."

"What show?"

"A new play."

"What's it about?"

"Marvin hadn't read the whole thing. It's set in Colorado, and it's about sick rainbow trout or something. I'm going to pick it up when I get back."

Renée gets so still when she's thinking that I thought she'd fallen asleep. After a few minutes, she said, "What are you afraid of, Jono?"

"Well, Jesus, there's some mass murderer running around."

"I mean about us living together."

"I'm not."

Renée sighed. "I think you're afraid, but I'm not going to talk about it anymore. I promise."

"You can talk about it."

I waited for her to say something until little snores bounced against my chest.

We got to the water tower ten minutes early, so I used the time to point out some snow-angel reference points to Renée. Kenny Snowden walked up at six-thirty on the nose. I introduced Renée, and he got down to it.

"Lou Adelman's the gunsmith we had look at the priest's trunks. There were sixteen weapons in each one." He read from a note-book. " 'Six Winchester Model 88 rifles in .243, .308, and .284 caliber. Three carbine versions of the 88. One Marlin 336. One Marlin 444. Seven Mausers, including two built in the Fabrique factory in Belgium. Four Model 70 Winchesters in .22 caliber and two Model 43 Winchesters in .22 caliber. The handguns were four modern .38 police specials and four of the earliest lock guns, all original. One matchlock, one wheel lock, one flintlock, and one percussion lock.' "

He looked at me. "Manny took the .22 rifles to the forensic guys. They didn't fire the slugs we've got. But Lou called me late last night with something. I'm meeting him at his shop. Care to join me?"

On the way to Adelman's gun shop, Kenny Snowden insisted on sitting in the backseat so Renée could ride up front. He leaned forward. "And where are you from, young lady?"

"Queens."

"Big-city girl."

"Yes, sir."

They both chuckled, and Renée watched East Providence glide by her window.

"Tell me, did your family drink water directly from the tap, or did you use bottled water?" Kenny asked Renée.

"We couldn't afford bottled water."

Kenny nodded. I waited. Tap water. Jesus.

"Anyone in your immediate family become forgetful?"

"No . . . wait . . . My great-aunt forgot stuff."

"She became . . . confused?"

"Absolutely."

"She developed symptoms like Alzheimer's, say?"

"Just like that. But the doctor called it something else, because she was about a hundred."

"Why do you want to know, Kenny?" I asked abruptly.

"I got theories about some things. I got a theory about water. Here's his place."

Lou Adelman was tall, thin, and bald. He seemed about Kenny's age. His left hand had a pronounced tremor. We followed him through his shop, past locked weapon cases in neat array and into a small open alcove office in the back.

"How's Lila?" Lou asked Kenny as we settled in chairs.

"Confounded and confused."

"I'm sorry."

Kenny nodded.

Lou opened a manila folder. "Manny told me he gave you the catalog of the weapons I reviewed in the trunks. Amazing, amazing collection. Two of the Mausers were actually built by Fabrique Nationale in Belgium, and one of the Marlins is vintage 1880s. Perfect condition."

"So they're valuable?" Kenny asked.

Lou Adelman leaned on the edge of his chair. "The handguns? The locks? They're not replicas, and they're perfect." He took a deep, dramatic breath. "There's a matchlock in there, I'm talking one weapon now, that might be worth, say, three hundred thousand to the right collector."

"Jesus Christ," Renée uttered.

"These are astonishingly restored. Museum-quality gunsmithing."

We were quiet for a moment, and we all looked at Kenny.

He thought out loud. "Now, how would a Catholic priest get ahold of a collection like that?"

"I don't have a clue," Lou said, looking into the manila folder, "but I sure know who restored them. Guy's been dead for thirty, forty years, but I grew up with his articles on gunsmithing in *Outdoor Life* and *Field & Stream*. You name it. He's a legend."

Lou stood and pulled a leather rifle case from a rack behind his desk. He removed the rifle.

"He was also one of the country's foremost engravers. His mark was always on the floor plate. Like this."

He flipped the rifle over; Kenny and I both reached for our glasses. A tiny, oblong, frosted, nickel-plated engraving had been placed under the stock so smoothly it seemed a natural part of the wood. A man in armor raised a sword. It was microscopic art.

"That's his mark. His initials are on the figure's chest plate."

I couldn't see the initials even with my glasses.

"It's beautiful," Renée said.

Lou added, "Problem is, it can't be Gunny's, that was his name, because it's a newly restored Sako Finnwolf. Fella purchased it off the Internet and brought it in to see what I think."

"So it's a fake," Kenny said.

"Like I said, it's newly restored, so Gunny couldn't possibly have done it. But . . ."

"But what?"

"But it can't be a fake. It's exactly Gunny Persico's work."

"Gunny *who*?" I mumbled.

Lou called the rifle's owner, and he gave us the Web site where he had purchased it. We brought it up on Lou's laptop. Gunny's Smithery was located on Block Island off the Rhode Island coast. Kenny called and asked to speak with Gunny. He listened, said thank you, and set the receiver down.

"His business is located at the Narragansett Hotel on the island. Fishing tackle and firearms. During the winter he moves his shop to Fall River."

"Fall River." Lou nodded. "Gunny had his shop there in the forties and fifties."

Kenny dialed the number Block Island had given. He held the piece of paper with Lou's trunk catalog at arm's length.

"Hello? . . . Yes. Is this Gunny's Smithery? . . . Yes, I've just purchased a Mauser from an estate sale. . . . That's right. . . . Well, I really don't know anything about them, but it needs some cleaning up. . . ."

Kenny listened.

"Uh . . . let me . . . Here it is, yes, it says Fabrique Nationale on the—Yes . . . oh, good. No, tomorrow morning is fine."

Kenny wrote down the address and hung up the receiver.

"Tomorrow at ten."

"You think he knows something?" Renée asked.

"I think every piece of the puzzle has to be assembled."

Except for me occasionally pointing out some landmark of my East Providence history to Renée, the drive back to Kenny's home on Wampanoag Trail was made in relative silence. When I pulled up in front of his neat little Cape Cod cottage, he didn't get out right away. He leaned forward again. He didn't speak for a long time.

"I would greatly appreciate you coming to Fall River with me tomorrow, Jono."

"Shouldn't the police do it?"

"They won't. There's no crime."

"But Gunny Persico died years ago."

"That's the mystery."

We let that thought dangle in the air like gossamer.

Renée turned around. "Can I come, too?"

"Of course."

Kenny got out of the car and leaned into Renée's window. "Pick me up at seven-thirty. That will give me time for my walk and to arrange Lila's home care. I'll bring the coffee."

He started to push away, stopped, and said pointedly, "I make it with bottled water."

27

The Friday after Hickey and Rickey were rubbed out, Bobby made his final trawl of his summer job. Getting back to dock about six at night, he packed his deck gear into a paper bag and began walking home to his mother's house on Brightridge Avenue in East Providence. He knew he could have called Billy or Cubby, who had been using his mother's old Volkswagen, for a ride, but he felt closed up from being on the boat all day. He crossed over the Barrington River and into Barrington. Even though the fishing was grueling, constant work from four in the morning on, he wasn't the least bit tired. In fact, Bobby Fontes never was tired, even at bedtime. He was never hungry either and only ate when someone put something in front of him. Half an hour later, he could see the top of the roller coaster at Crescent Park. There he'd pick up Pawtucket Avenue, walk it through Riverside, and take it into East Providence.

Tall and razor thin, Bobby walked without swagger. His engineer boots with his jeans tucked into them pounded on the asphalt in syncopated rhythm. It was a cool night, but Bobby had his T-shirt off and stuck in his back pocket. He felt as if he were breathing through his nut-brown skin. Before his mother had been stood up at St. Martha's, she had been after him to cut his hair and shave his sideburns. Now she didn't seem to care about it, and his long black hair sailed out behind him. He felt the patch over his eye. His mother had also been on him to not wear the patch, but the dead eye was his father's signature. He shook his head to clear his mind and turned onto Pawtucket Avenue. Seagulls swirled over the houses closest to the bay. A fine, misty rain began. It felt good that it wasn't salt spray. It felt clean and new.

Bobby saw them before they saw him. They were coming out of the New York System hot-dog joint next to Bucci's Tailor Shop on Riverside Square. Jack Crosby, his brother Howie, Connie Dwyer, and little Allie Ponserelli. There were three girls, too. Mondos. Pretty in tight pedal pushers and high hair. Bobby didn't alter his stride and was twenty feet away when they saw him coming, glistening from the rain. He passed them without a blink.

Massive Connie Dwyer snickered. "It's raining, fuckface."

Bobby stopped but didn't turn around. There was a trigger inside him, and he didn't like it. When he finally told me this months later, he said he wished he *had* called Billy or Cubby for a ride. It was quiet behind him now, and he turned into it. Connie Dwyer could have been subdivided into at least two Bobby Fontes. Jack Crosby hadn't been there for the Petey Maloney deal, but he heard about it. Connie Dwyer *had* been there. He regretted the "fuckface" remark as soon as he said it, but now it was water under the bridge. Bobby slowly put his paper bag on the wet sidewalk without taking his flat eye off Connie.

"Don't touch him, Connie," Allie said quickly.

Connie nodded, and the group started to follow Jack to his car. All but one girl, a redhead with a heavy slash of crimson lipstick on her face. She looked at Bobby's sinewy torso sparkling under the corner streetlight. She turned back to her group.

"Chickenshit!" she shouted.

Now it was Connie Dwyer's turn to stop. His stomach leaped, but he coolly turned and pointed. "He's not worth it."

She put her small white hands on her hips. Lacquered finger-nails flashed red.

"How come everybody else you beat up is worth it?" she taunted.

"Shut up, Colleen," Howie said. "C'mon, Connie, fuck him."

"Yeah," whined Allie, "fuck him. C'mon, let's go."

Jack watched, leaning against the hood of his car. Jack was a good leaner and a better watcher.

Connie pointed again. This time at Colleen.

"I'm not chickenshit, okay? I've got things to do."

Connie could feel his heart racing. Earlier in the day, him and Allie had taken Jimmy Carmichael's Timex. Took it right off his wrist, and then Connie had slapped the shit out of him. Carmichael was a pussy. Connie didn't have to think about that one like he was thinking now. He hated to think. Thinking added dimension to the encounter, and the dimension was always something bad. Bobby still watched him with a disquieting ease. He didn't appear to be breathing.

"Just get in the fucking car, Colleen!" Howie shouted.

"Who's gonna make me? Chickenshit Connie Dwyer?"

Connie's umbrage instantly turned to rage, and he charged Bobby with a growl. Bobby sidestepped and connected three times hard to Connie's passing right temple. Connie settled onto the side-walk with a thump.

Bobby watched him for five seconds to be sure, picked up his paper bag without looking at the others, and began walking again. Ten minutes later, at the Socony-Mobil entrance, he stopped and turned. Colleen stopped, too.

They were quiet, and, of course, Bobby accepted the pause as his own. Her high red hairdo sagged in the rain. Mascara ran in black lines down her freckled face.

"How come you wanted that guy to fight?"

She shrugged. "I don't know."

Bobby watched her eyes. "I'm walking home from my job. I worked on a fishing boat in Warren. Today was my last day."

"Is it fun?"

He thought about this. "No, but we took some haddock. We took some cod."

He oddly felt like saying more.

"I don't have to walk. My friends would've got me, but I wanted to walk."

"I wanted to walk, too. I wanted to walk with you."

She walked forward, and they were on the sidewalk together.

"I'm . . . Bobby Fontes," he said awkwardly.

"I'm Colleen Crosby."

If the name gave him dismay, he didn't show it, and they walked into East Providence.

28

Kenny Snowden had called Father Oscar the night before for permission to pick up one of the Fabrique Nationale Mauser rifles on our way up to Fall River. We stopped for breakfast in Swansea off I-195. Kenny insisted on drinking his own coffee.

"I've lived in East Providence for sixty-seven years, and I've never been to Fall River, Massachusetts. Driven through but never stopped."

" 'Lizzie Borden took an ax / And gave her mother forty whacks,' " Renée recited with toast in her mouth.

Kenny joined her. " 'When she saw what she had done, / She gave her father forty-one.' "

"I brought her up on the Internet last night," he said seriously. "After seeing Gunny maybe we can take a tour of her house. It's a museum now."

"That would be so cool," Renée said.

Fall River is a city of about one hundred thousand. It sits on two hills above Mount Hope Bay, which really is part of Narragansett Bay. When I was a kid, Fall River had lost most of its fishing and manufacturing base, and except for the Fall River Knitting Mill, with an outlet where East Providence would go for cheap sweaters, the place was pretty well down-and-out. Its comeback was truly remarkable, and the bleakness I remember had given way to a sense of industry. Abandoned mills had been turned into fancy apartment complexes, and the port was full of naval and whaling vessels that were used as floating museums.

Gunny's Smithery was on the second floor of an old brick three-story, over a Portuguese restaurant. The sign on the door was fading badly. I wondered again why I was here. Kenny rapped on the glass.

Thirty seconds later an elderly but firm voice spoke on the other side. "Yes?"

"I called you yesterday . . . about my Fabrique Nationale Mauser."

The door opened, and the man who owned the voice immediately held his hands out for the rifle. He turned and walked to a wooden table. He flicked on a surgical operating light. Except for a slight potbelly, the man was gaunt. His fingers were long and delicate-looking. He sported a full white beard and a full head of white hair cut in a military buzz. He wore a black turtleneck sweater and khaki slacks. He laid the rifle down and spread out several vials and spray bottles of solutions. After he slipped on white cotton gloves, he brushed the mechanisms with a fine artist's paintbrush. He leaned in close with a magnifying glass but became instantly still when he reached the floor plate. We waited. He didn't move.

Kenny leaned down with him. "Recognize the work?" he whispered.

Kenny straightened, and the old man did, too. He kept his eyes on the Mauser, and they became moist, then wet. He dabbed at them with a handkerchief.

"This is my father's. This is Gunny Persico's."

I knew the voice, even with the years on it.

"Father Al?" I asked.

And he began to cry.

★   ★   ★

He took another sip of water and continued his debriefing.

". . . And it was all too much, that's all. After my father . . . after Gunny died and I had brought his legacy back to St. Martha's in the trunks, nothing was the same. I was floating. No anchor. I couldn't concentrate. I felt as if the world was closing in on me. The diocese had counseling, but that was more or less pep talks, and I needed more than that. One morning a little voice told me to run away."

"That's when you buried all of your belongings," offered Kenny.

Father Al nodded. "Even the keys to my old Ford. Even left my father's beautiful guns. I took a bus to North Stonington—"

"Selling insurance," Kenny interrupted.

Father Al looked surprised. "How did you know that?"

"The police found your things buried in a duffel bag there, too."

"Oh."

We waited.

Renée sat beside Father Al and put both of her lovely arms around him. "Are you tired? Want to lie down?"

He smiled sadly and shook his head. "One day I saw an old parishioner and thought she might have recognized me. And also I was worried about having my Social Security number traced. So I ran to Block Island."

He gestured to his shop. "This is cash and carry. On Block Island I barter, too. There I'm just old Gunny. I apprenticed to my father before I was called to God."

"Why didn't you just quit the priesthood?" I asked. "Priests can quit."

He looked at his long fingers. "It's complicated. Everything gets complicated."

We waited.

He took a deep breath and sighed it out. "There was a woman."

We left the Mauser with him and his secrets. He asked about the others, and Kenny said they belonged to him and he'd see that he got them. I didn't tour Lizzie Borden's place with Renée and Kenny. My mind was thumping into places it shouldn't have gone, so I walked for a half hour, hoping the cool breeze off the water would blow these disquieting thoughts away. More than one theater director has accused me of overanalyzing the strange and stranger parts I've played. Of building puzzles with the components of character until the essence of that character is hopelessly lost in the vast maze of my minutiae. Of course, there *are* infinite ways to play any role, and it may be that I have discovered a technique for not finding any of them. I read too much background. I study too much historical perspective. Maybe because of a small education, there's a part of me that overcompensates out of some intellectual inferiority complex and drives me to search for the orbit of a person and not for that person himself. I was distressed that I couldn't turn my mind in another direction. Now I was applying my odd technique to a nonplay in real time, in a role I didn't want to perform.

29

When the first school day of our senior year ended, Cubby, Billy, and me waited for Bobby in the parking lot. It was a beautiful September afternoon, and the Marlboros tasted particularly good after we'd been cooped up in EP High for almost eight hours. We leaned against Billy's DeSoto, checking out the girls with a practiced aloofness. Sandy ran up, all hope and energy, and kissed me.

"Hey," I said.

I had my sunglasses stretched across the vast expanse of my face. I felt a definite Ann-Margret/Elvis moment and coolly took a drag of my butt.

"I got cheerleading practice until six, okay?"

I gave her my all-state blessing. "Sure," I said.

We watched her bounce away, then took in the parking lot and surrounding area of cars and kids. Cubby and Billy were both seeing chicks from Bay View Academy, a Catholic girls' school across Pawtucket Avenue from the Bradley Hospital for Emotionally Disturbed Children—or "wackos," as Cubby liked to say. The young ladies had been sent to Bay View to avoid the pitfalls of public education in general and public-school boys in particular, but all the Catholic doctrine in the world was no match for a '59 DeSoto.

Bobby was walking toward us when he got intercepted by a redheaded mondo girl. They talked for a minute, and he offered her a drag of his smoke. She inhaled deeply. They both began walking our way.

"What the fuck?" Cubby said out of the side of his mouth.

"What?" I asked.

"The mondo with Bobby. That's a Crosby."

I looked close. "A Jack Crosby?"

"She's bad news," Billy said.

Bobby walked up to us with the flat look we were used to.

"You ready to roll?" Billy asked.

Bobby took a longer-than-usual pause. "Can we give somebody a ride home?"

Billy shrugged. "Let's go."

Me and Cubby got in front with Billy, and we rolled out of the parking lot and headed for Riverside.

"This is Colleen."

"Hi," she said to the backs of our heads.

"Hi," we mumbled.

"She lives on the Terrace."

She directed us to the Crosby haunt and walked in.

Cubby pushed Bobby's shoulder. "Asshole."

"What?"

"That's Colleen Crosby."

"So?"

We all fell uncomfortably quiet as the car eased toward the Portuguese section off Grosvenor Avenue.

"She's a pretty girl," I said finally.

After a moment Bobby nodded and said, "I'm thinking of asking Colleen to the senior prom."

"She's a sophomore," Cubby snarled.

"She stayed back a year," Bobby countered.

"It's only September, Bobby," Billy said reasonably.

We pulled up in front of his tiny house. He didn't jump out right away. We waited.

"I love that girl," he stated softly. "I really, really love that girl."

30

We dropped in on Cubby early afternoon at Tasca's. He kissed Renée's cheek, then gave her a desk-photo tour.

"What's that?" she said, pointing to a picture.

"That's me," I said. "I was about ten."

"But what's that on your shoulders? A Volkswagen?"

"Ho, ho," I said.

"Jesus, you had a big head."

"His head only looked normal when he was playing hockey. He was great. Hey, Jono, remember this?"

I leaned close. Renée, too. There we were. Me, Billy, Bobby, and Cubby in our black tuxedo pants and white dinner jackets. We wore crimson cummerbunds and bow ties. Sandy Minucci and the Bay View Academy girls wore long white gowns. Colleen Crosby wore a short black dress and had a cigarette dangling. She looked defiantly at the camera. Riot to follow.

"Senior prom," Cubby announced. "Big Tony took it in front of Billy's house because Jono couldn't go inside."

"Why not?" Renée asked.

"I'll tell you later." I looked up at Cubby. "Whatever happened to the Crosby girl?"

"What didn't?" he said, shaking his head. "She's put him through hell. I'll never understand it."

He'd lost me there.

"Understand what?"

"Her and Bobby. She's run him around for more than thirty years. Now his mother's in a nursing home."

"Wait a minute. Bobby married Colleen Crosby?"

"No. They never got married. They lived together—what do you call it?—common law. She goes on a drunk and disappears, he dries her out, brings her home. She runs off with some coke-snorting scumbag, he always takes her back. She looks like death."

Cubby turned to Renée. "Have you met Bobby?"

She shook her head.

"He's as old as me and Jono, but he looks about thirty-five, doesn't he, Jono? I bet he wears the same size pants he wore in high school."

"Bobby never mentioned Colleen."

"Would you?"

I told Cubby about my ride with Poochy Ponserelli. I told him what he said about Bobby letting it go because Poochy already had apologized.

"The fat bastard thinks he's a politician. Know what Ponserelli is? He's a shakedown artist for the construction unions."

"But why do you think he's afraid of Bobby?"

"I don't know. But then I don't really know Bobby anymore. I had the kids and Bobby had Colleen and his mother."

I told Cubby we'd be heading back to New York in a day or two, and we made those sentimental vows to keep in touch. I hoped we would. I didn't think so, though. You sort of stretch life out and move on.

I called Kenny Snowden from the car. He answered on the first ring. I needed Poochy Ponserelli's address. I wanted to talk to him, but I couldn't even explain why to myself, let alone Kenny Snowden or Renée.

"You're not a policeman," Renée said pointedly.

We were crossing the Washington Bridge into Providence.

"Do you hear me? Cubby said this guy is like a goddamn mobster. This guy kidnapped you, Jono."

"I don't think it was technically a kidnapping."

"You told me one of them had a gun."

"True."

"So technically it *was* a kidnapping."

"But I didn't feel very threatened."

We turned toward the East Side and Blackstone Boulevard. The boulevard's two directions are halved by a two-mile-long mini-park, and at the end of it is Swan Point Cemetery. I pulled in front of an enormous white stucco house. Blinking Christmas lights were on, even though it was afternoon. A limousine was parked outside, and Howie Crosby sat behind the wheel reading a newspaper.

"I'm only going to be a minute."

"I'm coming, too."

"Renée . . ."

"I love you."

"Renée, you'll help me a lot more by waiting here. Please."

She pouted but stayed in her seat. I walked up the steps and rang the bell. A pretty, dark-haired girl about twenty answered.

"Yes?"

"I'd like to speak with Mr. Ponserelli."

"Daddy's in his office in the carriage house. It's around back."

I followed the long driveway to the rear of the house. A large garage built to resemble the house itself was set back on the property. Four late-model cars, a Mercedes, a BMW, a Volkswagen Bug, and a red Cadillac convertible filled the open bays. Stairs on the side led to a second floor. I walked up and knocked.

"Who?" he growled.

"Jono Riley," I said on the other side of the door.

The door flew open, and fat Poochy stood there glowering. He wore a gold jogging suit, too small in the waist and thighs. A diamond pinkie ring flashed in the sun.

"Who told you I was here?"

"The young lady who answered the front door."

"That's my daughter. You leave her out of this."

"Out of what?"

He pulled a cell phone from his back pocket and pushed some numbers. He held the phone away and screamed into it.

"You get that other fuckface out of the limo and you get your fucking asshole asses back here now!"

We waited, staring at each other, until Howie Crosby and Allie Ponserelli ran up the driveway gasping and disheveled. Howie had his handgun out, and Allie carried what looked to be a sawed-off shotgun.

"Stop!" Poochy screamed.

Now they huffed directly below us at the bottom of the steps.

Poochy pointed at me. "This fuck walks up to the front door, talks to Angela, walks back here, knocks on my fucking door. What are you fuckfaces doing? Whacking off?"

"He snuck up, the bastard," Allie whined.

"No he didn't, you dumb-fuck, asshole, cocksucking, dago shit. He walked up. He knocked on the fucking door. 'Who?' I said. 'Jono Riley,' he said."

"He thinks he's such a big deal. He's not!" Howie shouted, raising his gun.

"Put that fucking thing down, you potato-eating mick piece of shit!" He turned and looked at me, shaking his head sadly. "It's like they never got out of the Terrace. C'mon."

I followed him into his office. There was a large oak table with a computer on top. A thick shag throw rug separated several leather chairs and a couch. An enormous television screen dominated the back wall. A Jacuzzi was in front of it. Kenny gestured for me to sit.

"Beer?"

"Nothing, thanks."

He settled his bulk behind the table. He pointed to the computer.

"Can you use one of these?"

"Not very well."

"I can't even turn the thing on," he said woefully. "It fucking eludes me." He looked up and pointed at me. "But I don't need to. I make so much money I can hire some faggot to use it for me. Know what I mean?"

"You make a lot of money."

"Fucking-A. How about you? What's a big-fucking-deal actor get?"

"I don't make hardly anything."

"What about when you were that retard? I saw that show. *Blues and Whites.*"

I shrugged. "What the producers did was figure out a way they could pay me at a much lower rate than normal because I was autistic."

"You're, like, deaf? What are you doing, reading my lips?"

"I meant the character I played was unable to speak because of a condition of abnormal self-absorption."

"And so they wouldn't pay you?"

"Not much."

"Did you put their cocks in a vise?"

"I don't have powerful representation."

"I don't mean actually *crushing* their cocks in a vise, but just *getting* them in a vise sends a strong message that the next time they might really be looking at their cocks getting crushed."

"I'll pass that on to my agent. Look, I don't want you to think

I'm harassing you, because I'm not. I'm just trying to understand what's going on."

Poochy stood, waddled over to the picture window, and looked out over the driveway to the back of his house. I kept going.

"Know what I found out, Poochy? The rifle that fired the .22 into twelve-year-old Marie D'Agostino's back was used to kill three other people."

He turned and stared at me. "Three?"

"That we know of."

"Jesus Christ on a crutch."

"Now, I don't claim to be anything more than a sometime actor and a bartender, but I have to understand, you see, what's . . . going on."

Poochy walked back to the table and sat with a grunt.

"Like . . . what did you mean when you told me to tell Bobby Fontes to let it go? What did you mean?" I wasn't preparing a role, but I was gathering minutiae all the same.

Poochy took a deep breath. I waited. He shook his head, bewildered.

"Ever notice how he . . . never changes? You can see him one day and not see him again for years, he never changes. Everybody gets old, right? Not him. It's like his life is one long day for him. He starts out thirty and stays thirty." Poochy looked up sorrowfully. "It's not fair."

"But what did you mean?"

He looked over my head. "Fuck," he sighed. "Look, I'm associated with various trade unions now, which is how I earn my keep. Did you know that the fucking governor is a personal friend?"

"You told me."

He turned a framed photo on the table so it was facing me. "Check this shit out."

A smiling Poochy Ponserelli flanked by Bill and Hillary.

"I slept in the fucking Lincoln Bedroom. I went to a state dinner for some fucking Zulu king. So it's legit with a capital *L*. But you gotta start somewhere. You can't just waltz into being an independent contractor with heavy union ties and a house on Blackstone Boulevard. Did I tell you who my fucking neighbors are?"

"Yes."

"So I had to start small. I had to keep my dreams under my hat. My old man ran book out of the New York System in Riverside. Strictly small potatoes. I had to make my own way. Jackie and me did a little shaking down, a little collecting for the DeSimones in North Providence . . . and . . . Jesus, everybody was selling a little shit in the seventies."

"Drugs, you mean?"

"Just enough for walking-around money. We practically gave it away. Jackie, the asshole, didn't want us to sell to the Irish. You believe that asshole? What if I wouldn't sell to Italians? Senseless. We worked it out. Absolutely no heroin. That was the deal."

I saw him strike a self-righteous pose. I heard sanctity in his voice.

"We were not like the scum over on Elmwood Avenue in Providence. Those fucking spics would sell horse to their fucking grand-mothers. We did not sell horse. Anyway, she was always a cunt. Always drunk. Always—"

"Who?"

Poochy Ponserelli looked at me like I was an idiot. "Colleen." His eyes narrowed. "Don't tell him I called her a cunt. That was between you and me. I didn't mean it the way it sounded. Okay?"

My mind was racing.

"Okay?"

"Okay."

"But it's the God's truth. She was a fucking drunk since she was twelve years old. Jackie, my friend, Jackie Crosby, who could give a fuck about anything, actually has cried over his sister. Fucking crying like a big baby. When she got ahold of coke, man, she was fucking gone. Gone."

He shook his head sort of mournfully. "Whoever thinks a little tiny smell of that shit is gonna drive somebody nuts? One sniff, and bang, she's begging Jackie for more."

"Her brother gave her the cocaine?"

"You make it sound like it's fucking dirty. Maybe he thought it would help her stop drinking. Who knows what the micks think? But she went nuts. Then your friend comes over to Jackie's, three in the morning, Jackie's in the rack with some broad, he sits on the end of the bed and tells him to get everything together, all the loose ends, and say good-bye to everybody. Jackie says, 'Where am I going?' Your friend just gets up and leaves. Jackie comes over here scared shitless. I tell him, 'Hey, asshole, people are supposed to be scared of *us*.'"

"What happened?"

"Jackie got indicted for some bullshit federal thing and cut a deal. He's at the end of five in the Adult Correctional Institute."

"So nothing happened with Bobby?"

"Not until last week." Poochy Ponserelli swallowed. "Jackie's getting out in ten days. Last week your skinny fucking friend visited him. Asked him if he'd said his good-byes. That same night . . ."

Sweat appeared on the ridge where his hairline had been.

"That same night . . . what?"

"I get a call, late, it's him. He tells me he thinks my Angela is a very lovely young lady. That's what he said, exactly: 'She is a very lovely young lady.' I knew where he was going. I'm not a fucking moron. I told him I never gave any of that shit to Colleen. I told him I was sorry that she was into it, because I knew her when she was a little kid. Then there's nothing on the phone. I think he's hung up, but something tells me not to put the phone down. Then he says it again. 'Angela's a lovely young lady.' Jesus. Fuck."

He looked at me almost plaintively. "Did you tell him? Did you tell him to let it go?"

Renée drove us back to the Ramada. I dialed Bobby's cellular phone number on the way. The phone picked up, and I waited through the pause.

"Hello," he said softly.

"Bobby. Hey. It's me, Jono."

"How are you, Jono?"

"Great. Great. Listen, my friend Renée—"

Renée glanced at me.

"My girlfriend, Renée . . . remember I told you she was coming up?"

"The fireperson."

"Yeah. Well, she's here, so I wanted to see what you're doing for dinner tomorrow."

"Tomorrow?"

I waited.

"What about tonight? I'm sort of busy tomorrow."

"We're going to the theater tonight."

"I could meet you for a drink after."

"It might be late."

"That's okay."

"Sure, then. How about eleven? Where?"

"Merrill's Lounge."

"Sure."

I waited, but he didn't speak.

"Bobby . . ."

"What, Jono?"

"See you tonight."

I punched in Kenny Snowden's number and asked him for another favor. We were in the middle of the Washington Bridge heading into East Providence. I looked at the black river below. Renée continued on 195 into Seekonk. Two cars behind us, a blue-and-white van took the first exit into East Providence.

31

"All four of them live on the Terrace," Cubby said, popping open a 'Gansett.

"Deborah's not a mick or a dago either," Billy added. "I thought you had to be one or the other to live on the Terrace."

Cubby passed out the beers. "We got maybe three Jews in the whole town, and Billy fell in love with one of them."

"I fell in love with two of them. I think I love her sister, too. She's got a pair out like this."

I lit a Marlboro and passed the pack over to Bobby. "How come a girl with a name like Shapiro goes to Bay View Academy?"

Billy shrugged. "Beats the shit out of me."

The black stretch limo moved into traffic on Taunton Avenue and turned immediately onto Pawtucket for the pickup of our senior-prom dates. As we rolled toward Riverside Terrace, we savored the beers and the smokes. Big Tony had arranged for the limo and driver. Cubby had asked the guy if it was okay to drink some beers and smoke, and the guy said sure. He also asked him if he wouldn't mind not mentioning it to his old man. It wasn't as if Big Tony didn't know every little thing we were up to, but he wasn't about to give his approval to this coolly black-tuxedoed, crimson-cummerbunded, and bow-tied party of ladies' men.

We directed the driver past Crescent Park onto the Terrace horseshoe for the first stop on the loop, Maureen Moynihan's house. Maureen had dated Cubby all year long, and despite her being two or three inches taller, they looked good together. She was an only child in a neighborhood of people that worked overtime to keep their families under, say, twelve kids. We waited while he got out, sauntered up the walk, ran back for the corsage, and sauntered back for her. She looked beautiful in her long white gown, and when they walked hand in hand back to the limo, we actually watched them without snickering. Suavely he opened a 'Gansett and handed it to her.

Deborah Shapiro was next. Her mother had Billy pose with her for a photograph even though the Shapiros, like all the parents, were going over to Billy's for cocktails and photos. Or almost all the parents. Deborah also had on the requisite formal gown, and this one fluffed and dived wonderfully, and we were sensitive enough not to stare at her very nice tits.

It was a warm May evening, and the Minucci men were waiting for us on their front lawn. Every one of them was smoking. The five oldest ones had beers, too. I got out and started for the front door. While Alex, Hank, Brian, Dougie, Eugene, Billy, and crazy Jimmy got a tour of the limo, Larry fell casually in step with me.

"What's that you got on, Jono?"

"The tux?"

"No, the smell."

"It's Canoe for Men."

I got to the door.

"We use the Mennen stuff," he said, gesturing to the other Visigoths. "The Skin Bracer. The underarm deodorant."

I nodded.

He put his arm around my shoulders. "Big night tonight," he said.

"It should be fun."

"It's at Rhodes on the Pawtuxet, right?"

"Right."

"That's a great place. I had my senior prom there. Took Molly Milroy. A great girl. Jesus, we had a ball. It was absolutely the best blow job I ever had—up to then, I mean."

He nudged me, and we both laughed.

"Anyway Jono, listen. Alex, Hank, Brian, and Dougie told me to tell you that if you touch Sandy, prom or no prom, they are going to beat the holy shit out of you. Eugene and Billy told me to tell you if you are anything less than a perfect gentleman, they are going to kill you. And, hey, what can I say about Jimmy? He's my brother, I love him, but he's fucking crazy. You never know what he's gonna do."

I rang the bell, and there was amazing Sandy Minucci. I was taking this wonderful captain of the Townie cheerleaders to my senior prom. This was how life was supposed to work. She came toward me in a white chiffon gown. Pearl earrings dangled. Her blond hair shone and dipped. I pinned the corsage above her right breast.

"Easy there, tiger." Her father glowered and waved me over for his own parting death threat.

The Crosby lair was set back farther from the street than the other houses. There were no lights on except for the fluttering glint of a television set. Bobby stepped out of the limo. Me, Cubby, and Billy did, too. I hadn't noticed, sitting in the limo, how striking Bobby looked in the formal wear. His long hair was slicked back, and his razor-straight build gave him a tall, almost ethereal countenance. If he'd had a mustache, he could have passed for a fifties movie star. He stared at us.

"What are you guys doing?" he asked quietly.

"Stretching our legs," Cubby said.

"I can get Colleen myself," Bobby said evenly.

"There are no lights on," Billy said.

We all looked up the walk to the dark house.

"We're just gonna walk with you, Bobby," I said lightly.

After a moment Bobby shrugged, and we followed him up to the house.

What a family this was. What a clan. I mean, think about it, here we were picking up a girl for our last senior-high-school dance, and all four of us were expecting ambush. To put a little perspective on exactly how likely that was with the delightful Ponserelli-Crosby mob, some of our other friends thought we should bring Officer Snowden or even a gun with us when we picked her up. When we made it to the front door, we hung back, and Bobby pushed the doorbell. The door opened, and a shriveled little woman in her fifties stood facing Bobby with a can of 'Gansett of her own. She stared at him. We knew that even though Bobby and Colleen had been together all school year, he'd never been to her house before. It was much easier to meet on neutral ground.

"What do you want?" she said.

"I'm here for Colleen."

She looked him up and down. "What are you supposed to be? A waiter? Yeah, I know." She turned her head and yelled, "Colleen! Bring it down. Your Portagee's here."

We had always tossed off our ethnic designations in meaningless banter. Somehow it made us feel closer to each other. Her tone had me rethinking this. Bobby, of course, showed nothing and waited. A man appeared behind her. He looked exactly like a gone-to-seed Jack Crosby. He wore a wife-beater. Black suspenders held up his wide slacks near his chest.

"You the boy that took Bunny Soares in Warren last summer?"

Bobby nodded slightly. We knew there'd been some trouble on

the Fourth of July, but we didn't know what, and Bobby wasn't talking about it.

"Kicked that guy's ass pretty good, I heard. I know Bunny— he's a tough one. Kicked his ass, though."

Colleen pushed past the two of them and stood in front of Bobby with her little defiant look. She had on a short black dress that looked sexy and, I suppose, inappropriate for a prom. When we got into the limo, Colleen was cordial and chatty. She laughed easily and demurely turned down a beer. She held Bobby's hand, and he smiled. I could see some of what Bobby saw in her. Colleen wore her mondo armor as a defense against her impossible family, and as a little of it slipped off, a smart and compelling girl was revealed.

Big Tony was waiting for us in front of Billy's house. He had two cameras around his neck and a windup Canon 8-mm movie camera. We stowed the beer, popped some Sen-Sen, and posed in front of the limo. When they went into the house, I got back into the car so nobody'd think my feelings were hurt, even if they were. Big Tony got in with me.

"Smells like a brewery," he said, and winked at me. "Don't drink a lot. I'm serious."

"We won't, Big Tony."

We were quiet.

"You don't have to stay, Big Tony. I'm not sad or anything."

"I'm gonna go in in a second. He's my sister's husband," he said with a gesture toward Billy's house, "but I'm pissed at him, and I told him so. So you're thinking the army?"

"Yeah."

He nodded and looked out the window. He nodded again and opened the door. He leaned over and patted my fat cheek.

"I love you," he said.

"I love you, too, Big Tony."

I watched him walk up the porch stairs and into the house. Four years later, after a series of progressively worse heart attacks, Big Tony D'Agostino would be dead at forty-nine, and I'd be fatherless all over again.

Rhodes on the Pawtuxet was an enormous dance hall built in the twenties with a raised oval bandstand in the middle of a highly polished parquet floor. Couples would essentially dance around the band, which on prom night was Debonair Duke Bentley and His Swing Men, an eight-piece ensemble that featured Benny Goodman and Tommy Dorsey standards as well as up-to-the-minute vocal interpretations of the Beatles, Elvis, and the Fabulous Fabian.

We knew that the social organization of the evening was inescapable, and we made arrangements to meet up at eleven by the entrance. Cubby had just been named second-team all-state catcher and would have to spend some time with the baseball guys. I'd be visiting the hockey players, and Billy and Deborah gravitated over to some of her Bay View Academy friends. Bobby was only interested in doing whatever pleased Colleen, and what pleased Colleen were her close-knit and entirely alien mondos. He followed her over to their corner. The boys in pegged tuxedos and the girls in high hair and short dresses.

Cubby shook his head. "Jesus," he said.

"She seems like a nice girl," I said.

He looked at me and laughed. "What time is it?"

"Around eight."

"The night is still young," he said, and he and Maureen walked over to the ballplayers.

It was a very nice time. Sandy said it was "magical," but I didn't know about that. I danced and laughed and in general tried to drop a mask of knowing sophistication over my still-huge head.

Billy, Cubby, and I met up in the men's room for a smoke, but we couldn't find Bobby.

"Fucking mondos," Billy said.

We nodded although I wasn't so sure, as I didn't know anything about them except that they never participated in any after-school stuff and only spoke to each other. When we walked out of the men's room, Officer Kenny Snowden in a tuxedo and accompanied by a strikingly beautiful black woman cha-chaed past us.

"Good evening, gentlemen," he said.

We smiled and said hello. He introduced us to his wife and kept dancing. We watched them dance away. Except for a very small group of kids, most everyone was happy to see Officer Snowden there, blending security with pleasure. I guess that said everything about our high-school cop.

Cubby nudged me and gestured with his head.

Connie Dwyer in a four-sizes-too-small tuxedo was attempting to cha-cha with his date. She was tall and elegant, in sharp contrast to the marauding clodhopper who had escorted her to the dance.

"She's from Bay View," Cubby said. "Maureen said she was too nice not to go with the asshole."

He saw us watching and looked hard at us. He gave us the finger. We gave it back to him and walked over to our girls. We hadn't known for months that Bobby had hit Connie in front of the New York System, and most likely we'd never have known, as Bobby sure as hell wouldn't talk about it, if it hadn't been for Connie confronting him in the cafeteria right before Christmas. We were getting up from lunch, and there he was. It must have been eating at him.

"You hit me with a sucker shot, and you know it."

Bobby put down his tray and looked at Connie.

"Admit it," he said. "You know you did."

Bobby didn't say anything, and Connie took that as complete

vindication, happy to get it out of his system without getting publicly annihilated. Actually, Connie Dwyer had rebounded quite well from Bobby's summer KO. After a short period of emotional convalescing, he reemerged as the gang's enforcer. But what really brought him full circle as a self-respecting wrecking machine was the recognition bestowed upon him by none other than Poochy Ponserelli for personally masterminding the response to Parker's Newsstand for its refusal to pay protection money. Connie burned down the stand.

Now honored as a man of brains as well as brawn, Connie had assembled a cadre of beasts loyal to himself and his way of doing business: Donnie Newlove, a wiry junior out of East Providence, known for his signature *D,* placed prominently in red spray paint on all property he vandalized; Ernie Guthrie from the Terrace, who was nearly as big and intelligent as Connie himself and held the title of oldest EP sophomore of all time at nineteen; and KiKi Coulette, a disturbing Irish–French Canadian blend who was a senior and was rumored to hold a black belt in karate, a rumor he encouraged vigorously. These four caitiffs branched out from the confines of Riverside, making petty-criminal forays into Greater East Providence and bordering Barrington. Prowling through the after-school streets in Ernie's mother's Karmann Ghia, they sought out isolated misfit school chums and solicited whatever they might have with them. Money. Wallets. Watches. Hats if they liked them. On the rare occasion that one of their benefactors went to the police, Ernie and his tribe would tell the cops with sorrowful looks that they had been given the goods. Later, of course, they would deal with the poor sport. So life was moving pleasantly for Connie, and there didn't appear to be any reason it wouldn't continue indefinitely. Then he saw the first of many graffiti. Always in red. Always in small block lettering. BOBBY FONTES KICKED CONNIE DWYER'S ASS. Connie ran to the boys' room to get a wet paper towel to clean it off his locker. There it was again, only this time it was placed in several pivotal locations. He scrubbed away the slogans as best he could, then ran back and scrubbed his locker.

Over the next several weeks, so many slogans appeared that even with the assistance of his associates Connie could not stop the word from getting out that, indeed, his ass had been kicked. Not only that, but the ass kicker was a tall, skinny weirdo who never spoke and seemed to glide quietly through his life. Also, the bastard was always followed around by the little mondo Colleen Crosby. What was Jack thinking? The fucking guy was a Portagee, for Christ's sake. A sucker-shot Portagee.

One day at lunch, Bobby walked over to the Ponserelli-Crosby table. He stood next to Connie. He just stood there for a minute without speaking, then finally said, "Look, I'm sorry somebody's been writing that stuff. I'm embarrassed. I'm sorry." Then he walked away.

"I told you he was a faggot," Allie Ponserelli said.

"He thinks he's great. He's not great," Howie Crosby added.

They watched Bobby leave the cafeteria with Colleen close behind. Somewhere in the vacant chambers of Connie's mind, something resembling a plan must have begun to take shape. A plan that would restore not only his waning public image as a destroyer but also his private dignity, which was taking a pretty constant beating. There would be payback for the sucker punch and for provoking him in the first place. Howie Crosby's voice brought him back.

". . . and so this guy tells my old man that this other guy, Bunny Soares from Warren, used to be a professional. A great big fucker. My old man remembered seeing him fight in Providence. Anyway, Colleen's fucking freak was working on a fishing boat this summer, and my old man wasn't sure how, but Bunny challenges him to a fight. The freak doesn't want to fight. Soares keeps it going. Challenging him every day, calling him names. Freak just pretends he doesn't hear him—"

"Then Bunny touches him, right?" Allie cut in.

"He spit at him, so I guess that's like touching. This guy tells my old man that Bunny was in critical condition for almost a week. I mean, the fucking freak almost killed him."

Connie decided his plan might need refining. Time and place seemed crucial. Weapons and backup, too. His alleged mind drifted back to a week ago Sunday when he had asked Mary Agnes Donnelly to the senior prom. He had met this Bay View Academy junior at the Riverside New York System. She was from Barrington's lace curtain–Irish section by the Rhode Island Country Club and had stopped in for an after-school dog. So absolutely beautiful was this auburn-haired girl that Connie's gaze actually darted to her eyes before her chest. It was a sensation that Connie had never experienced before. He pretended to be a human being, even a modest and shy one. After she had left with her girlfriends, Connie walked thoughtfully back to the Terrace considering the thunderbolt that had hit him. He passed Tubby O'Brien on the street. So stunned was Tubby that the daydreaming Connie didn't shake him down for cash, he gave him some anyway.

The next day Connie cut his last three classes so he'd be sure to see Mary Agnes when she left Bay View. He pretended he was merely walking past and just by chance bumped into her. He walked with her to the Pawtucket Avenue bus stop and asked her if she'd like to "maybe see a movie or something, maybe get a dog or something, maybe," and as she was a nice girl and didn't want to hurt this hulking and shy boy, she said sure. The next day they met at the New York System, and she talked easily about herself, and Connie talked shyly about whatever lies he had planned to tell about himself. When she told him that even though she attended a Catholic school she wasn't Catholic but Presbyterian, he told her that it shouldn't matter what a person believes, that God loved everybody. She smiled, and he did, too, although he truly hated anybody that wasn't Irish Catholic except this green-eyed, auburn-haired, red-cheeked apple of a girl.

For their first official date that weekend, Connie had decided to drive a late-model Chevy Impala. He found a beauty in the Mammoth Mart parking lot. It was a convertible with a great AM radio. They went to the new Five Movieplex in Seekonk and saw *Our Mother's House,* a black-and-white English movie that Mary Agnes had heard was "magical." East Providence girls always thought things like movies or songs or dances were "magical." Apparently, Barrington Presbyterians, too. Her tears fell like rain as Dirk Bogarde moves into the house of the wife he had abandoned and abuses the five children there. Connie thought it was a piece of shit. Nor car chases. No horses. No John Wayne. Fucking English faggots.

"Wasn't it great?" she gushed as they walked to the stolen car.

"It was magical," he said.

He walked her up to her front door, and they shook hands good night.

"I had a really nice time," she said.

"I had a magical time," he said.

After abandoning the Impala behind the merry-go-round at Crescent Park, he walked into the Terrace. He experienced a peaceful satisfaction flowing through him that he'd never felt before. A contentment he didn't think possible lifted him. His eyes watered, and it was for joy. Just the nearness of her. Just the exquisite touch of their good-night shake. He could not place the feeling. Could this be romance? It was surely a sensation unlike anything he'd had before. When Bonnie Gogarty gave him that blow job over the Christmas vacation, he thought that was romance. Of course, he had paid eight dollars for it, so perhaps it only had the veneer of romance. Maybe romance was free. He walked down his driveway to the back door of his little frame house and for a moment wished he actually did live in the five-bedroom brick Colonial he had described to Mary Agnes. He paused for a moment, savoring the night's sweet memories. A soft breeze rustled the new leaves. Then a disembodied voice rang out from somewhere on the Terrace, a voice so disguised that Connie couldn't tell if it was a guy or a girl. It was a shout, clear and damning.

"BOBBY FONTES KICKED CONNIE DWYER'S ASS!"

A couple of months went by, and Connie's separate roles as grotesque terrorist and self-effacing scholar (for he had informed Mary Agnes that he'd been accepted by a "whole lot of really magical colleges and stuff") were paying handsome dividends. He had been tapped as official bodyguard to Poochy Ponserelli during his initial foray into the international business of narcotics and had convinced Mary Agnes Donnelly to go to the senior prom with him. It *was* magical, and maybe if the moment was right and the music was right and the cherry cola and Old Granddad he had secured in a wild flight of sophistication was right, then possibly on prom night he would fuck her Presbyterian brains out and stuff.

And now prom night had arrived. Connie was torn between a tan Lincoln Continental and a Volkswagen bus that were parked side by side at the Warwick Mall. After a cursory inspection, he chose the VW bus, because it ran on regular gasoline and had a fold-down bed. He picked Mary Agnes up at seven and was dumbstruck by her long, cream-colored gown and the delicate shoulder straps that held it to her. She had long white gloves, too, and a peach-tinted ribbon through her hair. Connie posed with Mary Agnes on his arm as her mother and father snapped pictures. He felt proud and, for a moment, proper in his Murphy-plaid bow tie and cummerbund. He drove to Rhodes on the Pawtuxet with high hopes for his future with the incomparable Mary Agnes Donnelly. He would win her completely with his shyness and gentleness and with the cha-cha he'd been practicing in his kitchen. And sometime soon after the dance was over, he would settle old scores with a freaky little Portagee who had plagued his life since suckerpunching him in August. KiKi Coulette, Donnie Newlove, and Big

Ernie Guthrie were waiting outside in Ernie's mother's Karmann Ghia for Connie to give the word. He smiled to himself and kept smiling until he saw the freak's asshole friends watching him cha-cha. Well, he had something for *them,* too. Only first he'd take care of the freak.

At exactly a quarter to twelve, the lights flickered up and down several times and bandleader Duke Bentley announced the last dance to a medley of "Stardust," "Chances Are," and the television theme from *Lassie.* Outside, we fired up our Marlboros and headed for the limo. Officer Kenny Snowden and his pretty wife waved to us, and we waved back. She got into their car, but Kenny continued standing by his door, watching closely until all his kids were out of the lot and on the way back home. Connie saw him, too, and decided to isolate his prey at a different spot. Isolate and destroy. It would be this final cap to the evening that would be irresistible to Mary Agnes, because if there was one thing he had learned from the Terrace girls, it was that kicking ass was the ultimate romantic gesture. The act that stood apart from the others and said, "I care."

Our limousine cruised quietly toward Barrington Beach, a traditional townie post-prom destination. We had some beers and told some lies. Our driver said he was going for a smoke and he'd be back at the limo in a half hour. Maureen and Deborah kicked off their shoes. Cubby and Billy followed them down to the water. A full moon was directly over our heads, its sparkles bouncing off Narragansett Bay like fireflies. Sandy held my hand, and we kissed. I had it in my mind to walk her down the beach to a quiet spot and go as far as we could without losing my life to crazy Jimmy Minucci. We started onto the beach with a wave to Bobby and Colleen, who stood next to the limo looking out to sea. I won't say that Bobby seemed content, because he never did, really. Not content or relaxed or even comfortable. But watching him standing close to his redheaded mondo, sharing a Marlboro, was probably the only time I could say that Bobby seemed untroubled by this world. Maybe he was seeing possibilities on the horizon. Hope in the distance. He put his arm around her, and she put her high head of hair onto his shoulder. They watched us disappear into the dark. A Volkswagen bus and a blue Karmann Ghia pulled in on either side of the limo. Connie Dwyer got out of the stolen bus. KiKi Coulette, Big Ernie Guthrie, and Donnie Newlove eased menacingly out of their ride. Connie had his tux jacket off and began to roll up his sleeves.

"Hey, look who's here!" shouted Connie.

"Who?" asked Mary Agnes, getting out on her side.

"Couple of mondos," he said.

"Four of you," Colleen said. "Pathetic."

"You shut the fuck up!" Connie yelled.

"What?" sweet Mary Agnes asked quietly.

"I meant shut up. To her. Because she's mean and stuff. See that guy she's with? He sucker-punched me."

Colleen snorted. "He did not. He kicked your fat ass. Everybody in the whole fucking universe knows it." She looked at Mary Agnes. "Didn't you read it at school?"

"I . . . I go to Bay View."

Colleen snorted again. "Figures."

"Shut up," Connie warned.

"See, Bobby Fontes kicked Connie Dwyer's ass, and he's all mad about it because it's hard to be a criminal if you get your ass kicked. Did you know Connie was a criminal?"

"Shut up. I am not, Mary Agnes. I'm shy and stuff."

Mary Agnes Donnelly tried to smile. "What a nice night. Let's just take me home." She looked at Colleen and said lightly, "I live in Barrington."

"Whoop-dee-fucking-do."

I had heard them and ran back. Cubby and Billy were too close to the whitecaps to hear anything. I told Sandy to stay on the beach, and I stood beside Bobby. He looked at me. I waited.

"I can do this, Jono."

I nodded. "I know."

KiKi moved closer to us. "You don't know shit," he said, pointing at me. He moved his finger in Colleen's direction. "And you don't know shit," he said, poking her arm.

Bobby attacked so quickly that the only reactions were open mouths. He grabbed KiKi's pointing finger with his left hand and punched him hard, twice, on his forehead with his right. KiKi was down. Bobby looked over to Donnie and Big Ernie.

"I'm sorry. This is between me and Connie, because I hurt his feelings. Tell KiKi I'm sorry. Okay?"

Big Ernie and Donnie mumbled something, and it was clear, especially to Connie Dwyer, that he was alone now.

"Oooooh, Bobby," Colleen snickered. "Watch out for Connie Dwyer. He's a big criminal from the Terrace."

"Will you guys please stop?" Mary Agnes pleaded. "Don't spoil a magical night."

And it *had* been a magical night, Connie thought later at the Rhode Island Hospital emergency room, where we had taken him and KiKi. It had been a moment frozen in time, a moment he would often recall with ambivalent emotions. The dazzlingly radiant Mary Agnes Donnelly and the elegantly tuxedoed neophyte gangster at the very crossroads of romance. Everything seemed possible. No hope unattainable. No dream too large. Even a blow job loomed in fuzzy potential. Well, he thought, as his head swelled alarmingly and the doctor put the last of seventeen stitches over his eyes and secured his four cracked ribs, it could have been worse. Couldn't it? Not really. Mary Agnes told the police at the hospital that she didn't know what to do with Connie's Volkswagen bus that was still at Barrington Beach. Connie was arrested three days later and plea-bargained the stolen-car rap to a sentence that required him to enlist in the army the day after graduation.

We limousined our girls home to the Terrace under moon and stars. Everything was changing, the way things are supposed to, even if we were too close to see it.

32

The play ran a little over two hours, including a fifteen-minute intermission. *Sandpilot* was performed in a cozy three-hundred-seat half circle with thrust stage that was intimate enough for a two-character piece set simply under the heavy limbs of an ancient apple tree. A forty-year-old guy arrives on the site of an old sanatorium where his grandmother was a patient seventy years earlier. Nothing left of the place but this visitors' bench circling the last apple tree of an orchard that was used for a kind of patient therapy. It turns out he's searching for clues as to why his grandmother was there and if what she had was like his own out-of-control manic depression, which isn't responding to medication. He meets a young woman, the Sandpilot, who may or may not be his grandmother. I was confused by some references and thought it might have been too long. Renée loved it.

"I loved it," she said. "How come this isn't in New York? This would be a great role for you, Jono."

"I'm too long in the tooth."

"But with the grandmother being younger, age isn't a problem. It'd probably lend more . . . what?"

"What?"

"What's the word? Lend more . . . oh, shit, there's a perfect word."

I was distracted. In fact, I'd been preoccupied the whole performance. I had told Kenny Snowden to call me as soon as he knew something. There was no message from him at intermission, and I was anxious to get to a phone.

"Immediacy!" Renée half shouted. "See, an older guy would add immediacy. See?"

"I guess. You see a pay phone?"

We were in front of the theater. A steady wind whipped down on Providence, driving the already cold night to a single-digit temperature.

"Where's your cell?" Renée asked.

"Car."

We crossed the street and headed down to the Biltmore Bar, where there was a phone next to the men's room. I punched in my calling card and my 917 service code. I had two messages. The first one was Randall Pound's soft voice.

"Hey, Jono. I finally finished all of the Sinclair Lewis canon. Just now closed *Our Mr. Wrenn* and wanted to tell somebody. I'm on to Fitzgerald now. Making progress. Say hey to Renée. I'm on my stool and we miss you at Lambs."

The second one was from Kenny Snowden. It was long, and after it played out, I pushed it up again and wrote some of it down.

"Jesus," I said.

"What?"

I shook my head. "Let's just go back to the hotel, get our stuff, and get back to the city."

Renée looked at me.

"C'mon, Renée."

We walked through the biting wind to the car and pointed it toward 195. We were quiet, the vibrant firefighter and the jittery actor. We packed our stuff quickly, Renée picking up on the bizarre urgency that seemed to overwhelm me.

"What are you going to tell Bobby?"

I stopped and looked at her.

"We're supposed to meet him, remember?"

"He'll get over it."

She got to it like I knew she would. "What's going on? Why are we running?"

"We're not running."

"Yes we are, and I've got a real bad feeling you're going to regret it. Like, what if that guy in *Sandpilot* didn't—"

"Renée, this isn't a play."

"I was just—"

"This is real life."

"I was just saying that what if the guy stopped asking the Sandpilot those questions, those important questions? What if he just left? Even if the things he learned hurt him and frightened him, it was important that he learned them."

My pipsqueak of a brain vibrated. It was getting hard to line up the thoughts in any order. The more I tried to organize them into linear ideas, the more confusing they became. All I had was a big head full of information I didn't want in there. I didn't want to add it all up. I sat on the edge of the bed trying to calm myself down. For some reason the mental exercises I used to center Jono Riley, Actor, would not kick in. Probably because they were bullshit. Renée sat next to me and held me.

"What?" she asked quietly.

The wind was hitting the room's windows in short punches, and light snow was beginning to swirl with it.

"I need to think some things through, Renée. I need to clear my head." I put my hand on her sweet face. "We'll take the rental back to New York and turn it in there."

Her eyes wouldn't let it go.

"I'm an actor. A fucking actor. That's what I am. Nothing else. I've *played* a detective, but I'm *not* one. Jesus Christ, I don't know what to do but get out of here. C'mon."

She waited while I checked out with the night clerk. He looked at me like I'd lost my mind, checking out at eleven in the evening into what promised to be a blinding snowstorm. Still, it made sense to me. I read once that between *life* and *plot* there is a *story*. It works on the stage, all right, but when it's you in the middle of it and nobody's acting, you need a little overview. Or a lot. Distance was the only way I could see to get that perspective. We pushed out of doors and leaned against the wind. I popped the car's trunk and put the cases in. I was at Renée's side opening her door when I heard him.

"Jono?"

He wasn't dressed for the cold. He wore black pants and a white shirt and a dark sports jacket. He also carried a rifle.

33

We looked silly in our crimson caps and gowns. Maybe not the girls, but it was my opinion that the guys certainly did. Except Bobby, that is. Bobby seemed to look good in anything, even the rented graduation gown. Like he belonged in it. Like he satisfied some unspoken requirement that made it special and right. Cubby looked shorter and fatter. Billy looked too serious and academic, which I'm sure his parents liked, but it just wasn't Billy. And because my graduation cap was two sizes too small for my already colossal noggin, the sight of the thing, protruding out of the gown, made my head, unbelievably enough, appear larger than it really was. We smoked by Billy's DeSoto, then skulked over to where our folks had congregated. I stayed away from Billy's dad and stood between my mother and Marie. Big Tony had the movie camera working hard. Bobby's mother had come with a new boyfriend and looked astonishingly lovely, as usual. Bobby appeared preoccupied and quietly scanned the sea of parents and seniors as they got ready to file into the gym for the graduation ceremonies. I knew what was up, because Bobby had made a rare phone call to me the night before. He hated the phone. It magnified his natural hesitation and made it seem more than just a Bobbyism. I was kind of startled to hear his voice.

"Jono?"

"Hey, Bobby."

I waited.

"I know . . . when I don't . . . you know . . . speak right away, it sounds bad on the phone, so I'm sorry."

"Nobody's perfect. Except me and my big fucking head. What?"

He laughed a small one. I waited some more.

"She's gone. Colleen. She hasn't been in school. I went over to her house. . . ."

"Alone?"

"She's just . . . gone."

"If you go over there again, call me and I'll go with you. Okay? Don't go over alone."

A longer than usual pause.

"Bobby? Okay?"

I could hear him breathing. Shit. I could feel him thinking.

"Sure, okay, but she's gone. I can't find her. She's just a little girl, Jono. I don't want her somewhere where I can't . . . you know . . . watch her and . . . and help her."

I felt sorry for my friend. I could hear things in his voice I'd never heard before. Even maybe a little catch in his throat. I didn't want to feel disloyal but she was a Crosby, and surely *something* had gone wrong somewhere back in that lineage to produce Jack and Howie. Why not Colleen, too?

"Are you at home?"

"No. I'm at the Creamery. I thought . . . I don't know. . . . I love that girl."

"I'll borrow my mother's car and be there in ten, and we'll check around. Want me to get the other guys?"

What a question. When we were hurting, we needed each other like oxygen.

"Of course," he said.

Twenty minutes later we pulled up to the Newport Creamery, and Bobby got in back with Billy.

I turned around. "Want to start in Riverside? Crescent Park? We'll do the Terrace again, too."

Bobby nodded, and I pulled onto Pawtucket Avenue. We stopped at Nardo's Liquors, Cubby picked up two six-packs of 'Gansett, and our tobacco-smelling, hops-burping ride headed into Riverside. We were extraordinarily quiet, concentrating on our Marlboros and beer. There was a lot working in the old Ford wagon. We surely picked up on Bobby's concern for Colleen and didn't want to compound his worry by making any snide remarks about that piece-of-shit family of hers. But more than that, I think we were realizing that we weren't going to be tooling around to-gether much longer. That the world wasn't going to let us take our sweet time getting into the flow of real life. It was a sledgehammer of a feeling, and we had seen it coming since spring. But we didn't make those silly vows that pass for promises in other places. We took the traditional East Providence route. We just pretended it wasn't happening. To us anyway.

I pulled in front of the New York System hot-dog joint, and we followed Bobby inside. Allie Ponserelli was sitting in a booth with a couple of onion-covered dogs and a huge coffee milk. The little prick hadn't replaced his enforcer at the moment and tried to pretend he wasn't there. Bobby stood over him at the table. He waited as usual. Little Allie washed down his bite of dog.

"What?" he whined.

"Allie," Bobby said quietly, "I'm looking for Colleen Crosby. She hasn't been in school. She hasn't been home."

"So?"

Bobby stared at him.

"*I* don't know where she is," Allie said. "She takes off. She always takes off. That's what she does."

Bobby watched him for a few more seconds, as though he were gauging the answer, weighing its truth, and then he left the System with us trailing behind. I pulled Mother's Ford Country Squire onto the Terrace, making a slow loop. Petey Maloney was walking home with two bags of groceries. I stopped a little ahead of him, and Bobby got out. Petey froze. In the throw of the streetlight, Bobby's stillness and pause could have been the opening of a Hitchcock movie. I got out, too.

"Hey, Petey," I said, "we're looking for Colleen Crosby. Seen her?"

Petey couldn't take his eyes off Bobby. I knew what he probably was thinking. Petey's complexion had cleared up, he had made friends in school that were decent, he had a sweet girlfriend, he was actually learning things in his classes, and now he was going to die at the stony hands of this nightmare. He actually shivered.

"I've been looking for her," Bobby said sadly. "I guess sometimes she takes off, but I'm scared about it. Can you help me, Petey?"

"Have you . . . have you tried her house?"

"Last night."

"I haven't seen her."

Bobby and I walked back to the car.

Just before we got in, Petey said, "She's nicer than the rest of them. The rest of the Crosbys aren't nice."

We drove on, past the marina, past the Minuccis', and stopped in front of the Crosby place. I know that memories, especially memories of kids, tend to set things into almost mythological proportions. Make events and people and places much bigger or darker or spookier than they ever were. That said, in retrospect and current dreams, the Crosby household gave off the smell of corruption like nothing I have experienced since. Even the overgrown yard and dying trees reflected the familial iniquity. We didn't speak. Bobby's pause extended into several minutes; still we waited.

"There's just . . . some people that . . . that need people to help them."

We didn't answer him.

"Ever notice that the people that . . . need us . . . don't know how to tell us that they need us?"

Bobby got out of the car, and we did, too.

"I can do this alone."

"Do it alone, then," Cubby said. "Only we're still coming with you."

We all walked toward the house and away from the comforting streetlight. Bobby rang the doorbell. He rang it again. He used the door knocker. After a long moment, the beast himself opened the door. Jack Crosby was dressed the way he had seen TV mobsters dress. A cheap black suit, black shirt, yellow tie. He had on red cuff links and high-heeled Cuban loafers. He was wearing sunglasses, and I wondered if the creep even knew that the sun had gone down.

"I'm looking for Colleen, Jack. Have you seen her?"

He looked past Bobby at the three of us. "What's this? This your faggot gang?"

Bobby turned and looked at us, too. A smile tried to show on his face. His eyes shone with something like pride. He turned back to Jack.

"These are my friends, Jack. You know these guys. I'm looking for your sister."

Poochy Ponserelli, dressed exactly the same, appeared over Jack's shoulder. "What the fuck's going on?"

"These faggots are looking for Colleen."

"Yeah? Why?"

"Yeah," Jack said to Bobby, "why the fuck do you want Colleen?"

I felt the words form in my stomach, and the anger that drove them up surprised and startled me. "So he can protect her from pieces of shit like you, you sorry-ass motherfucker. Now, answer the fucking question."

Everyone looked at me. I would've, too, but I kept the anger on my face even though now I felt ridiculous.

Jack and I faced off. His cheeks came red and his fists balled hard, but he knew where Bobby was. He could feel his breath. After a few seconds, he caved. I guess that's a fat portion of thug character.

"She goes to Crescent Park sometimes. The mondos."

We were almost to the car when he shouted, "Think you're so tough. You're not so tough."

"I can't believe you said that," Billy laughed.

Cubby spread his hands on the sides of his head so it seemed bigger. " 'You sorry-ass motherfucker,' " he said.

We all laughed, even Bobby. We drove off the Terrace and turned in behind the carousel. I idled the engine for a few seconds, then shut it down. Crescent Park in shadow was off. Just off. Not right somehow. The rides and game booths angled sharply against the clear sky hanging over the bay. We got out of the car and took it in. The roller coaster, a brittle-looking all-wood structure, loomed like a distorted skeleton. Billy had the plan.

"I'll go left, Cubby go right, you guys do the midway."

"What are we looking for?" Cubby asked, stubbing out his smoke.

Billy put his out, too. "Mondos, I guess."

We fanned out in our assigned sectors. I couldn't help thinking about my waterfront and our search for the missing troop. I thought that maybe Bobby ought to give a swim tag to Colleen, and she could put it on the board when she was in or take it off when she planned a disappearing act. But I had a feeling that even the small consideration of a tag would be too much for her. I stopped and listened. I could hear water lapping at the inlet behind the coaster. Cubby, Billy, and I met up ten minutes later. We saw the glow of Bobby's cigarette at the edge of the inlet and walked over. He was looking out into the narrow sections of bay. We didn't say anything. After a while I drove us home.

Now Big Tony was lining us up for the guy shot before we went into the ceremonies. When we put our arms around one another's shoulders, Billy's old man pretended to be looking somewhere else. Okay, so I lied. I do feel guilty. I do feel responsible. I told him I was heading into the service like my pop had done, and that was that. But I never talked Billy into it. In fact, I never mentioned it again. The East Providence Riley men do not cry. Not that we're insensitive to stuff, but that New England deal is very powerful in us. I mean, we feel really sorry for ourselves, but it usually manifests itself as a sort of self-deprecation. I never cried when I got hurt, even in the army. In fact, I can only remember three times I let it go. When Pop went, when Big Tony slapped me, and outside Billy's wake at Rebello's Funeral Home. Marie saw me through the window wailing on the grass. Cubby and her had to take me home.

Anyway, Bobby was still distracted when we filed in. We didn't sit next to each other, because we all had seat assignments in alphabetical order. Principal Nels Blair introduced the Reverend Robert Cryer from the First Baptist Church for the invocation, and we were off. Valedictorian, Merit scholars, DAR award winners, et cetera, were up first, followed by the athletic awards. When the Best Athlete Award was given to Neil Thomas, I could hear Cubby's signature cough, and Billy's, and, following a pause, Bobby's, too. Neil was a really terrific guy who played three sports, but yours truly was the only Rhode Islander ever to make Most Valuable Player *twice,* and it would have been three times if those French-Canadian Christian Brothers, who were prejudiced against me, hadn't taken away a hat trick I should have had. But that doesn't bother me. Although I clearly was not across the line, and they *know* it, wherever they are.

Then our graduation speaker was introduced. We had tried to get Ted Williams, but that didn't work out and so "Salty" Brine of radio, TV, and advertising fame brought it home to us.

"Hi, shipmates."

"Hi, Salty," we intoned.

He told us to work hard, pray hard, and get lots of rest. Finally it was time for our ticket out. Vice Principal Castro called out our names, Principal Blair gave out the scrolls, and Salty sealed the deal with a handshake. We filed out to "Pomp and Circumstance" played by the juniors and sophomores of the school band. It sounded like a Broadway orchestra tuning up. Our mothers were teary. Big Tony's cameras whirred and snapped in front of the East Providence High clock. We were posed in so many shots I can't imagine why I don't have any of the ones Big Tony gave me.

I saw her the same time Bobby did, moving through the crowd toward us. Or rather staggering toward us. Her matted red hair was pushed away from her forehead and stood up like the feathers on some angry woodpecker. Her black dress was grimy and stiff. She was as white as snow, only not new snow. She seemed hard and caked over. Sixteen-year-old Colleen Crosby, carrying a quart bottle of Narragansett, stopped ten feet away from Bobby. She smiled, I think, and some teeth were gone. Bobby moved calmly to her. I can still see clearly everyone stopping in stride and watching the drunk little girl and the man in robes who appeared to float to her. He put his hand on the beer, and she released it. He tossed it to the ground. She looked at him, shuddered, and began to cry. A small cry, small like the tiny thing she was.

Bobby scooped her into his arms and turned to Billy. "I have to take her home."

Billy began to move without thinking. I followed him. Cubby, too. We formed a sort of bizarre honor guard moving through the quiet, staring company of new graduates and their families. As we approached the car, I remember thinking that even in this supremely inappropriate moment, Bobby appeared somehow natural and correct. Bobby eased her into the back of the DeSoto and followed her in. We got into the front. On the way back to the Terrace, Bobby cooed and whispered softly to her. Before he helped her out of the car, he brushed his fingers over her hair.

"Who bought the beer?" he asked evenly.

"I don't know," she sniffed.

He paused, and she understood it, too.

"Was it Jack?"

"Uh-uh."

They got out of the car and walked to the house. We watched them but stayed on the grass. While he waited for the door to open, he brushed her cheeks and asked her questions. After her mother let her in, closing the door in Bobby's face, he glided pensively back to Billy's car.

"DeSimone," he said.

"Which one?" Cubby asked.

"Louie."

"Fucking mondo," Billy said.

Cubby lit a smoke. "A *connected* fucking mondo. My old man says Louie's father is Ray-Ray DeSimone's brother."

Ray-Ray DeSimone was Rhode Island's major representative to the New England mob. It's a little state, and he got a lot of play in the *Providence Journal*. I actually had met him at Boy Scout camp. He was one of the fathers who accompanied Troop 6 East Greenwich. He seemed like a great guy, the reports of him burning down South Providence for profit notwithstanding. Billy stopped at a phone booth, and Bobby checked for the address. He got back in.

"Twenty-eight Argyle Avenue."

Billy nodded. "That's off the Wampanoag Trail."

We got on the trail near the Barrington Bridge and headed into East Providence. It was only two in the afternoon, but some typical clouds had darkened things up. I was using my abstract reasoning that has continued to plague me and turn me ass-backwards to this day.

"Bobby?"

The Barrington River was on our right, new ranch-house developments on our left. They went by, or we went by them.

"Yeah, Jono?"

"Don't get mad at me, okay?"

Rivers and houses.

"I'd never get mad at you, Jono."

"Look, I think whoever bought the beer is a fuck, because a guy shouldn't give beer to . . . girls . . . or anybody who isn't old enough, okay? But . . . it's like both their faults. Colleen didn't have to drink it either."

I waited. We did a U-turn so Argyle would come up on our right.

"I think you're right, Jono. But I don't think she knows what happens when she drinks. That family, her family, they didn't teach her . . . anything. If . . . if a puppy eats something that it shouldn't, whose fault is it?"

Cubby turned around. "What if the puppy's owner didn't know he shouldn't eat it?"

Bobby shrugged and watched the river. "But what if the owner's given it to the puppy before and knows it makes it sick?"

"Then the owner is a sick fuck that ought to be killed," Cubby said.

Well, shit, I guess I couldn't argue with that logic. We pulled onto Argyle Avenue and stopped in front of the house. Bobby rang the doorbell. A pleasant, round woman answered the door, and invited Bobby in. A few minutes later, he came out and got back in the car.

"What?" Cubby asked.

Bobby looked at me.

"Nothing. Jono was right. Louie told me he gave the puppy the beer, but he didn't know it would hurt her and never did it before. I believed him."

"So you didn't hurt him?" Cubby asked.

"No," he said after his beat. "And I didn't kill him either."

34

We drove through the storm toward Shad Factory in Rehoboth. I was driving the van, and Renée sat up front beside me. Bobby sat behind us with his flat expression and his rifle.

"I moved out here about nine or ten years ago," he said softly. "Remember? We'd take our bikes or your mother would drive us? We'd fish beneath the Shad Factory waterfall."

"I remember," I said hoarsely.

Renée reached over and touched my arm.

"You can have a garden out here. You can listen to the birds. They shut down Asquino's, can you believe it? Everything good, they shut down. There was no reason to stay in East Providence anymore. It's an easy drive to the nursing home, even though my mother doesn't know me anymore. Did I tell you she just sits there and asks for him?" He turned to Renée. "That's my father. He took my eye, remember, Jono?"

"Sure."

Bobby paused. Snow was falling hard, and the windshield wipers slapped high.

"There's a road coming up on your left where Amaral's Turkey Farm used to be. Remember, Jono? Remember how we'd stop and

Old Man Amaral would let us dig worms out of the turkey manure for bait?"

"I remember."

"Turn on the road. About a half mile in."

We pulled in front of a weathered gray saltbox house. The property around it was mostly woods, with a small front yard. A Jeep was in the short driveway, covered with fresh snow. It looked like a Christmas card.

"This is what I'm going to do, Jono. I'm going to get out on Renée's side, and so is Renée, okay? I'm going to be there with Renée until you walk around the front of the van and join us, okay?"

"Okay," I said, as calmly as I could.

When I got to them, he motioned us up the driveway with the rifle.

"We can go into the house through the garage. I want you to see everything."

He opened the garage door, flipped on a light, and closed the door behind us. The long form of an automobile was under a huge tarpaulin. He grabbed a corner of it and peeled it off the car.

"Recognize it?" he said.

"Billy's?" I asked, stunned.

"I bought it back from the guy Billy's father sold it to after . . ." He looked at me sadly. "C'mon."

He opened the garage door to the house, and we moved into the kitchen. He switched on more lights.

"Look, Jono."

He pointed to an enormous blown-up photo of Cubby in his EP baseball uniform. He was in his catching pose. It filled almost an entire wall of the kitchen. Under the picture was the legend CUBBY D'AGOSTINO.

"And here. You look, too, Renée."

Around the corner of the kitchen, on the living-room side of

Cubby's photo, was a similar-size photo of me, in full hockey regalia, waving my hockey stick with one hand and carrying the state championship trophy with the other. Under my picture it read JONO RILEY, MVP.

"Recognize that, Jono?" he said, looking at it. Awe and pride seemed to swell in his voice. "You were great. He was great, Renée. Some nights I can sit here with you or in there with Cubby and I can go back . . . almost. Sometimes I can put on Billy's AM radio and go back to you guys."

He paused, and his eyes moved onto me.

"Ever . . . ever go back, Jono? Ever want to just go back and be on the beach one more time? And . . . and ever want to get those squeezes from Big Tony and eat all his macaroni?"

I looked at my Renée. "No, Bobby."

"No?"

"I have memories. That's what memories are. We're lucky because they're pretty wonderful, and I been going through them a lot since I been back in East Providence. Even the ones that aren't so good. But I wouldn't want to really go back, Bobby. No. I'm here now. I'm where I am."

He looked at me, and his eyes flashed. "I'm not. I'm not here now. I'm anywhere else."

I waited.

He came even again, almost embarrassed. "I mean, it would be nice to be all together again. Sit."

Renée and I sat on a green plaid couch. Bobby remained standing. We were quiet a long time. The wind and snow rattled the windows.

"What are we doing here, Bobby?" I finally asked.

"I was going to meet Renée, remember? You said you wanted me to meet your friend who was a fireman, and we were going to meet at Merrill's Lounge—only you were leaving."

I didn't say anything.

"Why were you leaving, Jono? Why didn't you want to see me?"

"Bobby . . . Renée, I haven't said anything to Renée. . . . Please. . . ."

"He likes you, Renée. He likes you better than any girl I remember him with. I can tell. You do, don't you, Jono?"

I looked over at Renée. I hoped fear wasn't spreading across my face like it was every other part of me. "I love her, Bobby."

Renée actually smiled. I'd said it before, of course. I guess this time it was truly unsolicited.

Bobby nodded and spoke barely above a whisper. "Love is hard, though, isn't it? Complicated, you know. And sometimes if you're not lucky you can love something that just can't love you back. Not the same. But that can be love, too, I think. You can't stop feeling things no matter what. You can't stop hurting if you're hurt or being afraid if you're afraid. So why should I stop loving her? Can you tell me that, Jono? How can I stop loving her?"

Renée leaned forward and spoke softly. "I don't . . . Bobby, I don't think any person can get inside any other person's mind, let alone inside two people's relationship. Everyone's is different. Every situation is unique. It's really whatever works for you."

"But it doesn't work for me. It never works," he said quietly, shaking his head. "It breaks me. It makes me feel old. It's awful. Awful. But it's something, isn't it? It's something when she's back. When I find her, wherever she's . . . I don't know. I wish it were easier."

"Bobby?" I said.

He came back.

"Renée. My Renée. I didn't say anything."

"About what?"

"About . . . anything."

"That's why love is so hard. I find her. I pick her up all dirty and crying, and suddenly she's little Colleen again, and I carry her home and I clean her and feed her and hold her and . . . then she stops crying and stops wanting to be held and— Say anything about what, Jono? You know, but you don't know."

I watched him. His good eye burned into my hockey picture. A smile sneaked across his mouth.

"God, you were a great player. We never told you, though. We didn't have to."

The smile receded. For some crazy reason, I knew what he was going to say next.

"When your father died, thank you for letting me sit with you and your mother. He was a good guy. I still think about how quiet he was. How much he liked just being in his house."

I didn't smile, but it was true. My pop believed in our house.

"Big Tony, too. Those guys loved being home. I always felt good knowing they were home. They were so nice. Good. My old man, that guy who lived in our house but was never a part of it, that eye taker, he made Mother and I not want to be home. We weren't allowed to like being home. Remember how my little mother looked sometimes after he got drunk and mad? Remember that? I'd try to get in between them, but I was small. I'd go down so easy, and I couldn't protect her. I couldn't protect myself."

Bobby ran a finger over his eye patch.

"He comes home one night with another drunk, he comes home and wakes us up and starts on us while the other one watches and drinks. Laughing, I think. Bang. He slaps my little mother. Bang. He kicks her. I go at him. She's my mother. Jesus. He grabs me by my hair and turns me around so I'm facing his friend. Watch, he says. He takes his fingers and starts on my eyes. He digs my eyes. Nobody knew that, but he almost dug it out. He did it to show his friend. Jesus, Jono, he dug my eye out."

Renée started to move off the couch to comfort him. He pointed the rifle.

"Please stay."

She sat back. He looked over our heads.

"I knew I had to . . . had to do something. I knew way before he took the eye. He had this in the basement. This rifle. I was nine when I found it. It was all dusty and in a corner, but there was a box of bullets with it, and I took it. I hid it in my room. I didn't want him to shoot my little mother, and he would have. Sooner or later he would have. I came home that summer without my eye. Big Tony brought me home with all you guys. He hid in the basement when Big Tony brought me home."

He smiled at the memory.

"He hid. A few weeks later, he comes home again. He's drunk. He's mad. He doesn't hit me, though, because Kenny Snowden knew about the eye and was watching, and he knew it. But he goes at Mother. I get in between, and he quits. He takes a bottle into the back and sits behind the garage. After my mother went to bed, I snuck out back and watched him. He was too drunk to stand. He fell back down and went to sleep."

He looked at me now. He spoke even and without any discernible emotion.

"I went into the house, put a bullet in the rifle, and went back outside. I had it up against his head . . . right up against that terrible thing . . . only . . . only I couldn't . . . I couldn't."

He shook his head.

"I went back inside, put the rifle away, took a pillow from my room and a sponge from the kitchen. I went back to him, put the sponge into his mouth, and put the pillow over his face and pressed down for a long, long time."

The story hung over us like basement dust. Renée breathed out heavily and slowly shook her head.

"I took the pillow and sponge back inside and went to bed. That was his heart attack. It was the first time I slept through the night."

We all fell silent. Motionless.

I tried to get his eye, but it was ogling his history. "Bobby . . ."

He snapped back on me. "I'm trying to say it, Jono. I'm trying to say it all."

The driving storm filled the silence. The picture window showed a blur of whiteness. I thought of snow angels and bullets. Bobby spoke to my photo as much as to us.

"Ever notice how we don't appreciate anything until we don't have it anymore? I'm going to start going to mass again. I'm going to go to confession and go to mass and . . . I could go during the week, early, some other church, though, not St. Martha's."

"I . . . I took mass the other day there."

"I know, Jono. I've been watching."

I nodded.

"I used to take Colleen . . . hoping, you know, that maybe . . . She tried, though, Jono. Renée, she tried to stop, but she got that powder one day and . . . Do you know who gave it to her? Do you?"

Renée looked at me.

"Yes, Bobby," I said.

"His . . . his own sister. I love that girl, and I can't . . . help her . . . at all. Sometimes when I find her, sometimes when I have her back and she's in her bed and she's clean and she's sleeping . . . sometimes I look at her and . . . and for a minute I don't know her, I can't recognize her. She's like half of something I remember."

He paused, and we waited.

"But that's love, too, I guess," he said with a sigh. "I guess not recognizing someone is part of it. Or part of our kind of love. Me and Colleen. We know who we are . . . and we don't know."

Now he looked hard at me.

"Mr. Holt," he said flatly. "The woodworking teacher. He was the first one I meant it for. He was the first one after the eye taker that it was meant for. I'd see him, you know? I'd see him at school, and I knew him but I didn't know him. It was a feeling of knowing him and . . . and my patch eye would hurt when I'd see him. One day I knew who he was. I just saw it clear. He was the other drunk. He was with him that night. He watched when he took the eye. He laughed . . . I think. . . . Holt . . . I took him, Jono. I took him for watching my eye go. It felt right."

Renée had both her hands up to her mouth. My mind raced in hurried prayers of being correct and speaking correct.

"Bobby," I said, "I'll be here for you, Bobby. We can—"

"And I didn't feel sorry for it. I didn't feel anything. . . . Did you ever look in Billy's glove compartment? God, he was so neat. Everything had a special place. I would say he was the neatest of all of us."

"I wasn't neat at all," I said quietly.

"But you were there, Jono. You were there whenever we needed you. Renée, he never let us down. Ever. You were the one who'd always be there when we needed you. Look."

With his free hand, Bobby turned a huge scrapbook that lay on the coffee table. I opened it. There were pictures and clippings from front to back.

"They're in order, starting in kindergarten. CYO, that big snow-storm. I have a lot of the ones Big Tony gave us after graduation."

I flipped the pages. Renée leaned in and looked with me. The unreality of the situation seemed bordering on a dream.

"Your mother." He pointed. "Your beautiful mother and your father. Billy's father. Cubby and Big Tony, Marie."

He stopped short. I looked up at him, and he backed up a few steps. His face lost any expression.

"I loved her, too," he said flatly.

"We all did."

"Yes . . ." He looked away again. "Vincent Mello," he said, letting the name hover over the coffee table.

"Who?"

"Nothing was the same after he didn't show for her wedding. You were there, Jono. Everybody was there, and my little mother was so . . . alive. She'd met him at St. Martha's. He was visiting his sister, and she introduced my mother to him. I was there, too. They'd go out to dinner. They'd go to a movie. He lived in Rockville and—"

"The mailman," I uttered.

Bobby looked at me and took his moment. "I know you know, Jono. I want to tell it all. . . . Yes, the mailman. It shouldn't be like that, I know. It's not my business, but . . . it bothered me. . . . No, that's not it—it worried me when she would stay in Rockville with him. And it wasn't just him, or . . . not him, I mean. It was the feeling that something wasn't right. It was how my patch eye would hurt again. I'm never sure of anything except when my patch eye hurts. Then I know something isn't right. I mean, I can be on a job, and when Colleen . . . when she goes off, I know. I know. But this Vincent Mello and Mother were going to be married. Remember how beautiful she looked? It was August, Renée, the end of August, and my little mother had made her dress herself. She could do that. She didn't need stores to do those things for her. She was amazing, I think. . . . So we sat in church and waited, and my patchy eye hurt, and we still waited until it hurt so much I thought I was going to have to run out of there. That's when we found out he wasn't coming. That's when he left my little mother all empty and sad."

Renée, of course, still didn't understand. Pointing to the scrapbook, she asked, "Is this your mother?"

Bobby tilted his head to see the upside-down picture. "That's Mother," he said, smiling gently. "That's my little mother. She was so young. Too young. And so much gets taken away, even from people you wouldn't think could lose things. Like Colleen. Jesus . . . sometimes I think it's her, but it's not. . . . So I waited, Jono. That's what I wanted to tell. I waited almost two years, and then I took him."

Renée's mouth hung open. "You . . ."

"Yes, Renée," I said. "Bobby . . . took him."

"Oh, God." She sighed, closing her eyes tight.

We listened to elements colliding outside and in.

"We had a dog once, remember, Jono?"

"I'm not sure."

"Or my mother and I had a dog. She found it. Black with white spots on his nose. A puppy. It just went under our porch and wouldn't leave, and she took it inside and we put it in a box with some water. We walked to Sunnybrook Farm for some dog food. She called him Fernando after somebody she knew in the Azores. He was a great dog. A nice dog. We had him three weeks. One morning I call Fernando, but he's gone. I knew the eye taker had gotten him, too. I would never want to be a little dog. If I had to be an animal, I'd be a big one. A strong one . . . a bear, maybe. A polar bear."

"A polar bear?"

"Maybe."

"Like Hickey and Rickey?"

"Who?" Renée asked.

"Polar bears, Renée," I said, still watching Bobby. "There's a little zoo on Newport Avenue, Goddard Park. There was a petting zoo there, and—"

Bobby laughed softly. "Jono? Remember what Cubby called those hairy Scottish cows? Those red ones that we'd feed? The ones that drooled?"

"I don't remember."

"He called them 'sloppy cows.' Renée, when we were little kids, they would take your whole hand in their mouths if you had an apple or something. They'd never hurt you. They'd just lick the apple out of your hand."

"They had two polar bears," I said, and turned to Renée.

"Hickey and Rickey were their names. They were famous in Rhode Island."

"Not famous enough to get fresh water," Bobby snapped. "Not famous enough to not be miserable. I'd go to see them in the summer after the fishing boat was in. I loved the park. I remember Big Tony taking us. Your father, too. . . . I remember everything, that's my problem. . . . Only a *few* things should be remembered, things that make you all right, or help make you all right. But I remember too much. It's like I'm watching a bad movie twenty-four hours a day. Sometimes I can't tell myself from the actors. Jesus." Bobby's eye watered, and he turned his head almost imperceptibly to the side. I didn't speak. I finally understood that I was there simply to listen. Renée held my hand, and we waited. He came back to it.

"That was a hot summer, a tough summer, all right. I had some problems on the fishing boat with a guy. I had some bad things working up, and I knew it. So on my days off, I'd sometimes go and see them. Sometimes I'd tell the animal keepers that they were sad and they were dirty and . . . Jono, Renée, I brought them some fish one day and threw it over to them, and they could not get up to get the fish. That's how much they hurt. These suffering, hurting, beautiful things. . . . I was coming to it on the boat, knew I'd have to fight this guy on the boat. . . ."

"Soares," I mumbled.

Bobby looked at me. "Yes, Bunny Soares. There was no way out. But Hickey and Rickey . . . One night I go, and Rickey had blood in his eye. Dried black blood. I asked the bastards why, and they told me it got poked out. Like no big deal. His eye gets poked out and it's no big deal."

He lit a cigarette. He offered me one. I took it, and Renée frowned.

"Marlboro," he said. "Big Tony."

"All of us," I said stupidly.

"Your father smoked Camels. He was great. I remember . . . yeah, Camels."

We smoked for a minute.

"I decided that if they couldn't help them or wouldn't help, then I'd help them. There's a heaven for animals. I know it. I never heard of a mean animal."

I thought of the four of us in our studied casualness puffing Marlboros as if it were some action essential to our actual lives. My casualness was no more.

"Soares," I said.

"Soares," he said. "We got along for the first few days, but he wasn't right, you know? He'd be drinking on the way back into harbor, and usually he'd be complaining or making fun of some-body, but he left me alone . . . at first. He'd always be talking about fighting. About boxing. He kept this old paper in his pocket. He fought professionally. I don't know. I can't get feeling clean after a fight. But Bunny would take out the paper and say, 'Hey, look, I beat this boy, and he was almost champion.' Crazy. A crazy man . . . One day he's staring at me and laughing and saying he heard I like to fight. I say, 'No, Bunny, I hate to fight.' But he keeps on. Day af-ter day he's calling me names. I don't care. Jono, you remember I don't care what assholes say."

"I remember."

"He was a man, Renée, he was this man, and I was a kid. We were seventeen, remember, Jono? Seventeen. I was worried about Mother. I was worried about things. I didn't want to fight, but he wouldn't let it go. So I'm walking off the boat onto the dock be-hind the Warren Fish House, and he follows me off saying things, and he slaps me. Here. In the back of my head."

Bobby slowly shook his head. Sadness flooded onto his face.

"Slapped me . . ."

He shook his head again.

"He was big and drunk. He could fight, I guess. But even

though he was drunk, he was thinking . . . or trying to. You can't fight when you're thinking. You have to trust everything around you is working separate from you. Your hands. Your feet. I learned that when I would stand there and take it from my . . . I mean, when my father would try for Mother. I would let him spend it all on me. All of his kicks and punches. I just would never free all those separate parts to fight. But if thinking doesn't get in your way, you can keep all of that little space around you as your own . . . but he slapped me."

He shrugged and took a shallow drag of Marlboro.

"He kept getting back up, even though every man on the wharf was telling him to quit. He'd get up, over and over. After a while he didn't get up. He quit the boat and went to another one. I was sorry, you know. I know he felt comfortable on my uncle's boat, and I went to him and I said to him, 'Hey, you don't have to leave the boat. C'mon.' And he says . . . he says . . . 'I'll get you. And I'll get your family.' . . . Jono . . . My little mother was my family."

All three of us looked in different directions, confined by the blast of snow and words.

"Couple of months after school, I come home and my mother gives me an envelope she found in the door. I open it, and all it says is 'I'm going to get you.' . . . I knew Bunny Soares was still in Warren, clamming for Charlie Vieira now. He'd take a clam boat and rake out alone off Prudence Island every morning. The next morning I was in the rocks when he started into the bay. . . . My mother, Jono. My little mother . . ."

I could almost hear Bunny Soares falling into cold water, rolling onto sea grass.

Bobby came back to me and read my mind. "I loved Marie, too," he said.

I nodded.

"She was like my sister. You know I loved her."

He shook his head slowly. Long, fine hair swayed with it.

"I was . . . eleven. Now, that's a terrible age, isn't it? You're in a hurry, but there's nowhere to go. You can't get out of his way. When you're eleven, he can always find you, and you're so small, too small to run and too small to help my little . . . I had the plan, or at least the part that had him gone, taken. It was how to get there. How to take him. It was all I thought about. Dreamed about. I would wonder what she'd look like without the broken noses and cheeks and patches of nothing where he'd take the handfuls of her hair. . . . I started to see myself with the rifle, the one I'd found and hidden in my room. I'd had it maybe two years. One day I stayed home from school, took it outside and shot at some trees. Later I took it to Kent Woods and practiced. But I knew it wouldn't be target practice, and I knew if I didn't do it right, it would never stop. He'd be killing us forever. Forever . . . So I had to know I could really do it when I had to. I had to know if I was strong enough. . . . Couple days after Christmas . . . remember that big snowstorm?"

"I remember."

He stared at me a moment. "Yeah . . . I know you do," he whispered. "I was helping with mass. Mother was with me at St. Martha's, because she was one of the women who decorated for Christmas. Remember all the wreaths and trees? I had brought the rifle with me. I had it in a blanket and told my mother it was a lit- tle hockey stick. In between services I thought I'd shoot in the woods by the water tower. I kept my black cassock on and held the rifle under it, by my leg. I crossed Pawtucket Avenue and walked over to Dover Avenue. The fence around the tower was locked. I climbed up a tree that brushed against the tower and dropped onto the catwalk from a limb. The top of the tower slanted out, but snow held to it. I cleared a spot and looked around. I could see the old foundry and St. Martha's. I could see all the way to the bay at Riverside. I was going to shoot at some trees again, that's all. . . .

Then I saw you and . . . Marie coming. I watched you coming. I saw her putting snow on your head. I saw you both stop and make your angels. . . . I thought . . . I thought if I could just . . . just wing . . . just scratch someone I really loved, then I could for sure stop him from killing my mother. . . ."

I was angry and sad at the same time. I wished his father were alive so I could kill him all over again.

"But you didn't just 'wing' someone you loved. You shot her in the back."

His lips quivered. He stared at me. "I wasn't aiming at Marie."

Our long silence was filled with windblown snow shuddering onto the window, shaking the house. My inappropriate brain jumped away from conclusions. It was not the time to think. I was empty. All I could do was turn to my firefighter.

"I *do* want to live with you," I said.

She looked at me and smiled.

"You don't . . . live together?"

I shook my head.

"Why?"

Renée looked at him now. Soft and fearless. "Because he was afraid."

We all entered Bobby's pause now. Perhaps it was the first time I ever understood it.

"Don't be afraid, Jono," he finally said.

He walked out of the room and into the kitchen. I heard the door to the garage open and leaped to the phone. I had barely gotten 911 banged down when I heard Billy's DeSoto fire up. Through the picture window, we saw it charge around the Jeep, turn back toward East Providence, and disappear into the storm.

35

After the two small tents were up and the beer coolers were unloaded from Billy's DeSoto, we fanned out for driftwood to burn. I
had closed up my final summer at the waterfront, and the guys had
picked me up for one last night at Misquamicut Beach. It had been
a gloomy, almost foreboding summer, with lots of rain and cold
Canadian air blowing down on Rhode Island. Today, though, sun
broke up the clouds around three and warmed the stretch of ocean
between our beach and Block Island. We swam, sniffed around some
girls, then settled back for Marlboros and 'Gansetts. Stars came out
early. The night stayed warm. We were quiet and thoughtful, I
suppose. At least, there was a sense of contemplation among us.

Cubby crunched a beer can in his hard hand and reached for
another. "When do you guys leave?"

"September fifteenth. Six A.M. We report in Providence, and
they bus us down to Fort Dix," Billy said.

"So, like, you guys can go through basic training together?"
Cubby asked.

"That's the deal," I said. "After basic they'll probably split
us up."

"Your pop's still pissed, huh? At Jono?"

"Yeah," Billy answered.

"Jono's a dumb mick," Cubby said.

"C'mon, huh?" Bobby uttered.

"What?"

"That's not nice."

Cubby nodded, pulled on his beer, and looked at me. "What kind of geese don't fly?"

"Portageese," we all said. Bobby, too.

Flames sparked out of the fire, into the night. We fell quiet again and listened to the sea rolling and rolling.

"I got engaged, I guess," Billy said.

We looked at him, glowing behind the flames, but none of us spoke.

"Yeah, I gave Deb a ring. I put thirty bucks down, I'll do eighteen a month for a couple of years. We aren't gonna tell our folks for a year. I'm just telling you, so it's kind of a secret."

I was embarrassed, because no one was filling the empty space with words of congratulations. But really, rings and marriages were far off in some distant place.

"Well, great, Billy, congratulations," I said finally.

"Yeah, congratulations," Cubby muttered.

We knew Bobby's voice was coming.

"I dreamed last night that Colleen was my wife."

We drank beers and waited, giving him some room.

"I dreamed we were at that Fourth of July picnic Big Tony had last summer. Remember that? All that food? Big Tony and your mom were standing by the porch holding hands. Remember? I dreamed Colleen and I were married and holding hands."

We let that hang awhile. I poked the fire, and new flames, blue and gold, broke through.

"We ought to promise to meet on the beach every year forever," Cubby said. "Get drunk and shit. Talk."

"What if we live somewhere else?" Billy asked. "I mean, I might move to Maine or Alaska."

"You'll be an adult, shithead. You can come back every year so we can all fuck around."

"I'm not going to leave," Bobby said after his beat. "My mother . . . So I'll be here. When?"

"Beginning of summer," Cubby said.

"Memorial Day or something?" Billy asked. "What if I'm in California or something?"

"What? They haven't got planes in California?"

"How long?"

"Shit, I don't know. Couple days, maybe. A campout. What do you think, Jono?"

I stood up and brushed the fine sand off my bathing suit and legs. "What if we're old and fat? You guys, I mean. What if I show up still cool and handsome like I am and Cubby weighs five hundred pounds and Billy's bald and Bobby hasn't got his *other* eye?"

Cubby tossed me a new 'Gansett. "That's true. What if we showed up one year and Jono's head had grown even bigger, like a Chevy instead of a Volks?"

We laughed. And the salty breeze took it out over the ocean toward Block Island. The lapping of waves filled our silence.

Bobby lay on his back, smoking and watching the perfect night. "It's a good plan," he said to the stars.

"Memorial Day," Cubby said.

"Memorial Day," Billy agreed. "Even if I'm in Australia or something."

"Hey, they got planes in Australia. Jono?"

"Memorial Day. Okay."

Cubby held his hand out, and we topped it with ours. "Like now, first one here lights the fire."

We held our oath hands in the air in solemn agreement. Unspoken vows, important and ironclad, rolled around our hearts and brains until, contained by firelight, we dropped our hands, sure of a continuing center of our lives.

A few months later, Billy would be dead and I'd be blown up.

36

Everything I wanted to keep after thirty years in New York City filled about half of the small van I had rented. Discards of my life flowed over cardboard boxes and plastic bags piled high in front of my old East Eighty-ninth Street walk-up.

I slid into the passenger side. "It's like I was never here."

Randall Pound nodded behind the steering wheel. "You were here, Jono. Things are things. They're not important. Remember what Mrs. Joad said when the preacher asked her why they had brought everything they owned to California?"

"What did she say?"

"She said, 'I don't know.' "

We took Eighty-sixth Street over to the West Side. The apartment was in a brownstone on West Eighty-seventh between Columbus and Central Park. It had taken the two of us all day long and ten trips, the van bulging, to get Renée's things up from Chelsea and a half hour for mine. I handed Randall a Coke. It became miniature in his enormous hands. I took one, and we drank in silence, our eyes swinging around the sunny rooms.

"It's a big thing. Moving," he finally said. "It's like death and it's like birth."

I laughed.

"No, really, Jono. Any way you look at it, it's something new. It's an adventure. Sandburg, in a lot of his work, points out the essential insignificance of people. In the long term, I mean. These are the kinds of things that put the lie to that. You and Renée moving in, I mean."

I dropped Randall off at his place and returned the van to a garage on West Twenty-third across the street from Pier 63. I strolled over to the long dock adjacent to the roller-skating rink and walked out until I was facing Jersey on the other side of the river.

It's surprising how clean and orderly things appear from a distance. The warehouses and apartments on the far bank all seemed shiny, sanitary. This kind of overview is necessary, I think. It's important for people to fool themselves into believing that order is possible, even if we know it isn't.

Several months had passed since Bobby disappeared. I'd talked with Kenny Snowden on the phone two or three times, and he had promised to keep me informed if he heard anything concerning Bobby, or Colleen Crosby for that matter. The truth is, the whole thing has become so surrealistic I can hardly believe it happened. It's as though I see it through gauze, the way they film old actors to blend away the wrinkles. The way they photographed Doris Day to smother her freckles.

Renée and I got back into our essential routines. She fought to keep the city from burning down, and I ensured that any adults entering Lambs Bar and Grill between 10:00 P.M. and 4:00 A.M. could put a liquid patina on their evening. By day I became Acting Man, a superhero without portfolio, unless you count the two Midas Muffler radio commercials I managed to fool some advertising company into giving me. Oh, and I think I might have struck gold with a new off-off-Broadway play that I begin rehearsals for the end of next week. It's a one-hander, and I portray Alfred Packer, the Colorado man-eater. Also forty-one other characters, including five prospectors who get cannibalized in the winter of 1873. That's right. I eat myself.

I stayed on the pier until ten to six, walked over to Engine Company 14, then walked with Renée over to the Seventh Avenue subway station at Eighteenth Street. She held my hand very tight. I could feel her brain waves flowing down to her little fingers.

"What?" I said while we waited on the subway platform.

She looked up at me dramatically, her brilliant eyes huge and shining.

"Last night when you got back from Lambs, the last night in my apartment?"

I nodded.

"You thought I was asleep, but I wasn't."

The crowded train arrived, and we were quiet all the way up to West Eighty-sixth and Broadway. When we climbed out onto the street, she held my hand again.

On the corner of Broadway and Eighty-seventh, before we turned toward Columbus, she stopped and squeezed my hand. "I heard you crying."

I laughed. "I don't cry, Renée. I'm from New England."

"I just have to know. Was it because we're moving in together?"

"I wasn't crying, for God's sake. C'mon."

"Because I thought about it hard all day, Jono, and if you really don't want to, I'll still love you and I'll still—"

"C'mon, Renée."

"I just have to know, so we don't do anything stupid."

We started walking again and stopped in front of the pretty brownstone.

"I'm not going in until I know that's not why you were crying."

I looked at her, then over her head toward Central Park. Renée's greatness as a human being is a result of her simple and simply impossible bravery to face every experience completely. To view with wide-open eyes the truth and lies of a moment. My courage left me somewhere between Misquamicut Beach and Billy's car accident. I have a theory that it is an indication of maturity to replace honesty and straightforwardness with a deep, vague inner monologue. A personal double-talk to fool yourself into thinking that if there are significant episodes in your time here, they'll go away by themselves. Renée would have none of it. I sat on the step, and my firefighter sat with me.

"I got to your place about quarter to five. I was meeting Randall at seven to start moving the stuff over. I thought maybe I'd medi-tate instead of getting into a sleep and then have to get right up."

"We should have got a mover."

"Yeah. It was a lot more than I thought. I'm beat. . . . But I sat in your kitchen . . . and I started to do this acting meditation where you concentrate on the beat of your heart and . . . and you move it around your body. Your shoulders, your hands, all over. It's an easy one. Even a dumb mick from East—"

"Jono . . ."

"Anyway, I must have drifted away a little, because when I opened my eyes, they were all at the kitchen table. Big Tony, Cubby, Billy, Bobby, my pop, Mother, sweet little Marie in pigtails. Me, too. I watched us from . . . from now, I guess. Then they were gone. And for a second, just for a second, I felt . . . lonely. So I guess I . . . maybe I . . . I don't know. . . ."

"Cried?"

I put my arm around her. "Yes. And then when I thought how happy I was that we were moving in together, I cried a little more. Only for joy. Do you think this means I'm in my second child-hood?"

"I love you," she said in her fierce way.

"I love you, too."

"You don't have to say—"

"Renée, let's go home."

37

Two weeks before I left for basic training at Fort Dix, Sandy Minucci broke up with me. She'd been acting withdrawn the past couple of days, but I only noticed in a sort of peripheral way, as if her
pouting and silence were running parallel to me instead of on a
collision course. Also, I was pretty preoccupied with my imminent
departure for the army.

We had been to a lousy movie in Pawtucket and were having a
roast beef sandwich at the Beefhearth Restaurant.

"You're not eating. Aren't you hungry, Sandy?"

"I don't know." She shrugged, not looking at me.

"Are you sick?"

"Uh-uh."

I chewed in silence. Sandy arranged her sandwich and fries.
The Beefhearth's roast beef sandwiches were what my old man
used to call "ten-napkiners." Juicy. Tender. I had to lean over my
plate so as to not drip a gallon of the delicious sauce down my
shirt.

"Good," I managed with my mouth full.

I watched her and her sandwich, too. The Beefhearth always
served it on top of a fat bed of crispy french fries, which added

greatly to its stout, overstuffed appearance. The heat from the fresh roast beef softened the kaiser roll nicely.

"Really, really good," I said again as I swallowed the last of my wonderful sandwich.

Sandy was going to attend Rhode Island Junior College in the fall. Her plan was to get some good college credits and transfer to Salve Regina in Newport and become a schoolteacher. Sitting across from her, seeing her all scrunched into herself, I couldn't imagine her a teacher. She suddenly seemed so young. So much younger than me. Heat still rose off her sandwich. I imagined warm, crispy fries underneath.

"I got . . . sort of asked . . . to go out," she said in a tiny voice.

I didn't hear exactly what she said, so I nodded and smiled at her and her roast beef sandwich platter.

"I mean . . . I mean, you know the guy, and he's, like, really shy now, and he asked me, but he wanted, you know, for me to, like, talk to you. Because—"

Now I heard her. "Wait. You got asked out?"

"Uh-huh."

"On a date?"

"Yeah."

I sat back in my chair.

"It's not a big deal," she murmured.

"What did you say?"

"I didn't say anything."

"You must have said something."

"Well . . ."

"Did you say yes?"

"No."

"Did you say no?"

"No."

I looked down, but all I saw was my empty platter. The roasts my mother cooked were mostly pot roasts, the Yankee pot roasts, or sometimes she wouldn't wait for St. Patrick's Day to boil up some corned beef, but she absolutely never slow-roasted a superior cut of meat, sliced it thin, and dribbled real au jus over it and the accompanying fries. I looked at Sandy's superabundant platter.

"I mean, I didn't know what to say."

I nodded.

Sandy placed her hands on mine. "I said . . . I'd ask you if it was okay."

"To go out with the guy?"

"Uh-huh."

We stared at each other. We knew that things were changing. They had to. Changing as surely as the fries underneath her roast beef were slowly cooling.

"Well . . . who . . . who is he?"

"He's nice. He's nervous."

"He's nervous about me?"

"He's nervous . . . you know . . . about . . . Bobby."

"What's Bobby got to do with anything?"

"Petey's just nervous about him."

I looked down at our hands, forcing my eyes not to drift over to her food. "Petey . . . Maloney?"

"I know he was a jerk, but he's changed a lot since Bobby beat him up and my brothers tried to kill him. He's polite and quiet, and he's really smart."

"Petey Maloney asked you out?"

She nodded slowly. "Just to . . . you know . . . a movie or something."

"Well . . . what do Larry, Alec, Hank, Brian, Dougie, Eugene, Billy, and Jimmy say?"

She shrugged. "He's just nervous about Bobby."

The thing about me was that I was only going through the motions. Trying not to leave a ripple in life's undulating ocean. I couldn't imagine myself being in love for the sake of love with anyone except Marie D'Agostino, and as I never had a chance, I never declared myself. Only felt it out there somewhere, hanging in the air like a promise never stated. I'm pretty sure if Marie was my steady and we had this conversation over roast beef and fries, I wouldn't have been able to finish even my own food. That's the mystery of passion. At least I knew that much.

"Look . . . I want you to do what you want. I mean, I'm going into the army. I might even get killed and stuff."

She smiled and nodded despite teary eyes. "I've got to go pee," she said.

I watched my little blond cheerleader walk away from me with both regret and relief. The future loomed as challengingly as Sandy's untouched roast beef platter, and so I slid it boldly in front of me.

38

Renée gave him my number at Lambs. It was just after midnight.

"Mr. Jono Riley, please."

I recognized the voice. "It's me, Officer Snowden," I said.

"Kenny."

"Yes, sir."

"Sorry to bother you at your place of business and so late, but I thought you'd want to know."

I waited. I could hear some papers being shuffled or spread out.

"My former partner sent me over some police materials. Colleen Crosby, forty-seven years old, of no permanent address, died the day before yesterday—that would be Saturday—the twenty-fifth of May, of an apparent overdose of cough suppressant. Her body was slumped on a bench inside the Providence train station."

"Bobby . . . ?"

"No, nothing new there."

I felt a bizarre sense of relief. "Well, I . . . I suppose if he were around, she wouldn't have been on cough syrup."

"I suppose."

"Is there an obituary or anything?"

"Just an announcement in the *Journal* and the *East Providence Post.*"

"Funeral?"

"No information on that."

We were both quiet and thinking.

"Renée mentioned that you run the bar at the restaurant," he said finally. "Do you mix with tap water or springwater?"

There it was again. Jesus.

"You see, I've recently been forced to institutionalize my wife, as even home care was becoming overwhelmed, so naturally water has been on my mind. Fluoridated water, I mean to say. There is a link, you know, to Alzheimer's. I'm positive of that."

"I'm so sorry, Kenny."

"She was some lady. Yes she was. Keep in touch, Jono Riley, and remember to keep a fresh supply of springwater in your home."

"Yes, sir."

I mixed a tray order, then took some seltzer for myself and walked down the bar to Randall Pound. I talked it out, and he listened hard. Listening is something that's becoming a lost skill. Randall has it raised to an art form.

"Poor little girl," he said, shaking his head.

"I guess."

"Now his anchor is gone. His meaning. Faced with an inability to deal with what fate had lined up for him, Bobby essentially organized his world around someone more wounded than himself."

I nodded, but Randall had lost me. Bobby Fontes was still too flesh-and-blood to categorize so simply and neatly.

"It's not over," he said.

I crawled into bed at sunrise and slept poorly, in and out of dreams that did not feel like dreams at all. Bobby continuously swirling off the old water tower and Marie's snow angel taking on a life of its own. Renée woke me at noon.

"Kenny's on the phone."

I sat up and held the receiver with both hands. "Officer . . ."

He jumped in crisply and businesslike. "Jack Crosby was shot to death around seven this morning."

My mouth was caked with the night. "What . . . ?" I managed.

"He'd been back at the Terrace since he got out of the Adult Correctional Institute. Back strong-arming for Ponserelli. Police found his body in the library parking lot next to the water tower."

"Oh, Jesus."

"A .22," he stated.

He waited for me. I could hear my own amplified breathing over the receiver. I looked up at Renée.

Kenny's voice softened somewhere between West Eighty-seventh and the Wampanoag Trail.

"Are you all right, Jono Riley?"

"I . . . yes, yes. Thank you for calling. I don't know what to do."

"Nothing for you to do. There's an all-points for New England and that will stretch out to other jurisdictions. I would say it's only a matter of time before he's caught. He may have a leg up, because it's the Memorial Day weekend and most local forces will concentrate on traffic problems, but after that . . ."

"Will you keep me informed?"

"Absolutely. Oh, and, Jono?"

"Yes, sir?"

"Remember that there's a link between tap water and Alzheimer's."

"Yes, sir. I'm getting springwater. You bet."

39

The cab pulled in front of Rebello's Funeral Home in East Providence, and I struggled out. I still needed a cane while the last of six operations on my right leg healed. My army uniform, so snug before the grenade wounds, hung baggy over the spaces left by a forty-pound weight loss. My head had not, of course, shrunk like the rest of me; in fact, it seemed actually bigger than usual, a continent of confusion.

A fine, misty rain fell in swirls, and the June dusk grew colder. I had come directly here from Hillsgrove Airport, having arranged with my CO at Fitzsimmons Army Hospital in Denver to take personal leave time before reporting to my new base in Petersburg. On the drive to the funeral home, I noted how unfamiliar Rhode Island had become in the nine months since I had been gone. There was a stillness, a kind of patience, to the state that I just didn't share anymore. I was visiting in some peculiar way, and not simply coming home.

I limped off the sidewalk onto a patch of lawn and lit up a smoke. Several people left and several entered the front of the large white Colonial home. A hearse had parked at the side door, and the driver also smoked by his car. I noticed that the parking lot was full, as were the side streets. My cap felt soggy, floating as it was on the ocean of my head, and I took it off and hung it over my belt.

Mother had called me in Denver with the news that Billy had been killed in an automobile accident just outside of Fort Gordon, Georgia, where he was in the Quartermaster Corps. There were two other GIs with him, and the one who was driving had flipped the car. They were all killed instantly. Now I was standing outside Rebello's trying to figure out how something like death could touch any of us. I didn't want to see him there in that finality. I wanted him alive, at least inside the vastness of my head.

Large bay windows were on either side of the front door, but light was coming only from the left-hand side. That was Billy's room, I assumed, and watched it closely for answers to questions I had asked myself over and over since Mother's call. Was I responsible for Billy going into the service? And if laying out my plans over Cubby's mother's pasta had inspired Billy to take the same route, then was I by implication responsible for his accident and death? All of my upside-down, convoluted, near logic ponged inside me like heavy pinballs until nothing was clear. Nausea began to creep up out of my stomach and into my diaphragm. Breathing became spasmodic, like I was coming up for air in Yawgoog Pond and then diving back down into a weedy bottom. I looked at the window again, and Billy's father stood staring out at me. It seemed I had faced off with him right here on the funeral-home grass, many times before. That's how clear it was that somehow we had already played this awful scene. Like a clod, I dumbly pointed to the entrance. He shook his head no. We had done this before, I was sure of it. Plea and rejection. Again and again.

So things had fallen back onto themselves—or something like that. Drips of the mind seeming as tangible as the rain that suddenly broke into a downpour. I lowered my noggin, shook the big thing sadly, and as much as I resisted the common emotion, began to blubber. I leaned a hard angle onto my cane, giant head balanced on a pin. An olive drab statue of soggy remorse.

And then they were with me, of course. Bobby looped his shoulder under my cane arm and straightened me. Cubby took my other side. Marie, in her sad, perfect black dress, held my head and eased the impossible thing onto her shoulders. Big Tony ran up behind her and began cooing quietly.

"Aww, Bozo. It's all right, Bozo. It's all right."

And for a while it was.

40

I pulled the rental onto the deserted parking lot and drove it to the remembered corner where cold dunes abutted the pavement. I turned the ride off, and engine noise was replaced by easterly wind and driving surf. What had begun as a glorious afternoon had fallen to a sullen, gray dusk. A storm threatened in the mantle of inky clouds falling low over the Atlantic. People had abandoned the beach early for a movie or maybe an indoor picnic. I stepped out of the car, pretending the weather was somehow appropriate for the shorts and T-shirt I had worn up from New York. I grabbed a Styrofoam cooler from the backseat and headed toward the ocean. As soon as the beach leveled and I could see past the cover of salt grass, I caught a flicker of light between some dunes about fifty yards ahead.

We saw each other at the same time. Me moving toward the light, Bobby coming over the dunes with a fresh supply of driftwood for the fire. I didn't say anything, put the cooler down, and went off for wood myself. Fifteen minutes later, with the fire strongly working toward coals, I sat down and poked at it. Bobby let his hands hang by his side, looking up and down the expanse of beach. While I waited through his pause, I saw how much more suitably he had dressed than me. Jeans and a brown watch sweater. His Red Sox baseball cap was on backward.

"Yeah," he sighed. "Yeah, I think this is about the spot. The last time we were all together."

"I don't know. Maybe. Close though."

He looked at me. A thin smile spread onto his dark face, then flattened out. "I knew you'd come, Jono. We could always count on you."

I nodded and stood out of my crouch. "I'm so sorry, Bobby. I'm so sorry about . . . Colleen."

"I knew it didn't make sense, me loving her. I knew it was impossible . . . but when she was Colleen . . . well, I don't know. She was everything. That make sense?"

"Sure."

He looked back out toward Block Island, hidden in the darkness. While I waited again, I glanced around for the .22. I didn't see it.

"How's Renée?" he asked softly.

"Happy, I guess. We moved in together."

"She loves you."

"I hope so."

"You love her."

"She's it, all right."

Now I looked out to sea with him. "I brought some 'Gansetts. I brought some sandwiches."

"Have some."

"I brought them for you, too."

"I'd take a 'Gansett."

I gave him a can and held up a sandwich.

"Later," he said. He rolled the cold, wet can against his neck and closed his eyes. " 'Gansett isn't really 'Gansett anymore."

"I know," I said.

"Falstaff bought it."

I nodded.

"They brew it in Indiana or Milwaukee or somewhere. Nothing stays the same, Jono."

"Things change."

"Yeah."

"That's life."

Bobby shrugged and closed his eyes. I could feel the words coming, and while I waited, I thought about this drive to Misquamicut and the oddness of my decision making. It's a headfirst dive with me. It's those half-sure instincts that, once acted upon, leave me talking to myself. I have second-guessed a life, and it played over me now on the cold sand. And not just the obvious hesitation of whether or not I should have shared our beach vow with Renée or Kenny Snowden but the whole ridiculous journey into a profession I had neither the training nor the capacity to succeed in. Yes, I actually began to feel sorry for myself. I'll say it again: Actors! Jesus!

"I thought Cubby might come," Bobby said sadly.

I watched and waited.

"I loved her too, Jono. Will you tell Cubby I loved her, too? I didn't know it was a . . . a . . ."

"Traveler," I said.

"A traveler."

We popped our beers and drank them, listening to waves. Sparks jumped off the driftwood.

He looked at me. "Jack was the end of it. Colleen's gone. Mother's some other place inside her head. Before you got here, I was thinking about all of it. Everything. Jono, I can't believe anything has happened. I don't believe in it."

"It did happen, Bobby."

"Yeah."

"Bobby, I came to the beach because you're my friend. All I can do as a friend is tell you to call Kenny Snowden. Remember Kenny? I'll go with you. I'll go with you the whole way."

More pause among the wind and waves. I waited.

"I know. I'll do it now. Where's your car?"

"Where we always parked. By the big dune."

He nodded.

"We can call Kenny from the Misquamicut Beach house."

"Okay," he said, standing.

"C'mon."

"I'll meet you at your car. I just want five more minutes."

I stepped closer to him. Things needed to be said, but Jono Riley was probably not the one to say them.

"I'll be there, Bobby. I'll be there the whole way."

We both smiled a little. I picked up the cooler and began walking to my car. Should I say I was surprised to hear the distant pop of the .22? Or that I put the cooler down and walked back to the fire instead of running? Even now there is a blunting of memory. I will say this, though: Fear and expectation seem to go hand in hand with me.

Bobby had sat down and leaned against the straightest dune. The small rifle was easily short enough for him to trip the trigger after he had put the business end into his mouth. The rifle had slid down onto his chest. His head was pushed back on the sharp dune grass. He looked out at the water and Block Island.

I called Kenny from the pay phone at the public beach house, then went and sat with Bobby, trying to see what he saw.

41

The last day of March, and because winter had been unusually mellow, new buds were already popping a chlorophyll green on the maples and oaks surrounding Pierce Field. My old man had the ball in his right hand and his Ted Williams–autographed bat in his left. He pointed to the sun, low in the sky, and shouted, "Last one!" He hit a hard grounder to third, where I picked it, scooped it to Bobby, watched him toss it to Billy at second, who fired it to Marie at first. She picked it out of the dirt, turned, and winged it to Cubby, who stood in front of my father at home plate. We were still in our school clothes, and we'd talked that tired old guy into some after-dinner grounders. We'd been there maybe an hour and could have shagged them all night if he'd let us. Cubby turned, handed Pop the ball, and we began to follow him to our station wagon. Marie ran over, got between me and Bobby, and dropped her long, slender arms over our shoulders, her glove lying on my twelve-year-old chest. Her tight black pigtails were finished with green bows, and a tiny crucifix on a braided gimp cord lay at the top of her breastbone. I got into the front with Cubby, and Marie sat in back between Bobby and Billy. Right before he fired up our Ford, my old man sniffed and looked at me.

"What's that smell, Jono?"

"What?"

"That smell. What is it?"

I caught my Marie D'Agostino's exquisite eyes in the rearview mirror, and she smiled the smile I can still savor decades after the fact. She looked serious for a second, then smiled it again.

"Roses, Pop," I said, my eyes still on her. "That smell is roses."